TARGETED

HOSTAGE RESCUE TEAM SERIES

KAYLEA CROSS

TARGETED

Copyright © 2014
by Kaylea Cross

* * * * *

Cover Art & Formatting by
Sweet 'N Spicy Designs

* * * * *

ISBN: 978-1500924676

Dedication

To my amazing readers, who support me and encourage me to listen to the voices in my head so I can write their stories. From the bottom of my heart, thank you!

Kaylea

Author's Note

Welcome to book two of the **Hostage Rescue Team Series!** In this one I've pitted Agent Celida Morales against her sexy and unattainable former partner, Tuck, so expect plenty of fireworks as these two struggle to find their way to one another.

Up next will be Bauer and the girl he swore he'd never fall for. The bigger they are, the harder they fall, and I can't wait to make Bauer fall flat on his face. *chortles*

Happy reading!

Kaylea Cross

Prologue

———•————————•———

Nineteen months ago

Special Agent Brad "Tuck" Tucker shifted his brake hand on the rappelling rope and spoke quietly into his microphone. "Saber one and two in position." His voice barely carried in the cold November air, his breath fogging in the frigid night.

"Roger that. Stand by," the commanding officer replied from inside the mobile command center.

Tuck glanced beside him at one of his teammates as they hung suspended on the side of the five-story building in the darkness, and received an affirmative nod in response. The hostage-taker inside had an automatic rifle, two handguns and a machete he'd already used to kill his father-in-law a day ago. The standoff had gone on for two days before Tuck and his team had been called in to end it.

The gun-toting asshole inside that apartment had no idea what was about to happen to him.

Tuck stayed absolutely still in the harness, the soles

of his boots flat against the brick siding as he waited.

"Execute."

At the quiet command through the headset, Tuck and his teammate automatically rappelled two leaps down the building. A split second later the sniper team on an opposite rooftop activated the charges on the apartment's front windows. The sound of shattering glass surrounded him an instant before he and his teammate swung through the busted windows, feet first. He landed inside the unit with his MP5 up and ready and lobbed in a flashbang.

The other five members of the assault team breached the apartment door a heartbeat later as it exploded and added a few of their own, filling the small space with blinding flashes and smoke. The back bedroom door flung open. "FBI, FBI, everybody down!"

Through his NVGs Tuck could see the perp standing in the doorway, the automatic rifle in his hands aimed at the entry team. He was wearing a ballistic vest and they'd already received clearance to take him out if he refused to surrender. Before the guy could move Tuck already had the red laser dot from his weapon aimed at the center of the guy's face.

"Hands up, hands up!" the team leader shouted as more laser dots appeared on the suspect.

The perp's face twisted into a mask of rage, his face slick with sweat as he let out a scream of rage. "I'm gonna kill you motherfuckers!" He started to raise his weapon. Before the muzzle had even moved two inches, Tuck fired a double tap, hitting him in the face. The guy fell backward, dead before he hit the floor.

"He's down. Move, move, move," the team leader said, ushering the rest of the team past him. They all rushed to the back bedroom to retrieve the hostages while Tuck covered the team leader as he walked up to the tango and kicked the assault weapon aside.

2

Following protocol, he put two fingers beneath the man's jaw to check for a pulse. "Dead."

Tuck and another teammate cleared the rest of the small apartment. "Clear," he reported.

"Clear!" someone shouted from the back, confirming the threat was neutralized.

Tuck lowered his weapon as the others came out of the room carrying the two females and one child. *Mission accomplished.*

As the team filed out of the apartment, the team leader went to one knee and slapped a good natured hand on the man's chest. "Very convincing," he said with a chuckle.

The "suspect" reached up a hand to shove the now yellow-spattered protective visor up, revealing one of their teammates. Vance grinned up at them, his teeth startlingly white against his dark skin. Currently out with a badly sprained ankle, he'd volunteered to be the perp for this exercise "Well, I'm definitely awake now. And I'm also glad Tuck remembered to load simunition into his magazine."

Tuck chuckled, slung his weapon across his chest and reached down a hand to help his teammate up off the floor. They almost always used live ammo during their exercises, just like Delta did, so that was nothing new for him. "For a second there I couldn't remember if I'd loaded the simunitions or not," he teased. "Glad it all worked out."

Vance grunted and slapped him on the shoulder by way of a thank you, hobbling a bit on his bad foot. "Me too."

"Nice touch with the rage yell, by the way," Tuck commented. "Really added to the atmosphere."

Vance shrugged. "I do what I can. Don't mind taking one for the team every now and again. But you just killed me with two shots to the face, man, so I'm not talking to you right now. And you owe me a fucking beer," he said as he walked past him.

"Yeah, all right." Tuck followed the others out of the "apartment" on the infamous Hogan's Alley and back to HQ for debriefing. This place felt like home to him. He'd spent countless hours here back in his Delta days, and because the Hostage Rescue Team routinely used Delta's ranges and shooting houses, he'd be spending a lot more time back in his old stomping grounds.

And damn, it felt good to be back after two years in the field as a regular FBI agent where he'd put his recently earned degree in criminal justice to good use. Having come from his elite, tier one unit to the FBI after his knees had healed up from the last surgery, the switch to investigative work and the lack of action had damn near killed him. He'd never been cut out to be a desk jockey.

Now he was finally back in his element, doing what he did best: Kicking ass and taking names.

The training and op tempo for the HRT was a huge step up for some of the guys on the squad, but for him and the guys who'd served in tier one military units prior to joining the FBI, this was status quo and they wouldn't have it any other way. The constant training kept them sharp.

After they were dismissed for the night he showered and dressed, then checked his phone. He'd missed a call from his partner, Celida, but she'd left him a text.

Well???

Smiling a little, he typed back his response. *Well what?*

She responded a few seconds later. *You know damn well what! So?*

Sorry, you'll have to be more specific.

He could just imagine the scowl on her pretty face

as she answered. *It's been two weeks since selection. Did you make it or not?*

Chuckling now, he replied. *Meet me for dinner and I'll tell you. My treat.*

His phone dinged a few seconds later. *Fine, if you're buying. When?*

Damn he loved that sweet/tart mix of her personality. Even though he was excited about the future, the truth was he was going to miss working with her. It was for the best though. He was already thirty-one and she was twenty-nine. They both needed to move forward in their careers.

Now, he answered. He texted her the name and address of an Italian restaurant near the Baltimore field office. Once he received her reply that she'd meet him there, he climbed in his truck and headed north.

She was there waiting for him when he pulled into the parking lot, leaning against her four-door sedan with her arms folded across the chest of her cream wool coat that highlighted the sexy, full hourglass curves beneath it. Her coffee brown hair was pulled back into a sleek ponytail at the back of her head, a few tendrils blowing around her face in the slight breeze.

She lifted a dark brown eyebrow at him expectantly when he climbed out of his truck. Her cheeks were pink from the cold, highlighting the lightly bronzed skin tone of her Cuban heritage, and her deep gray eyes were fixed on his face. "So? You gonna tell me now?"

Not until he got to spend some time with her. They'd always kept things strictly professional, a little harmless flirting aside, but they had no such restrictions anymore. Made it damn hard to stay patient, not plunge ahead, but he knew he had to go slow with her. He didn't want a fling and then be done, and that's exactly what he was afraid would happen if they rushed things and acted on the attraction they'd both tried to ignore the past two years.

Because he was well aware that in terms of relationships, she only did short and sweet with guys. At least the ones she'd hooked up with until now.

For damn sure Tuck wasn't going to be like the others. "After dinner. Come on."

He took her upper arm and pulled her away from her car. And he didn't let go. She cast him a sideways glance but didn't comment or pull out of his grasp. She stood five-six but in her heels she was tall enough to look him dead in the eyes. The hostess sat them at a table for two near the wood-burning brick fireplace. The setting was decidedly romantic, way different than any of the places they'd eaten at together before now, both on and off duty, and he wasn't sorry for it.

Tonight marked a new chapter in their relationship and he wanted to lay the foundation for that transition. He'd had a few serious relationships over the years, but none of the women could hold a candle to Celida.

She was a former Marine, for starters, which was just flat out sexy, and during their time as partners her shooting had improved to the point where she was now damn near as good as him with a handgun. Her mind was quick, she was driven and focused, and fucking loyal to the select few she included in her inner circle. She'd earned his trust within two weeks of leaving the Academy and though nothing hairy had gone down during their partnership, if it had Tuck knew without a doubt he could've counted on her to have his back.

In short, it was a goddamn miracle he hadn't made a move on her up 'til now.

The waiter brought them a basket of freshly baked bread and took their orders. He brought their drinks next and the moment he left Celida leaned forward and put her slender hands on the table, narrowing her eyes at him. Smalltalk was over.

"You made it. I know you did."

Hiding a smile, he sipped at his beer and shrugged. "Maybe."

She snorted and eased back into her chair. "No maybe about it. With your experience? Come on. They'd be freaking brain dead not to sign you, so just quit with all the humble bullshit and tell me already."

He set his beer glass down, met her eyes and nodded once. "I'm in."

A flash of triumph entered those deep gray eyes, but he also caught the flash of sadness there. "Knew it." She brushed aside a wayward lock of hair that had escaped the sleek ponytail, and blew out a breath. "When do you start?"

"Already did, couple days ago. Did a training op today with the guys. The unit I'm in is on training cycle right now, but there's talk we might be sent overseas for a protective detail soon."

She nodded, grabbed her glass of red wine and looked away while she took a sip. "God knows there's enough hot spots in the world right now. You guys'll never be short on work, that's for sure."

"Nope." And though the FBI's Hostage Rescue Team's operational tempo was only slightly less intense than what he'd experienced in Delta, he was still looking forward to this change of pace. Most of the time he'd be working stateside, with only the occasional training or mission overseas.

Which was good, because he was sick and damn tired of working in the Middle East. He'd had his fill of chasing militant assholes in some of the toughest terrain on the planet. He'd much rather hunt them down here in the States where he at least had home field advantage.

"Bet you make team leader soon, too." She looked at him over the rim of her glass.

He wanted that but had to pay his dues first, no

matter what his background was. "We'll see."

The waiter brought their food and things got quiet as they ate. A little awkward even.

Tuck picked up the thread of conversation in between bites. "Heard you've got a new assignment too."

She shrugged, didn't look up from her lasagna. "You know I always wanted domestic terrorism. Fits well with my criminology degree." Now her eyes flicked up to his. "And I hear someone passed along a glowing letter of recommendation on my behalf to Greg Travers."

The agent heading up the domestic terrorism department in Baltimore. "I'm the one who's worked with you the closest these past two years, and he wanted to know what I thought of you."

Her expression softened, an embarrassed flush creeping up her light bronze cheekbones. "Well, thanks."

"Just told him the truth." And the truth was, she was fucking amazing.

The meal ended all too quickly and he grabbed the tab before she could. He walked her out to her car in the cold, at a loss about how to make this transition with her. She'd never completely let her guard down around him but he figured she'd let him in as much as she had anyone else in her life.

At her car she unlocked the driver's side door and paused, turning to look up at him in the dim glow of a nearby streetlamp. In the silence that stretched out their gazes locked. Their parting of ways hung between them, heavy and colder than the frosty air.

She was the first to break the tension, putting on a smile as she adjusted the red scarf she had wrapped around her neck. "So. Don't be a stranger, okay?"

That sounded way too much like a goodbye. Because he was an inch away from throwing all caution aside and taking that full mouth in a kiss that would leave her gasping, he stuffed his hands into his pockets instead. "You either. But don't worry, I'll be around."

"Hope so. And for the record, you were the best damn partner I could've ever hoped for and I was lucky to be paired with you. You taught me a lot, and for that I'll always be grateful. I'll miss you."

"Hey." Dammit, he didn't want her pulling away from him. He couldn't not reach for her after that, not when she'd just showed him more emotion than he'd ever seen in the two years on the job with her.

He caught her shoulders, pulled her to him and wrapped his arms around her, his cheek pressed against the side of her head. She felt good, all soft, generous curves melding into his body, and she smelled even better. Sin and temptation. "You act like I'm gonna up and disappear into thin air on you or something."

Celida returned the embrace, gave a tight shake of her head. "You're moving on. You'll be busier now than ever and we'll live an hour apart. It's not like we'll be bumping into each other."

"So we make the effort," he said, his voice nearly a growl at the thought of losing her now.

"Right," she said, and he wasn't sure if it was cynicism or not. She pulled away to stare up at him for a long moment, and Tuck took all his will not to cradle that beautiful face in his hands, glide his thumbs across those high cheekbones and kiss the hell out of her. "Talk to you later, then," she murmured.

He nodded, jaw set. "Yeah. Drive safely, sunshine."

She paused at the endearment, then climbed behind the wheel. As she drove away, Tuck was already certain of two things. One, she still wasn't ready to give him what he wanted.

And two, if there was going to be any keeping in touch going on from this point forward, he knew it would be up to him to make it happen.

Chapter One

Present Day

O f all the challenges she'd faced throughout her life, she had a feeling this was the one that would either make her or break her.

Special Agent Celida Morales took a deep breath and squared her shoulders as she paused before the door that led into the FBI's Domestic Terror Division offices in Baltimore. The name held a wealth of new meaning now, because for her, the job had become personal.

Very personal.

In the glass panel set into the top of the steel door she could see her reflection in the bright fluorescent lights above. Other than the deep pink, two inch long scar on her right cheek from where a bullet had grazed her two months ago, she looked normal enough on the outside. But inside, that day had changed her forever.

Domestic terror had left its mark on her a few short weeks ago. Now more than ever, she was determined to leave her mark on it.

She pushed the metal release bar and strode down the brightly lit hallway, her footsteps muffled by the carpeting. It felt strange to be back here after all this time off. At the second office from the end on the left, she opened the door and switched on the light. Her office was exactly as she'd left it.

The desk was clear except for a framed photo of her and her mom, and one of her and her best friend. Zoe had stayed with her for the first few weeks after the attack and was due back in town tonight for another visit. She was the sister Celida had always wanted, and it didn't matter that they weren't related by blood. Though the family bond Zoe did share with the man who'd introduced them proved to be an ongoing complication for Celida.

She wasn't going to think about him right now though.

In her top desk drawer she found the files she'd been working on before her forced leave of absence. She pulled them out, her fingers pausing on the top manila folder marked Xang Xu. The man responsible for what had happened to her. He was currently behind bars in between trials and looking at a life sentence rather than the death penalty because he'd agreed to a plea bargain.

Now he was helping officials with their investigation into the radical Islamic sleeper cell activated here on command from its leaders back in mainland China. Xinxiang province, to be precise, where the ethnic and mostly Muslim Uyghur people were engaged in a struggle for independence from China's unyielding response to religious groups within its borders, made worse by the recent terror activity there by Islamic extremists.

She flipped open the file and looked at Xang's picture, the first time she'd seen it since the day she'd been wounded. Her body didn't react. No elevation in her heart rate, and none of the fear she'd braced for came. But then, Xang had merely ordered the attack and hadn't been one of the men who'd come to kill her that day.

She should have died in that hotel room. She knew that. She'd let her guard down too far, hadn't anticipated that the cell members knew of Rachel Granger's location. If not for Rachel, they'd have put a bullet through Celida's brain while she lay helpless on the floor, bleeding and concussed and immobile, praying for the backup that had arrived too late.

Pushing those thoughts aside, she booted up her computer and entered in the last of the information into the case file, officially closing her part of it. Even though the case had been in full swing for some time and she'd already given her reports and testimony, she might still be asked to help out or confer on certain aspects of the case. But unless new activity occurred with the Xinxiang terror cell or more members were discovered here in the U.S., she would be moved onto a different case.

She turned when someone knocked on her partly open door. Her boss, Special Agent in Charge Greg Travers, stood in the doorway, his six-foot and muscular frame filling the space. A handsome and well-built man in his mid-forties with a healthy dose of gray sprinkled in his chocolate brown hair and dressed in his standard uniform of slacks and a button down, he gave her a smile. "Welcome back."

"Thanks. Good to be here." She'd seen him a handful of times since the attack, had spoken to him plenty over the phone early on but it felt good to be back here in an official capacity again. All that time off had driven her nuts and given her way too much time alone in her head. The concussion and other injuries had healed up within the first few weeks. After that she'd been forced to stay sidelined at the recommendation of the agency shrink she'd been assigned to. Thankfully her appointments with him were few and far between now.

Without waiting for an invitation Travers came in and shut the door behind him. He took a seat in the chair opposite her desk, leaned back and put his hands behind his head, apparently getting comfy because he intended to stay for a while. "You get the flowers I sent last week?"

She smiled. "I got them. Thanks." He'd been a regular visitor for those first few days after the attack when she'd still been in the hospital, had called to check up on her every so often after that to make sure she was doing okay.

His sharp, pale blue eyes studied her. "How's your head?"

Travers walked the fine line between blunt and tactless, and she wasn't sure which side the question landed on. If he meant her mental state, she wasn't telling him shit. The agency shrink and medical personnel had cleared her mentally and physically for duty, and all anyone needed to know was that she was ready to get back to work.

No one but her needed to know the intimate details of the lingering effects the attack had wrought.

She gave a decisive nod. "Good. Barely get headaches anymore." Night terrors, insomnia and depression? Yep. Self doubt? Oh yeah. Physically, however, she was good to go.

"I talked to Rachel Granger the other day. She said you met her and Evers for dinner last week." Jake Evers, another member of the HRT and Tuck's former roommate, also known as "farmboy". Tuck had given him the nickname because of his Iowa roots. He and Rachel had been college friends, and when she'd realized she might be in danger she'd contacted Evers. They'd been together ever since and now shared a luxury condo in D.C.

"Yeah, it was good to catch up with them." They'd talked a bit about Tuck during dinner and they'd both seemed surprised that he hadn't been in contact with her much lately. "So, what do you have for me to work on?"

Travers's mouth twitched in amusement, the corners of his dark eyes crinkling. "Ready to dive back in, are you?"

"Damn straight. Got anything substantial for me?" She wanted to sink her teeth into something meaty, something with plenty of investigative work to do.

"Just so happens I do." He removed his hands from behind his head and leaned forward, bracing his elbows on his knees. "Got a suspect in custody who's linked to the Xinxiang cell. He's being held down at Quantico. So are the two assholes who attacked you."

He measured her with his stare and she didn't outwardly react to his words. Inside, anger and determination boiled in her gut. Every day she'd waited to hear that they'd finally been captured. Now they had been. "We've got some new intel that should help us round up more sleeper cell members here in the D.C. area. You wanna sit in on the interrogation?"

Celida kept her expression impassive even as her heart rate punched upward and her fingers clenched in her lap. She'd thought about how she would react to seeing them in person. The natural reaction of fear was there, yes, but so was the need for justice. They'd nearly killed her. Had kidnapped Rachel and would have killed her and her brother had the agency not gotten a break in the case and the Hostage Rescue Team not gone in to extract them both.

There was only one answer she could give him. "Hell yeah."

He nodded once in satisfaction, the side of his mouth curving up. "Figured you would. First meeting's in just over an hour. Wanna drive down with me?"

Well she didn't have anything else to do here. "Sure, but I'll take my own car. Have to pick up a friend at the airport at five." She stood, picked up her purse and briefcase and rounded the desk. "How long have they been in custody?"

Travers waited for her by the door. "Since last night."

She cut him a sharp glance. "Was it us, or the cops?"

"Us. We got a good tip. HRT went in and served the warrants, brought them in. Tuck's team."

Tuck.

A myriad of emotions flitted through her at the mention of her sexy former partner's name. All so complicated she didn't know how to make sense of them anymore. She had no idea what his schedule was these days but he might be on shift right now. Quantico was a big place, but she definitely didn't want to run into him while on base. Not when he posed the biggest threat to the emotional shields she'd managed to erect around herself over the past few weeks.

"I want to see them," she said.

Travers nodded and held open the door for her. "After you."

She followed him during the hour long drive back to Quantico while he filled her in on the investigation over the phone via her car's hands free device. Apparently Xang had given up everything he knew soon after capture and was going to testify against the men who had attacked her and Rachel.

The agency was closing in on other sleeper cell members here in the States, and they had several leads to investigate in China if government officials there cooperated. The Chinese had already executed several raids that had netted them some of the main players in the cell, mostly in Xinxiang and Beijing. Pinning everything on the men bankrolling the cell was proving harder than originally thought.

Fifty-two minutes later they arrived at Marine Corps Base Quantico. Having served in the Corps for five years before entering the FBI, coming back on base always felt a little bit like coming home for her. She parked in front of the detention center and followed Travers inside. Two uniformed Marines escorted them to the interrogation room at the back of the building. More FBI agents stood outside the room, waiting for them.

Travers kept his voice low enough that no one would be able to overhear as they approached. "Ready?" he asked her.

"Yes," she answered, ignoring the heavy thud of her pulse. She needed to see the men again, needed to know they were behind bars and would pay for what they'd done. Closure and all that shit.

When they reached the long, rectangular window set into the wall, she stopped in front of it. Travers nodded at one of the other agents and the man hit a switch that erased the digital frosting on the glass, giving them a clear view of those inside while the prisoners would only see a mirror from their side.

Celida folded her arms across her chest and forced herself to breathe slow and deep when the men came into view. They were seated on the far side of the table in the center of the room with their lawyer, facing the window. Eurasian features. Short, stocky, muscular builds. They wore orange prison jumpsuits and their hands were cuffed in front of them on the table. She knew their ankles would be chained as well.

The sight of them in chains soothed her, but didn't take the vivid memories away. She struggled to keep them at bay as Travers entered the room with an interpreter and took his seat across the table from the two men.

Images flashed through her brain. The bullets tearing through the door. Slicing into her arm and face. Her falling. Blindly returning fire. Screaming at Rachel to hide. The door slamming open, smashing into the side of her head.

She blinked, forced herself to focus on what was being said inside the other room. Travers was talking about the attack. The men confirmed that Xang had recruited them for it by offering extra money. She listened as Travers got the details out of them. It all sounded so remote and clinical. Made it sound as if what they were describing had happened to some random, nameless victims out there.

Not even close. A surge of raw fury shot through her as she listened to the translation of their story.

It happened to me, *assholes*.

When Travers finished questioning them, he exited the room and met her gaze as the door shut behind him. The locking mechanism slipped into place with a solid *thunk*. It took a moment for her to realize her fingers were digging into her upper arms and that she was holding her breath.

"You want a turn?" he asked her, pale eyes steady on hers.

She shook her head. "You were thorough." She didn't want them to see her. Not because she was afraid, but because she didn't think she could control her reaction if one of them did something stupid like smirk at her. Or worse, laugh at the damage they'd done to her face. The scar didn't make her self-conscious per se, but the thought of having those men see it bothered her. She was hanging onto her composure so far but didn't want to push it here in front of her boss and coworkers.

Travers nodded at one of the guards standing by the door. "We're done. Leave them in there until we're out of the building."

Celida knew he'd ordered that for her benefit, and while the thought of him trying to shield her would normally piss her off, this time she appreciated his consideration. She fell in step with him as they headed back down the hallway. "Where to now?" She wanted to be put to work.

He cut her a sideways glance. "Higher-ups want me to review your statements with you. Once we're done you can help me do up some reports and start pulling on some of the threads we've uncovered. We've got files on over a dozen more cell members in the area."

"Sounds good." She just wanted to dive back into her job and have something else to focus on other than worrying she didn't have what it took anymore. She wanted to do something meaningful again, something that mattered. These past few weeks awaiting clearance from the doctors for her post-concussion syndrome had been the longest of her life.

"Can you work late tonight?" he asked as they reached the elevators.

"No, the friend I'm picking up is staying with me, so I can't just ditch her."

"Zoe? Tuck's cousin?"

She wasn't surprised he'd guess that. It was no secret how close she and Zoe were, least of all to Tuck. Fate continually brought him in and out of her life. "Yeah."

Celida had first met Zoe through Tuck back when they'd been partnered together right after graduating from the Academy. She and Zoe had stayed close ever since, even though she and Tuck hadn't kept in contact much.

She wished it were different, but in truth his mixed signals drove her freaking crazy. She knew he was as attracted to her as she was to him, yet he wouldn't go there. Not even once they'd stopped working together and he'd moved on to HRT, removing the professional reasons for him keeping his distance.

She never knew how he'd be when they saw each other. He'd flirt with her one minute and be remote the next. It drove her insane, so she'd stopped tormenting herself and limited her contact with him for the past year. She was sick of being in limbo with him.

"He was pretty torn up about what happened to you, you know," Travers said.

She nodded, surprised he'd say that to her, or why he'd even care. She *did* know Tuck cared, however. It was his refusal to move beyond friendship that baffled her.

Whatever had happened in the hours after the attack was fuzzy for her, but she distinctly remembered Tuck being there with her in the hotel room at some point, his ruggedly handsome face leaning over her when she'd been on the stretcher, the deep blond waves gleaming in the artificial light overhead. His chocolate-brown eyes had assessed the damage to her face as he spoke to her in his deep Alabama drawl, those powerfully defined arms braced on either side of her.

They worked you over pretty good, huh, sunshine?

Coupled with the obvious concern on his face, that endearment, something she'd only ever heard him use with her and not very often, had nearly made her burst into tears. She didn't remember much after that except waking up in the hospital later that afternoon, alone. She hadn't remembered seeing Tuck there, although he'd apparently come by to visit her once more before she was discharged. He'd told her she'd been sleeping and he hadn't wanted to wake her.

Celida sighed inwardly. Maybe the truth was he'd been relieved at not having to be alone with her.

Since then he'd called her a couple times but the

conversations were kind of awkward because she didn't know what the hell to say and wasn't going to make herself more emotionally vulnerable to him than she already was. The one time she'd skirted the issue of their relationship status—or lack thereof—he'd said something about things in his life being complicated, but hadn't elaborated. And once he'd found out Zoe was staying with her when she was discharged from the hospital, he'd rarely called, apparently finding it easier or more comfortable to pass messages through his cousin instead.

She'd flat out asked Zoe what was going on in his life that was so damn complicated it prevented him from spending time with her, but her friend had refused to answer, instead saying she would have to ask Tuck herself. Whatever the complication was, she knew it had to be significant. She'd been driving herself nuts ever since, trying to figure out what the hell that cryptic comment meant.

Celida shook her head at herself. The man was former freaking Delta, for Chrissake, as badass as they came. Why the hell wouldn't he just tell her whether he was interested or not, once and for all, and put her out of her misery? He wasn't the type to string a woman along, so she knew he must have his reasons.

"I'll meet you back at the office," Travers said as they headed for the door to the parking lot.

She pushed it open and stepped out into the bright June sunshine with Travers right behind her. They split up, him going to the opposite side from where she was parked. Her vehicle was to the left of the main entryway.

She started up the sidewalk, adjusting her grip on her briefcase as she passed the first car parked along the curb—

A loud boom shook the air. A pressure wave slammed into her, the explosion close enough that it felt like someone had kicked her in the chest with an assault boot. Heat blasted her. The air whooshed from her lungs as she fell backward, her left arm and hip taking the brunt of the impact as she hit the sidewalk.

Fighting for breath, heart racing, she rolled onto her stomach to assess the situation. Footsteps pounded on the sidewalk behind her. Hard hands gripped her beneath the armpits and hauled her to her feet, dragged her back to the building entrance. Travers.

"Are you all right?" he demanded.

"Yeah," she mumbled automatically as she scrambled to gain her footing, ears ringing from the concussion.

The uniformed Marines were running toward them, weapons drawn. The front door and windows on the first two floors of the detention center were blown out. Their shoes crunched on the broken glass.

Before they slipped inside the building she dared to look back to see what the hell was going on. What she saw made her stomach clench.

A tall plume of black smoke boiled up from the end of the row of parked cars, like a mini mushroom cloud. Beneath it, her vehicle and dozens more near it were blackened hunks of twisted metal, completely engulfed in flames.

Chapter Two

Tuck hopped out of his truck and slammed the door behind him. Heart hammering, he headed over to where the MPs had set up the secure perimeter around Quantico's detention center. The passenger door slammed shut a second later, followed by quick, hard footfalls that told him Bauer was right behind him.

A small group of their other teammates were waiting by the line of police tape set up in the middle of the parking lot, keeping everyone out of the area. Tuck got his first real view of the damage as he passed by the end of a fire truck and saw the blackened, twisted remains of the vehicles littering the front of the lot, and the shattered glass in the lower stories of the building.

The EOD guys were still in their ballistic suits but they were gathered around their command truck, so they must have already deemed the area clear of further devices. Emergency crews were still on scene putting out the last of the fires from the explosion and treating the walking wounded who hadn't already been transported to the hospital.

His buddy and former roommate, Evers, saw him coming and called out as he approached. "I just talked to Travers," he said without preamble, pushing his shades up to rest in his short, dark hair. "She's okay."

Tuck expelled a breath and slowed, practically sagged in relief. He didn't have to ask who Evers meant and was grateful that his buddy had checked for him.

He ran a hand over his face as he halted beside the others. Bauer stopped next to him, grimly silent as he towered over everyone else with his jacked, six-foot-four frame and surveyed the damage. Tuck was just a shade under six feet and broad through the chest and shoulders, but whenever he stood next to Bauer he felt small.

"God," Tuck muttered. Looked like something you'd see in Baghdad or Kabul, not here in Quantico. He was so done with scary shit happening to Celida.

Evers clapped him once on the back. "Yeah. Blast wave knocked her down, but the EMTs checked her out and she's fine." He glanced from him to Bauer and back, his deep brown eyes holding a trace of amusement. "You guys made good time getting here."

Tuck nodded. "Thanks, farmboy."

"Hey, just trying to pay off some of my tab," Evers teased, referring to the imaginary debt they joked about that he'd accumulated from Tuck doing him a series of favors over the past few months.

"Well you can consider it paid in full now," Tuck said.

When Evers had called him with the news of the bombing and that Celida had been there, Tuck's heart had nearly stopped. He'd called Celida repeatedly but she hadn't answered any of them or his texts. He'd yelled at Bauer to get his ass out of bed and meet him in the truck, assuming they'd likely be called in on standby with the rest of the team because the attack happened on base.

Then he'd broken no less than a dozen traffic laws getting here as fast as he could. "Where is she?"

"Giving a report. Travers said she'll be in there for the next hour at least." Evers nodded at the building.

Tuck surveyed the scene again, watching the fire crews. The fires appeared to be out now, so they were busy cleaning up the area. Damage was pretty damn extensive. It was too early to tell what kind of explosive had been used, but he guessed it was plastic explosives. And if it was only one bomb, it had been big. How the hell had someone managed to plant a bomb that size here on base in broad daylight without anyone noticing?

Fucking ballsy, whoever it was. "Any idea who did it?"

"No, not yet."

He put his hands on his hips and studied the blast radius. It chilled him to know Celida's car was one of those twisted hunks of metal. If she'd been any closer to it when the bomb went off, she'd likely be dead. He couldn't even fucking stomach the thought of losing her.

The bombing was his second hard kick in the ass where she was concerned. If he could go back and do things differently between them these past few weeks, he would.

"Think it's the Uyghur cell?" he asked to no one in particular.

"Could be," Schroder, the team's medic and former PJ said, removing his ball cap to run a hand through his short auburn hair before tugging it back on. "I heard the two assholes who shot Celida were inside at the time. Apparently Travers had just finished questioning them a few minutes before the bomb went off."

Tuck wouldn't put it past the bastards. With the amount of pressure the U.S. intelligence community was putting on the cell, it stood to reason they'd be getting desperate to act before the entire cell was brought down.

And they'd already proven their penchant for using explosives, as evidenced in the twin hotel attacks two months ago.

The same day Celida had been shot and Tuck and his guys had been called in to the primary target, revealed only after Evers and the other team had gone in to rescue Rachel Granger and her brother from another explosives-wired building. Now his buddy and Schroder were back on Tuck's squad. Evers and Rachel were now living together and Tuck had never seen him happier.

Seeing Evers and Rachel together was yet another smack upside the head that said he'd better make a move and find out where he stood with Celida. Soon.

At movement in his peripheral vision he turned to see his direct boss, Agent Matt DeLuca, former member and now commanding officer of the FBI's Hostage Rescue Team striding toward them from the detention facility, his thinning brown hair covered by a Chargers ball cap. A former FORECON Marine, he kept in good shape and his bright green gaze was laser sharp. "You hear anything new?" Tuck asked him when he was close enough.

"Nothing yet. You find out about Celida yet?"

He nodded. The guys all knew he and Celida had been partners fresh out of the Academy and worked together for the two years he'd been required to serve before applying to the HRT. A couple of them even knew he was hung up on her. Namely Evers and Bauer.

"Evers spoke to Travers, who said she's okay." She had to be shaken up after this incident though. Dammit, this was her first day back on the job after nearly being killed in the line of duty two months ago.

"Good," DeLuca grunted, staring past Tuck's shoulder. His jaw flexed. "Fuckers blew up my new ride."

Tuck darted a glance from him to the smoking

wreckage behind him and back. "Seriously?"

DeLuca nodded. "Just picked her up two days ago, too. Brand new, had a custom paint job and tow package on there and everything." He shook his head as he gazed at the charred remains of his truck.

It was impossible to tell what the true target was yet, but both Celida's and DeLuca's vehicles appeared to be near the epicenter of the blast. "Were you in on the interrogation?"

"No, I was upstairs filling out more damn paperwork about the arrest warrants for the two assholes who got Celida when the bomb went off." He looked at the others standing around, all members of his hand-picked team. "So one of you's gonna have to give me a lift home sometime tonight."

"No problem," Evers replied before Tuck could. "We still on standby?"

"For the time being. Don't think whoever did this has the balls to try more right now, but you never know." He turned to address the rest of the group and clapped his hands once. "All right, nothin' to see here. Everybody back to work."

Bauer looked at Tuck, vivid blue eyes studying him. "I'm heading to base. You heading in, or…?" He raised his dark eyebrows.

Due to their rotating shifts, this was supposed to be a day off for them both, though it didn't surprise him that Bauer was reporting in after this. They might get called out to go hunt the bastards responsible for the bombing.

Tuck shook his head. "I need to see her." He'd put it off far too long already, and he'd almost lost her yet again less than an hour ago. Two scares like that in such a short time span were more than enough to make him take action.

"'Kay. I'll get a ride home with one of the guys

later if I don't see you."

If they didn't get called in for a mission before that, Bauer meant, since their team was part of the HRT unit currently on the four month long ops cycle. Another unit was on training cycle and the third unit was on support cycle. "Thanks."

Bauer slapped him on the shoulder once. "Tell her I said hey."

"Will do."

"Yeah, give us a shout if you need anything," Evers added before leading DeLuca to his truck.

When his teammates were gone, Tuck stared at the mess before him and took a moment to reflect on his life. The past few months had been tough, but they'd also forced him to take a long, hard look at himself and re-evaluate what his priorities should be.

Due to the nature of his job, his work, his team, had to come first. He'd known that from the outset and made that choice when he'd applied for the team and he'd gone into this knowing full well what kinds of sacrifices would be required of him. As a result, family had to come a close second, something that was especially hard now because his relentless schedule meant he didn't get to spend a lot of time with his dad. With each passing day he was increasingly aware that time was running out.

And Celida... Shit, he just needed to see her and make sure she really was okay. Because he was willing to bet she wasn't, and would rather die than admit it, even to him. Maybe especially to him.

His FBI ID got him through the layers of security posted around the facility and allowed him to gain entrance into the building. An agent posted near the elevators told him where Travers was, and since they'd followed protocol by locking down the elevators, Tuck took the stairs up to the fifth floor. The hallway was swarming with people rushing back and forth carrying files and evidence kits.

He pushed his way through the stream of bodies to the office he'd been told to go to and his heart leapt in reaction when he caught sight of Celida there, her dark head bent as she spoke to Travers and two other men. Her back was to him but he didn't see any bandages on her and she seemed to be alert enough. Thank God.

Travers saw him through the window and Celida turned her head and met his gaze. Tuck saw the flash of surprise and relief that crossed her face when she saw him, but then she offered him a tight smile and dismissed him by turning back to her conversation.

Finally able to take a full breath now that he'd seen for himself that she was okay, Tuck waited outside the room and leaned against the wall. It took over forty-five minutes for her to come out with Travers. Tuck nodded at the other agent in acknowledgement, then focused exclusively on Celida.

She wore a snug pencil skirt that hugged the rounded curves of her hips and a no-nonsense white top that stretched across the generous swell of her breasts. A two inch long pink scar marred her right cheek where one of the bullets had grazed her back in April.

Her lightly bronzed skin seemed unnaturally pale and the shadows beneath her eyes looked like bruises, but that could have been due to the fluorescent lights overhead. He ran his gaze over her as she approached, noting the scrapes and cuts on her arms, hands and bare knees where she must have fallen during the blast.

She and Travers both halted in front of him but he had eyes only for Celida. And now he could tell it wasn't the unforgiving lighting that made her look so stressed. He could clearly see that she was exhausted. She'd just been cleared to return to duty after healing up from the attack, and now this. It pissed him off. She'd had more than her share of shit to deal with already.

"You okay?" he asked, wanting to hear it from her.

"I'm fine," she answered, tucking a stray lock of her dark hair behind her ear in a rare gesture he knew meant she was either nervous or uncomfortable. Shit, he hated to think he made her feel either of those things. "What are you doing here?"

"Evers called me to tell me what happened and said you were here when the bomb went off. You didn't answer my calls so I came down to make sure you were all right."

Her expression softened. "Oh."

Yeah, *oh*, he thought, still holding her gaze.

In those first moments after Evers had informed him about the bombing, he'd flashed right back to when she'd been attacked at the hotel, when he'd seen her lying so pale and still on the stretcher, all bruised and bloody and defenseless. All those things had hit him hard, but it was the last part that had been the toughest to take. She was such a fireball, so fierce and beautiful and strong, seeing her that way had sliced him up inside.

God, he wanted to touch her right now. But he knew if he tried it she'd probably go all stiff or pull away, especially since Travers was standing right there. *Go away, Travers.*

"She's gonna need a lift home," the other agent said, as though reading his mind. "I've gotta stay and work on this, probably right through the night. Can you take her?"

"I can stay for a few hours. And don't talk about me like I'm not even standing here," she said, shooting a glare at Travers.

"You're done for the day," he said, glaring right back at her. "And there's a reason I didn't ask for your opinion just now."

Tuck shifted his gaze to Travers, a little surprised

that the man was giving him the perfect excuse to seize the opportunity he wanted most. Time alone with her. "Yeah, it's no problem. What about her security situation?" If there was any hint that she was a target, he wouldn't take her anywhere without a security detail to back him up.

"Nothing's come in so far about motive or intent, and since she only decided to come down here with me at the last second, I'm confident that she wasn't the intended target."

"And *she* is standing right here and more than capable of answering that herself," Celida pointed out, a warning edge to her tone.

Tuck hid a smile as he turned his attention back to her. God, she was sexy when she got fired up like that. "I know it, sunshine. Sorry."

The endearment just slipped out, but it did the trick because her eyes turned soft for a moment before she caught herself. "Can you drive me to the Baltimore office first then? I have some paperwork there I want to go over at home."

"Sure." Any excuse to spend time alone with her right now, he was taking.

They said goodbye to Travers and Tuck automatically took her by the upper arm to steer her through the crowded hallway. He knew the gesture was possessive and yeah, territorial, but he didn't give a shit. He just needed to touch her.

He kept his grip gentle, mindful of her scrapes and bruises, and was thankful that she didn't try to pull out of his hold. She was so dead set on not needing anyone for anything, and while he liked that independence to a point—because a clingy or needy woman would drive him freaking bananas—sometimes he just wanted her to drop her guard down around him and let him in.

He took them out the back exit rather than the front,

so she wouldn't have to see the carnage all over again. Once was more than enough. "I'm over there," he said, nodding at where he'd parked beyond the security perimeter.

"Thanks for this." She still hadn't pulled her arm free. Taking that as a good sign, he released it and put his hand on her lower back instead. She shot a sideways look at him through her lashes but didn't say anything.

"It's no problem." And Christ, this whole too-polite and awkward thing between them had to stop. For two years they'd worked together, trusting each other with their lives. That bond was still there, but faded now. Even still, he'd trust Celida to have his back in any situation. "Helluva first day back, huh?"

She snorted. "Yeah. Never knew this job would be so exciting."

He glanced down at her face as they neared his truck. "Did you hit your head when you fell?"

"A little, but the EMTs said I'm fine. No concussion this time."

Yeah, but even a moderate bump was cause for concern because of the cumulative effects of post-concussion syndrome. "I've got some ibuprofen in the truck."

"I won't say no to that."

Good. God knew the woman had rarely let him or anyone take care of her even that much during the time he'd known her. He opened the door and boosted her into the front passenger seat, unable to keep from staring at the way her pencil skirt hugged the round curves of her ass and inched up her bronzed thighs to reveal those gorgeous, toned calves. She had the kind of curves that made his palms itch with the need to stroke them.

In his fantasies she'd melt and purr under his touch. The reality was she was just as likely to deck him for trying.

After climbing behind the wheel he reached over to fish the bottle of pain killers out of the glove compartment. He and the guys he worked with were pretty much always working injured to some extent, and some over the counter meds helped make the aches and pains a little more bearable so he always kept them on hand. He handed her three tablets along with a bottle of water he always kept in the cupholder, and started the engine.

"I see you still love your country music," she said in a wry tone as the stereo came on.

One side of his mouth quirked. "Yep. You don't love it yet?"

"Nope. Still a rock or pop kinda gal."

"Well, nobody's perfect."

Her lips curved in response as she stared straight ahead out the windshield.

As he steered them out of the parking lot, he saw her looking at the wreckage behind them in the side mirror. "So, Zoe's coming in tonight?" he asked.

Celida faced forward once more, staring through the windshield a moment before looking over at him. "Yeah, at five. I'm supposed to pick her up. She told me you guys have some sort of plans tomorrow night?"

"Just dinner. You can come too, if you want." He'd like that, spending time with both of them in a relaxed setting, getting to see Celida smile and laugh a bit.

She looked back out the windshield. "Maybe."

Wasn't a flat out no, so that gave him hope that she wasn't averse to spending more time with him. "How long's she in town for this time? She never said."

"Until Sunday." She shot him another glance. "It's not a problem for you that she stays with me while she's here, is it?"

"No, 'course not. I like knowing that you guys are still tight after all this time." They'd hit it off right away the very first time Tuck had introduced them, a couple months after he and Celida had been partnered together.

"She's awesome."

"Yes, she is." A little unorthodox, maybe, but that was one of the things he loved most about his cousin. Zoe was definitely unique.

"Don't know what I'd do without her. She was amazing when I first came home from the hospital. She dropped everything, literally, even took two weeks off work to take care of me."

"And I bet you hated every second of her fussing over you, too," Tuck said dryly.

A half-smile stretched her lips. "Well, I didn't hate *all* of it. Probably a good thing she left when she did, otherwise I could've gotten way too used to it."

That surprised him. "Really?" He glanced over at her, wishing again that he'd told his cousin to take her earlier advice and shove it where the sun don't shine, and insist on taking care of Celida himself after she was discharged from the hospital. Ever practical and the living embodiment of a steel magnolia, Zoe had pointed out how fucking dumb that plan was because of how thin he was spread already.

His work and training schedule weren't exactly conducive to playing nurse, and he'd seen the painful reality of that firsthand over the past few months. Plus Celida would have freaked if he'd suddenly gone all protective caretaker with her, even if he'd done it because he cared. So he'd done the best he could with phone calls and occasionally stopping by over the past few weeks while juggling everything else going on in his life.

That was the thing that bugged him the most about all this. She didn't realize how *much* he cared. She couldn't have, because he'd only just figured it out himself the day she'd nearly been killed in that hotel room. He'd had feelings for her back when they were partners that he'd ruthlessly ignored for professional reasons, but the day of the attack had crystallized everything for him.

After nearly losing her this morning for the second time in two months, he wasn't wasting another day without laying it all on the line. If she flattened him for it, then she flattened him for it. But he didn't think she would. At least, not initially.

He was pretty sure she'd fight the idea of a relationship early on, but he hoped that part wouldn't last long. God knew he'd waited long enough for her already.

At the Baltimore office he escorted her inside, again with a supporting hand on the small of her back, ignoring the pointed I'm-not-an-invalid looks she gave him. He waited while she gathered what she needed and spoke to her worried coworkers who came to see her, assuring them that she was fine. From there it was less than a fifteen minute drive to her townhouse complex, tucked into a quiet residential neighborhood on the south side of the city.

"By the way, how's your dad doing?" she asked as he turned into the complex's lot.

The question caught him so off guard that his hands tightened on the wheel. He considered his response for a moment and avoided looking at her as he answered. "Not good."

A surprised silence filled the cab. "Why, what's wrong?" He could feel her stare as she watched him, caught her frown out of the corner of his eye.

"It's a long story," he said evasively as he parked out front of her unit. Toddlers and preschool-aged kids were running around on bikes and scooters on the paved roads in between the townhouse buildings.

"Tuck, seriously. What's wrong?"

The true concern in her voice made him look over at her. For some reason, the way she was gazing at him right then made his chest ache. This soft, caring side of her had always tied him in knots. The truth was he missed her, so fucking much. And shit, his throat felt all thick as he tried to force the words out. There was so much he had to tell her.

"Ask me in and I'll tell you."

She studied him for a second with a worried expression, then nodded. "Yeah, of course, come in."

Tuck got out and followed her to the front door, mentally gearing up for what was coming. Because he was about to make himself more vulnerable to her than he had to any other living being on earth—even the well-armed insurgents he'd spent most of his career in SF and Delta chasing.

He just hoped to hell she wouldn't make him regret it.

****

Ken Spivey tugged the brim of his ball cap lower on his forehead and drove at a steady pace north toward Baltimore through the mid-morning traffic. When the local news radio station interrupted their broadcast for breaking news, he turned up the volume.

"Authorities at Marine Corps Base Quantico in Virginia are confirming that a large blast rocked the detention center there less than an hour ago. Preliminary reports are saying that at least two people were injured in the explosion, one critically. Both were immediately transported to the hospital and authorities are working to secure the base and ascertain whether the threat of more attacks is still ongoing. No one has yet claimed responsibility for the attack and as of now the motive behind it is unclear. For live coverage we now go to

Peter Rivoli, who is standing by at Quantico."

Ken turned the volume back down and tuned the reporter out as the man detailed the scene for the listeners. No, the authorities wouldn't know who'd done it or why yet. And they wouldn't. Not until he sent them the ninety-two page manifesto he'd prepared.

Two casualties, the woman had said. He hadn't intended to kill anyone in this attack but if someone died because of his actions, then so be it. They would only be the first of many more casualties.

He drove west of the city to a poorer section of town and to the rundown neighborhood he'd visited earlier. In the parking area for a housing project he parked the car in the spot he'd taken it from this morning. The vehicle was nondescript enough to escape notice and it belonged to a single mother who worked the night shift as a janitor at a local high school.

He'd chosen her specifically because after watching her for the past week he'd been able to track her routine with ease. She rolled in at a little after seven each morning and whoever took care of the daughter overnight arrived with the child at seven-thirty sharp.

In the whole time Ken had been watching the family, the mother had never once emerged from her apartment earlier than three o'clock in the afternoon. He'd already filled the car with enough gas to replace what he'd used, and when she climbed into her car to go pick up her daughter later, she'd have no clue that he'd ever stolen it.

After peeling the military ID sticker that had granted him access to the base from the inside of the windshield and giving everything a wipe with a microfiber cloth dipped in rubbing alcohol, he got out and removed his latex gloves, carefully disposing of them in a Dumpster at the end of the lot.

Nobody looked twice at him. And they wouldn't;

not in this neighborhood where everyone was too busy going about their daily lives just trying to scrape out a living. He'd worked neighborhoods just like this plenty of times back when he'd been a member of the force, and society in places like this hadn't changed in the years since. In fact, he'd say the situation was worse than ever. More poverty, more drugs, more weapons. A very dangerous combination not only for the residents who lived here, but for the country in general.

The crimes in places like this hadn't changed, but he had. If anyone here somehow noticed him from his job as a local janitor they'd never recognize him. Even someone from back home would have trouble recognizing him now. He was a mere shadow of the man he'd once been.

He kept his stride unhurried as he walked down the cracked sidewalk past the dilapidated playground where the children played and the teenagers hung out along with the drug dealers and the pimps. A one-stop-shop for anyone who wanted to buy some entertainment or a distraction for the afternoon.

The happy shriek of the little ones playing on the rusted swing set didn't even touch him anymore. Another symptom that showed just how far the decay had spread inside him. They'd told him the worst of the grief would fade with time, but it hadn't. It was always there, every bit as intense as it had ever been. He was just too dead inside to feel it the way he once had.

He crossed the street and headed for the busy intersection two blocks down, then flagged down a cab and got in. After directing the driver to take him back into Baltimore, he leaned his head back against the seat and watched the world pass by, thinking of what he had to do next.

Most people would call him a monster for what he had planned, but he'd stopped caring what people thought of him long ago. And they could go fuck themselves, because none of them had a clue what it was like to breathe in needles of broken glass every minute of every day for the past four years.

But none of that mattered now. He'd waited so long, planned this carefully. In a few days his suffering would all be over. He'd be dead, finally at peace or at least beyond the ability to feel pain anymore.

And better yet, those who were left behind would finally understand his pain firsthand.

Chapter Three

"You want anything to drink?" Celida asked Tuck as she set her work files on her kitchen table.

"No, but I feel like I should be asking you that. You've had a rough morning," he finished, that sexy Alabama drawl of his like a caress to her senses.

She looked at him over her shoulder. God, the man was hot. And built. The finely honed muscles in his chest, upper arms and shoulders stretched the soft fabric of his T-shirt in a most distracting way. Having just under six feet of gorgeous, powerful male in the middle of her tiny galley-style kitchen went a long way toward taking her mind off the bombing. It felt nice to know he cared but if he went all gentle caretaker on her right now she was done for.

"I told you, I'm fine." Shaken maybe, but unhurt. Though she was sure today's events would give more fuel to the insomnia train she'd been riding for the past few weeks. All part of her brain's attempts to make sense of and deal with the trauma of her attack, the agency shrink had assured her. Her constant fatigue was also partly due to the after-effects of the concussion.

Tuck studied her with those melted-chocolate eyes that missed nothing while she drank her fill of him. It had been too long since she'd been able to admire him up close. He wore his hair longer than the other guys, the dark blond waves framing his masculine features and ending just above his collar. He had a few dings here and there on his face, small scars amongst the deep gold stubble on his cheeks and jaw, a slight bump near the bridge of his nose where he'd broken it long ago.

Those imperfections only made him more gorgeous to her.

"Okay," he said.

Okay was right, because she *was* fine, and she was determined to be even better, to return to the person she'd been before the attack. She went to the cupboard next to the sink. "Coffee?"

"If you're having some."

Oh, caffeine was definitely called for right now. She might even be able to get through the afternoon without wanting to collapse on the desk in her home office and sleep the day away. "Go ahead and take a seat on the couch. I'll bring it in when it's ready."

"I'd rather wait in here with you."

She paused in the midst of pulling out a coffee filter. "Suit yourself." Damn she was tired of always having her guard up around him. If he hadn't seemed so upset about whatever was going on with his dad, she would have confronted him about exactly what the status of their relationship was.

She couldn't keep up the "just friends" thing with him, it was too exhausting. She needed to know once and for all where she truly stood with him. If he wanted her, she was more than ready to get it on with him, because sex with him would be both mind-blowing and therapeutic. If he didn't want her, she was prepared to cut him out of her life for the sake of her sanity.

He didn't speak as she finished making the coffee, keeping her back to him while she got everything ready. All the while she was acutely aware of him behind her, though, watching. His stare was like a low-level electric current traveling over her skin, crackling with sexual awareness.

She's always known they'd be good together in bed, right from day one. Make that freaking fantastic, actually. And maybe once they got all that pent up lust out of the way then *maybe* they could truly be *just* friends.

All she knew was, she didn't want to do anything that would jeopardize that friendship. Other than Zoe, he'd been one of the most important people in her life. That's why it had hurt so much when he hadn't made more of an effort to see or talk to her when she'd been laid up.

When the coffee was done she poured two mugs, added cream and sugar to both and handed him one. His long fingers brushed hers and lingered on the transfer, his eyes locked on hers in that intense way that set off a hum of arousal deep in her belly. "Thanks," he murmured, standing so close she could smell the woodsy scent of his soap.

Air. She needed air. "Let's go sit."

She led the way into the living room and chose the far end of the couch. He took the opposite end, his big body curled into the corner of it as he cradled the mug between his large hands. The man had outrageously sexy hands. Clean, hard, powerful. She knew how lethally efficient they could be in the line of duty, how capable they were when he fixed or built something, but she'd also felt how gentle they could be whenever he touched her. What she wouldn't give to feel them gliding over her naked skin.

That line of thought was *so* not helping her feel more relaxed with him sitting four feet away.

She cleared her throat and shifted on the cushion, giving him her full attention. "So, what's happening with your dad?" She asked it gently but he immediately looked away and sighed and she could see how hard it was for him to talk about.

She waited in silence for him to speak, her heart going out to him. Tuck was a soldier through and through, one of the toughest men she'd ever met, and never showed weakness of any kind. The thought of him hurting cut her inside.

"You know he was starting to become kind of forgetful."

Oh, damn. Already afraid she knew where this was going, she nodded.

She'd met Al at least a dozen times while she and Tuck had been partners. The last few times she'd visited him with Tuck almost three years ago now, Al had seemed a little dazed. Slower. Forgetting where he'd put something, or spacing out in the middle of a conversation. At the time she hadn't thought much of it. "He's worse now?"

"Turns out it's not simple dementia, it's Alzheimer's."

Celida hid a wince. "How bad is it?"

He expelled a breath, his gaze fixed on the mug in his hands. "Bad. I had to move him from his assisted living place into a full care home. In his more lucid moments, I think that's the hardest part for him—the times when he realizes what's happening to him. He always told me he'd rather die than wind up in a care home. It hit him hard when he had to start using diapers. Begged me once to take him outside and put a bullet in his head to end it all and save him the humiliation of having people have to change him like a baby."

He paused again, swallowed, and she could see the tension in his shoulder muscles. "His pension and what money I can give to help pay for private care wasn't going to be enough long-term. He needs round the clock care now. I was afraid it would kill him, going into a place like that. On the days when he has some awareness still, I know he fucking hates being there. I held off on pulling the trigger on the care home as long as I could, but…" He shook his head, and she could see the guilt and sadness etched into his face.

Celida drew in a slow breath. The thought of a strong, proud Army veteran like Al winding up in a place like that, totally dependent on strangers for basic necessities like food and personal hygiene, pierced her. And Tuck was right, his father would hate it.

"I'm sorry," she said, meaning it. Tuck and his dad were close. The kind of close father-and-child relationship she'd only ever read about or seen in movies before meeting them and seeing it firsthand. "When did this happen?"

He glanced over at her, his eyes full of torment. "Three months ago. He's gone downhill fast since then. Most of the time when I go in there he doesn't even know who I am anymore."

Oh, God.

His pain made her heart hurt. She eased forward down the length of the couch to wrap her fingers around his hand, tug it free of the mug and squeeze it. "I'm so sorry." It sounded so lame, but it was all she could think of to say, and it was from the heart.

Tuck gave her a stiff smile and nodded, focused back on his coffee. "Thanks." He took a breath, that broad chest lifting and falling, seemed to be gearing up for whatever he was about to say next. "The doctors say he doesn't have much longer. A few weeks, maybe a couple more months. I found out a week before you were injured."

"Oh, no…" Saying she was sorry for the third time seemed excessive, but she was. So damn sorry. He looked so sad she ached to wrap her arms around him. But at least he hadn't pulled his hand free so she rubbed her thumb across the back of his hand in silent sympathy.

"That's why I wasn't around much," he continued. "Work's been pretty great about giving me time off here and there so I can be with him, but I know things are just going to decline pretty sharply from now on. I know I should probably bank the time for later when it's close to the end, but I want to be with him now, before he's too far gone to even talk. His good days are rare, but damn, I don't wanna miss any of them. When the nurses call to say he's having a good one, I try my damndest to get in there."

Celida nodded, not knowing what to say. She'd had no idea things had gotten this bad, and she completely understood why Tuck hadn't been there for her more after the attack. She just wished he would have told her so she could have helped, or at least been there to lend an empathetic ear, but maybe he hadn't been comfortable with it.

And Zoe. She had to know all of this. Why hadn't she told her anything? Celida would have at least reached out to Tuck to see if there was anything she could do to help.

His expression turned wistful, his eyes holding a faraway look as he gazed across the room at the mantel where Celida had a few framed photos displayed. Some of her and her mother, others of her and Zoe. "How old were you when your mom died?"

"Twenty." She'd died in a car accident on an icy January night on the way back from the store to pick up milk for Celida's breakfast, her thoughtfulness ending in tragedy. "You were eight when your mom passed away, right?"

"Yes. I remember her though. I was as close to her as I am to my dad. He never got over her. Still talks about her on his good days."

Celida's gaze strayed to the photos on the mantel. The rest of her place was decorated in neutral tones, splashes of color in the ruby throw tossed across the chaise in the corner and in the artwork on the walls she'd bought during a shopping trip with her mom soon after moving in. "I still miss her."

"You've told me a few times you guys were really close."

She nodded. "Not nearly as close as you and your dad, but yeah, I was closer to her than anyone." More like best friends than mother and daughter, which in hindsight maybe hadn't been the healthiest thing. Still, her mother had loved her, done her best and made many sacrifices to provide Celida with the life she'd never had.

His gaze shifted to hers. "What about your dad? You've told me some stuff but you barely ever talk about him."

There was a reason for that, and a reason why she didn't have any photos of him. She'd always been private about her family life, even with Tuck, and apparently Zoe had never told him anything. That loyalty just made her love her friend even more.

"He wasn't a good man. He's *still* not a good man," she corrected. "I think I told you that he brought my mother to Florida from Cuba, got her pregnant with me and basically treated her like shit until I was nine and he finally took off with one of his girlfriends."

"Yeah, and that makes him a fucking asshole in my book," Tuck muttered, making Celida smile at the fierceness in his tone. "You been in touch with him recently?"

"Nope. Not since he remarried about six years ago now. He'll never change and I finally realized that so I made the decision to cut him out of my life and move on."

"I don't blame you. I feel bad for him in a way though. He missed out on knowing you."

This time she was the one to look away, down at her own mug, fighting the twinge of pain at the thought of losing her father. Shitty as he was, he was still her father. But she knew she was far better off without him and didn't regret her decision. "I'm glad your dad was always there for you. You're both lucky to have that kind of bond. It's special. And rare."

"Yeah, I know it. Every once in a while he'll recognize me. Some days when I go in his eyes are bright and alert and he'll smile when he sees me. That's what I live for right now. For those days when I walk in there and I know he still remembers me," he finished in a husky voice and her heart broke in two.

Fuck her pride, and fuck his too. She put her mug on the table, put his there too, and got on her knees beside him to wind her arms around his wide shoulders. For a moment he stiffened as though she'd taken him off guard, but then he returned the embrace and rested his chin on the top of her shoulder, the stubble of his beard catching in her hair and his warm breath caressing the side of her neck.

Celida closed her eyes, savored the feel of him, all warm, hard muscle against her. "I didn't know," she whispered, squeezing him tight, the soft blond waves of his hair brushing her cheek. "I wish I could have helped."

He squeezed her in response, holding on just as hard for a second before releasing her and sitting back. He cleared his throat, wouldn't look at her as though he was embarrassed. "I haven't told many people. Guess part of me isn't ready to accept this is it."

"I can understand that." But Zoe must know. Why the hell hadn't her friend told her? Celida was going to ask her tonight. "Can I do anything now to help?" She wanted to ease the burden for him, even if it was in a small way.

He gave her a little smile, his chocolate eyes warm with gratitude. "You just did."

Her heart squeezed. Aw, hell, how was she supposed to keep her feelings to herself when he said sweet things like that? She eased back to her place at the opposite end of the couch. "You'll let me know if you need something though?"

The smile disappeared. He nodded, then looked away and surged to his feet, rubbing a hand over his face. "Okay, damn." He put his hands on his hips and faced her, his stare intent, a powerful alpha male on a mission. "Look, I didn't come in here and tell you that to make you feel sorry for me."

She blinked at the curt edge to his tone, but before the surge of temper starting inside her could gather any steam, he continued. "These past few weeks have made things real clear to me. I don't want to have any regrets when I'm on my deathbed, so I wanna spend as much time with my dad as I can before he goes, and you know what my commitment to my team takes. But I can't pretend there's not something else missing."

She stared at him, trying to fill in the blanks.

His gaze bored into hers, focused, intent. "You."

Speechless, her anger evaporating, she could only stare at him while her heart thudded against her ribs. She'd thought she would have to be the one to initiate this conversation, then pry this response out of him. She'd never expected him to say any of this to her voluntarily.

He kept his eyes locked with hers, his resolve clear

in his expression and in his body language. "The day you were wounded it scared the hell out of me that I'd almost lost you. You matter to me. Always have. I want you. To be with you."

Holy hell.

Every nerve ending in her body lit up, a wave of heat flooding her so fast that for a moment it felt like she was drowning. She couldn't believe he'd just admitted all that without being under torture. Though knowing Tuck, his training and experience in the years he'd spent in Delta, even torture wouldn't have made him say it if he didn't want to.

"I want to be with you too," she said softly. So much she could barely breathe right now.

His gaze sharpened, heated. "I mean for more than sex, darlin'."

Oh, man, he'd never called her that before. The way he said it in that deep drawl, the look in his eyes, made her all melty inside.

"How much more?" she managed to get out, loving everything about this conversation but balking at the thought of being locked into something she wasn't ready for.

Being exclusive, she could totally handle, because there was no way she would share him. Ever. But the long-term commitment she sensed he wanted from her still scared her a little, even though he was the best man she'd ever known. The truth was, she wasn't sure if she had it in her to make something last long-term.

His gaze never wavered from hers. "As much as you'll give me."

Her heart did a weird little roll at that simple statement, like it had fainted. Seriously, it was a freaking miracle that she didn't just slide right off the couch into a puddle on the floor in front of him. He wanted everything, but wasn't pushing her for more than she could handle. And damn, if that didn't make her slide a little further into love with him.

"Okay." It came out all breathy and soft, but it was the best she could manage when drawing in oxygen seemed impossible. She was on her feet without realizing it, already reaching for him when he held out a hand to stop her. She froze, looked at him questioningly.

His face was so serious. "All or nothing, Celida. If you want me that's the way it's gonna have to be. I can't do it any other way with you."

She heard the warning note in his voice, knew it likely was because he knew she didn't do long-term, but it barely registered above the territorial vibe he was giving off.

"Okay," she repeated, willing to examine the implications of her decision later if it meant finally feeling that mouth on hers, those hands all over her body. He was standing in front of her telling her he wanted her and there was no way she could say no.

His expression relaxed at her answer, the tension in his shoulders easing. Without a word he took the remaining step to close the distance between them and took her face in his hands. Such a powerful man, yet capable of such gentleness too. The tender, possessive gesture nearly undid her.

She gazed up at him, her heart fluttering wildly as he stared down at her, his gaze so hot on her face it burned. She slid her own hands up the back of his neck to thread into the silky waves of his hair. As though it was the signal he'd been waiting for, Tuck bent his head and kissed her…cheek.

Just as confusion and disappointment registered, he spoke. "I've wanted to kiss this better from the moment I walked into that hotel room and saw you on that stretcher," he murmured, his lips following the scar with tender kisses.

"It doesn't hurt anymore," she whispered back, her heart swelling with emotion. But she'd wanted him to kiss her for too long and she didn't want to wait anymore. Turning her lips toward his, she shivered in relief when he finally covered her mouth with his own.

Heat exploded inside her. Her nipples stiffened, a delicious thrill sending a hot wire of pleasure from her breasts to the pit of her stomach and down between her thighs. She increased her hold on his head and kissed him back, reeling from the intensity of it.

Tuck moved closer, pressing his chest against her breasts, the feel of those rock solid muscles making her light-headed. His body was so hard, the kiss demanding, but his lips and tongue were so soft as they caressed hers.

A delirious moan slipped free as she slid her tongue over his, rubbed against his body in an effort to ease the ache he'd ignited. Tuck made a low sound in the back of his throat in response and removed one hand from her face to wrap his arm around her waist. He hauled her up tight against him and turned them, moved back a few paces to the wall where he pinned her with his weight, the solid length of his erection lodged firmly against her belly and his hard muscles pressed all over her front from chest to hips.

She shuddered in his arms, everything in her turning liquid at the mind-blowing display of hunger from him. They were still clothed but this was almost as good as sex. And it was already so much more intense than she'd ever dreamed it would be.

Hungry for more, Celida slid her calf up the back of his, her range of motion restricted by her snug skirt. Tuck reached down to grab her thigh and pull it upward. She heard a seam rip and didn't care, focused only on the feel of his erection now pressed between her thighs, the slight friction frustrating because of the layers of cloth separating them.

Fists clenched tight in his hair, she kissed him with all the pent-up longing she'd hidden for the past three years and rolled her hips against his. Tuck hummed in approval and kept on kissing her, rubbing that denim-covered ridge right where she needed it.

She tore her mouth free and sucked in a breath, the back of her head hitting the wall with a slight thud as pleasure shot through her. His mouth blazed a scalding path of kisses down her jaw and the side of her neck, one hand buried in her hair and the other squeezing her ass to hold her close. Celida shivered, her moan drowned out by the roar of blood in her ears.

Tuck made a negative sound and raised his head to look at her, face taut with desire, eyes burning. "No sex tonight."

Blinking up at him, she wasn't sure she'd heard him right. Her body was on fire, pulsing with an arousal so strong she was literally trembling, and he wasn't going to put out the flames?

"What?" She couldn't keep the disappointment out of her voice.

A smile tugged at his full mouth, his expression softening. "No. I'm not stupid. I'm not gonna make it easy for you to make this all about sex, and I'm sure as hell not gonna give you what you want right now just so you can walk away after."

That sobered her. "Who said I—"

His lips stroked over the corner of her mouth. "I want you to wait for it, fantasize about it tonight after I'm gone. I'll make it worth the wait."

Something flipped low in her belly at the promise in that low, sexy drawl. But she already had years of fantasies stored up about the man. "Tomorrow then?"

He chuckled at the hopeful note in her question but didn't answer as he leaned in to kiss her again. A ringtone went off.

Tuck growled in protest and made no move to answer it, his tongue sliding wickedly across a sensitive spot on her neck. Her eyes fluttered shut, her body craving an end to this incredible torment, when something buzzed against her inner thigh at the same time that ringtone sounded again.

His phone. They might be calling him in. Maybe something to do with the bombing.

The thought was like a bucket of ice water dumped over her head.

He must have felt how stiff she'd become because he raised his head and looked down at her. His nostrils flared with each unsteady breath, his eyes burning with unfulfilled need. The ringtone seemed overly loud in the sudden silence.

"Go ahead," she whispered, easing her hands from his hair and lowering her leg from where she'd wound it around his.

With a hard sigh Tuck stepped back and dug his phone out. She caught his frown as he checked the call display. He hit dial and put the phone to his ear, his gaze finding hers. God he was sexy like that, his hair mussed from where she'd been gripping it, big body tense with sexual frustration and his eyes ablaze. "What's up?" he said into the phone.

Whatever the answer was, it wasn't good. His face turned blank for an instant, then a hard expression took over. "Okay. I'll be there within the hour." He lowered the phone. "They're calling everybody in," he said to her as he tucked it back into his pocket. "No new threats or anything, just some possible warrants and arrests. Not sure if it has anything to do with this morning."

She nodded, wrapped her arms around herself because she suddenly felt cold and vulnerable without his heat to warm her. "Okay. I've got some work to do and then Zoe—" Shit, she didn't have a vehicle anymore, did she? "Zoe'll have to take a cab over." While she called the insurance company and dealt with that headache.

"What time's she in?"

"Five."

He checked his watch, frowned. "I'll pick her up if I get off in time, or maybe Bauer can swing by to get her if he's off before me. I'll let you know once I get down to base and find out what the story is."

"Thanks." She didn't know what the hell else to say to him. She'd mistakenly thought this lingering awkwardness would vanish once they cleared the hurdle about their relationship. Despite that knee-weakening make-out session, she was still uncertain about where they stood. "Be safe."

"I will." He gave her a lopsided smile, an amused glint in his eyes that told her he'd picked up on her nervousness. Setting his hands on her waist, he tugged her close. "I was going to try to see my dad tonight, but—"

"No, you still should. Like you said, you don't want to regret anything later on. And besides, Zoe will be here, so it's not like we could just pick up where we left off." Even though she desperately wanted to.

He grinned, showing off even white teeth. "I'd kinda love to see her expression if I walked in and started making out with you in front of her."

She huffed out a laugh and slid her arms around his waist, feeling more at ease again. "How about you let me ease her into that idea first?"

"She'll be thrilled."

"I think so too." Lifting a hand, she brushed back a wave of hair that had fallen over his forehead. "So. See you later?"

"Hopefully sooner than later, sunshine. Think about

me tonight," he added in a husky murmur that made her toes curl, made her think of him whispering hot, filthy things in her ear as he plunged in and out of her willing body.

"I will." Not thinking about him, about how it would feel when they finally got naked together, wasn't even an option at this point.

He gave her a slow, lingering kiss before leaving. When he was gone she stood in the middle of her empty living room, simultaneously filled with excitement and dread as his words played in her head.

All or nothing, Celida.

The prospect was terrifying. She'd never given herself like that to any man. And yet she'd dived in headfirst with Tuck anyway. Probably because at the deepest level she knew he was worth the risk. But hell, was she ready for this?

For better or worse, things had just changed between them forever. Only time would tell what the consequences would be.

Chapter Four

Man, Tuck *so* owed him for this.

Special Agent Clay Bauer chose a spot against the wall near where everyone else on the flight from New Orleans was gathering around the luggage carousel and waited there with his arms folded across his chest. Crowds drove him batshit crazy but at least here he had clear lines of vision and with his back to the wall he didn't have to worry about watching his six. His spatial and situational awareness was so deeply ingrained into his psyche that he positioned himself automatically, the product of years spent in the SEAL Teams before he'd joined the FBI and made the HRT.

He scanned the crowd as more and more people came off the bottom of the escalator. His height gave him the advantage of being able to see over most people and the moment he spotted the garish red and black pigtails moving toward the baggage claim, he knew he had his answer to the question he'd asked Tuck earlier, when his buddy had asked him to pick Zoe up.

What color's her hair this time?

She was tall for a woman, around five-ten or so but

even without knowing that she would've stood out in any crowd because of her neon-red streaked hair, the black gothic-style skirt and snug black T-shirt that read Keep Calm and Save Bats. The dark clothing and harsh hair color made her fair skin look even paler, and the heavy eye makeup and glossy red mouth were way over the top.

People stared at her as she sauntered across the floor but she didn't seem to care—probably because she was so used to it by now, and because she was confident enough about herself to not give a shit what others thought about her. And Clay realized he was staring too. At the way her shirt pulled taut over her small but firm breasts, and the snug skirt hugging her full, rounded hips.

She looked around and when she caught sight of him her face broke into a great big smile that suggested she was excited to see him. Why the hell that would be, he didn't know.

She lifted an arm over her head to wave, totally uncaring of the stares she was getting, then rushed over to him. He'd just uncrossed his arms and stepped away from the wall when she reached him and threw her arms around his neck, engulfing him in a floral and musk-scented hug. The perfume was a bit much, but he couldn't complain about the way she felt against him, tall and firm with just the right amount of softness.

"Hey," she squealed, squeezing him tight for a second before easing away to beam up at him, her golden eyes seeming even brighter with all the garish black makeup she'd surrounded them with. The little diamond stud at the side of her nose winked in the light. "Thanks so much for picking me up—it's great to see you." Her south Louisiana drawl was slightly husky, as sultry as the city she lived in.

"You too," he answered automatically, edging back

a step to put some distance between them. Zoe was a hugger. Didn't matter if she'd just met you, she'd still hug you, and hug you hard, like she meant it. Something else he found weird about her. He tried to think of something polite to say. "Your flight good?"

"Yeah, it was great. I sat next to this really interesting guy and we talked nineteenth century romantic poetry the whole time."

God, he'd rather take a turn in the gas chamber without a mask than be subjected to that. "Good. Got any luggage?"

"Just one checked bag," she answered, shifting her carryon bag and drawing his attention to her black-painted fingernails and the black leather satchel covered in white and silver skulls. The skulls weren't so bad. He far preferred those to the weird-ass bat on her shirt. Though its silver wings stretched quite nicely over the center of her chest, emphasizing the curves of her breasts. Breasts he should *not* be noticing, let alone staring at.

"I'll grab it," he said gruffly after tearing his gaze away from those tempting curves. "What's it look like?"

"Smallish black, hard-sided case with a picture of Dracula on it."

Of course it was.

He strode to the carousel, saw her bag as it came around the curve of the conveyor at the far end. He grabbed it and turned to put it on the ground, aware that she was right beside him, still smiling up at him. "I'm parked in the lot across the street," he said, because he didn't know what else to say and didn't want to invite more conversation than necessary. Zoe was a hugger *and* a talker.

Either oblivious to or ignoring his brusqueness, Zoe slipped her arm through his and walked beside him toward the exit. "God I love that y'all have no humidity up here at this time of year," she said as they stepped out into the night air. "I've already got the A/C running full time at home, and by the time noon hits I always need another shower. Not that I mind because I love my showers, especially since I re-did mine. Blood red tiles with a few black roses on them for accents. It looks awesome."

He grunted to show he was listening, but wondered why she was telling him all this, and walked faster. As they crossed the street he could see the back end of his silver truck parked near the elevator. Rush hour was in full swing, so that would add another twenty to thirty minutes to their trip, but he should still be able to get her to Celida's within the hour. His social skills were rusty, be he could be civil that long.

"So," she asked when he stopped to load her bag into the bed of the truck, "how are things with you?"

"Good." He slammed the tailgate shut and went around to open her door for her.

She beamed up at him again. "Who says only southern men have nice manners anymore?"

As a Yankee from Pennsylvania, he didn't know.

She slid into the front seat and her skirt rode up her legs a bit, revealing the black spike heels he'd never noticed before. Those were actually pretty hot, and showed off the muscle definition in her sleek calves. He couldn't see them being very comfortable to travel in, but what did he know?

Behind the wheel he started the truck and pulled out into the flow of traffic, glancing at the clock on the dashboard to start his mental countdown. *T minus sixty minutes, give or take.*

"Is Celida really okay? She and Tuck didn't say what was going on but I heard about the bombing on the news."

"She's fine."

He could feel Zoe staring at him and for some reason it made him want to fidget, which annoyed him. He *never* fidgeted. "I bet she's not fine," Zoe said evenly. "How could she be? This was her first day back and she's still not totally recovered from the concussion."

Clay resisted the urge to rub a hand over the back of his neck. He didn't feel comfortable talking about this, and he didn't consider it any of his business. "She's tough. She'll be all right." She was a former Marine and an FBI agent, so that said plenty, at least in his book.

"And what about Tuck?"

He frowned, never taking his eyes off the road. "What about him?"

She made an exasperated sound. "Hello, you're his roommate, aren't you? How's he doing, really? Is he sleeping?"

"'Course he sleeps." Everyone did.

She rolled her eyes. "I mean, is he doing okay with everything that's going on with his dad? And Celida?"

Clay suppressed a grunt of irritation. How the hell was he supposed to know any of that? Guys didn't talk about that kind of shit. "He seems fine."

Zoe snorted. "God, you guys are brutal. Do you ever talk? I mean about anything besides work?"

He frowned harder. "Yeah, but not about that kind of stuff."

"Of course not." She sighed, shook her head and turned her head to stare out the windshield. "He's got a lot on his shoulders. I wish I could get here more often to help out."

"I help out," he couldn't help saying, unable to hide the defensive note in his voice. He'd picked her up at the airport just now after working all day on his day off, hadn't he? Both he and Evers had asked multiple times if there was anything they could do to help with Al's situation, and every time Tuck had said thanks but no thanks. And Clay did lots of stuff around the house so Tuck wouldn't have to worry about things like the lawn or the gutters or grocery shopping when he wanted to go see his dad.

Jesus, he was the guy's roommate, not his mother.

"I bet he still doesn't take any time for himself," Zoe said.

"We went out dirt biking a few weeks ago." Sure the day had been cut short when farmboy had called them back to the house because of what had happened with his girl Rachel, but whatever, at least they'd still gone.

When Zoe didn't answer he glanced over to find her watching him with an almost pitying expression. He shot her a scowl. Obviously she didn't realize that SEALs didn't deal well with pity.

Gripping the wheel tighter as he merged onto the highway, he forced back his annoyance and reminded himself that this would be over soon. He didn't know why she seemed to irritate him so easily.

Since he'd first met her through Tuck last year he'd seen her maybe a handful of times. She was only a couple years older than him, maybe thirty-three or thirty-four, but she had this way of making him feel dumb and confused all at the same time, and without any effort on her part. Maybe because she had a law degree and knew shit about everything from literature to architecture and wasn't shy about expressing her opinion, which he actually respected a lot.

He flat out didn't understand her though. The woman had a freaking law degree from Tulane and had given up practicing as a lawyer—along with the six-figure-a-year salary it had given her—to write romantic horror full time.

Romantic horror. What the fuck was that even?

How was horror remotely romantic? Granted he'd been out of the whole dating scene for a long time and still hadn't gotten back on that horse even though his goatfuck of a divorce had been finalized ten months ago, but he had no clue how to even relate to someone like Zoe.

The confusion part was compounded when he found himself looking at her without meaning to, or watching her for longer than was considered polite. She'd caught him doing it a few times too, but had never called him on it. Which was good. She wasn't his type, not even close, and checking her out made him feel creepy considering she was like Tuck's little sister rather than his cousin.

"Okay, and what about you?" she asked him now. "How are you doing?"

Huh? "Fine." Was there some deeper meaning she was after that he was missing?

"Yeah? Work's going okay? I know they push you guys really hard. Must be exhausting sometimes. I bet some days you'd love to take off and just lie on a beach someplace."

"No. I love my job."

"I know, but you must still get tired."

He shrugged. They were all tired and usually beat up to some extent, but they'd known what they were signing up for when they first applied. Almost all of them had come from a Spec Ops or at least some sort of military background. The job was demanding and exhausting, but none of them would have had it any other way. Just like with the SEAL Teams it was an honor and a privilege to make, let alone to serve on, the HRT.

A blissful few moments of silence passed before she spoke again.

"Does it hurt?"

He looked over at her. She was studying him with an openly curious expression on her face. He bit back a sigh. "Does what hurt?"

"Having that bug up your ass."

His teeth clacked together as he jerked his head back around to look at the road. He clenched his jaw and squeezed the steering wheel until his knuckles were white, then stole another glance at the clock. *T minus fifty minutes.* He could totally do this.

"Okay, that wasn't very nice of me, especially when you're doing me a favor by picking me up and taking me to Celida's, but you do realize I'm not the enemy, right?"

He didn't answer, mostly because right now he didn't think he could open his mouth and say something nice.

Zoe didn't seem to care. "Look, Tuck told me about your divorce, but I don't think you're aware that I knew your ex."

It surprised him so much that he glanced over at her again. "How?"

She raised her eyebrows. "How do you think?"

Duh, he reminded himself, she'd practiced family law in Shreveport, where his ex-wife was from and where they'd been married. It was also where he'd filed for the divorce.

"Did you work on our case?" His face started to heat at the thought. There was shit in those legal documents that he didn't want anyone to know about other than his superiors, who'd been apprised of everything because they'd had to be. And a good thing, too, since they'd saved his ass by fighting to keep him on the team after he'd been arrested. Without Tuck and DeLuca having his back at the time, his career—his life—would've been over.

"No," she said and he relaxed. Even if they didn't

62

know each other much, he didn't want Zoe to form an opinion of him based on what was in those documents.

Because anyone who read them without knowing him would either judge or be afraid of him. Zoe didn't seem to do either of those things, and he was surprisingly relieved about that.

"She tried to retain me for her legal counsel initially but after meeting with her a few times I refused representation. I knew after two hours that she was manipulative and mentally ill, not to mention a pathological liar."

Holy shit.

Clay was too stunned by that shockingly accurate summation to reply. Barely anyone had been able to see any of that in Eve—least of all him, until it was too late—not even her own parents. Only his closest friends had believed him, and a few of them only after accidentally witnessing one of her episodes when they'd dropped by for an unannounced visit. He wouldn't soon forget that humiliating experience.

Zoe continued. "I'm sorry you went through all that and I'm sorry for what she did and how she treated you. But you made the right call in getting out and ending the marriage because I honestly don't think she's ever going to change. Narcissists never do. They can't. And that's not your fault. Staying with her would have been like serving a life sentence and you deserve way better."

Wow. The agency had sent him to a therapist for an entire year after he'd separated from his wife and never once had she said anything as remotely comforting as Zoe just had.

"Anyway, I just meant that I hope you know not all women are like that. Truly." And then she shocked the hell out of him by reaching out and rubbing his shoulder with a gentle hand, as though to soothe him. Her touch sent unwanted sparks of heat along his skin.

He inclined his head, trying to ignore the feel of her hand on him but it was damn distracting. "I do know that. But thanks." Though yeah, it was a struggle sometimes to shake himself out of his cynical mindset now, especially when it came to women. And he knew there was still no excuse for what he'd done to land him in jail. Even though his record had been cleared of all charges, that incident was something he still wished he could go back and change.

"You're welcome." She gave him a gentle smile that stirred something inside him he'd thought long dead and kept her hand where it was, cupping it around the ball of his shoulder as though she didn't want to lose that simple connection with him.

He glanced at the clock again.

T minus forty-five minutes.

Clay mentally shook his head at himself. Jesus, he was gonna need an appointment with another therapist at the end of this trip.

****

Celida opened her apartment door and grinned as Zoe threw her arms around her and squeezed. She smiled. Zoe gave the best hugs in the entire universe.

Returning the strong embrace, she looked over her friend's shoulder at Bauer, looming behind her like a gruff grizzly bear with his rich chocolate brown hair in need of a cut and a face full of scruff that hadn't seen a razor in at least a week. His bright blue eyes held a slightly wary look.

"Good to see you, Zozo," she murmured into her friend's hair, currently dyed a shocking combo of fire hydrant red and jet black.

"You too, *bébé*."

God, she'd missed that NOLA accent and the

musky scent of Zoe's perfume.

Zoe released her and stepped back to look at Bauer. "Are you coming in?"

"I gotta head out," he said, and his refusal didn't surprise Celida in the least.

Zoe tilted her head. "Are you sure you don't want at least a beer or something?"

"Nah, I'm good." He looked like he was desperate to escape, which Celida found funny since he was nearly six and a half feet of raw, badass alpha male and apparently couldn't handle the thought of being alone with her and Zoe for twenty minutes.

"When's Tuck off work?" Zoe asked him.

He shrugged his impossibly wide shoulders. "Not sure. Depends."

"And even if they let him go, he was going to try and stop by to see his dad after," Celida answered.

Zoe's head snapped around, her black-ringed golden eyes wide with surprise. "Oh." It was clear she hadn't expected Celida to know about Al's condition. "He told you?"

"Today." Along with a whole lot of other important things Celida was still wrestling with. "You sure about that beer?" she asked Bauer.

"Yeah, but thanks."

"Okay, well, thanks for driving her over."

"No problem." He looked at Zoe, seemed to hesitate for a second before blurting, "See you later," and turning to go.

"Hey, wait." Zoe dropped her bag and turned to him, going up on tiptoe to wrap her arms around his neck and hug him. Bauer's discomfited expression was so priceless Celida had to fight back a laugh, but he patted her back gently with one big palm. "I'll be by your place to visit you guys in a day or two," Zoe added as she stepped back.

Bauer seemed frozen by the announcement for an instant. "Uh, okay. See you."

When he turned to go Zoe picked up her bags and entered the apartment. "He's a hard one to read," she muttered as she shut the door and wheeled her suitcase into the kitchen.

That surprised her. "You think?" Stoic, grim and anti-social. Didn't seem that hard to read to Celida.

"I think his divorce fucked with his head. Well, his ex sure did anyway," she amended.

"He was married?" Celida found that idea both shocking and fascinating. Bauer didn't seem the marriage type at all, let alone the kind of guy a woman would want around long-term.

Zoe waved her words away. "Forget I said anything. Okay, you look good. Are you good?"

"I'm good," she replied with a grin. Just a few scrapes and bruises and a faint ringing in her ears. She loved that Zoe cared so much. Maybe if she kept saying it out loud she'd actually *be* good. "You want coffee?"

"I'd kill for a beer," Zoe said, dropping into a chair at the kitchen table. "So, Tuck told you about his dad, huh?"

"Yep. How come you never told me?"

She sighed. "He asked me not to. Said he didn't want anyone else to know and that you were going through enough of your own shit anyway."

Yeah, that was something Tuck would say. Celida twisted the top off the beer and set the cold bottle down in front of her. "I wish I'd known. I hate that he's been going through all of that without anyone but you to talk to."

Zoe raised a sardonic eyebrow. "Gee, that sounds like someone else I know and love."

Touché. Celida hid a reluctant grin. "Hey, I lean on you, don't I? That's a big step for me."

"You kind of lean. But not really. Which is why I have to keep flying up here to *make* you lean for a couple days every few months. Stubborn girl."

"Well, you know how it is. Some lessons learned the hard way never die."

"True." Zoe took a long swig of her beer, her eyes assessing Celida. "Very interesting, how Tuck spilled his guts to you right after what happened this morning on base. He say anything else?"

Leave it to Zoe to cut to the chase. "He did."

Zoe set her beer down and leaned forward, her expression eager as a puppy's. "And?"

Celida scratched the back of her neck, which suddenly felt hot. "And he... We're kind of in a relationship now. I think."

Her friend's face had lit up initially, but at the last part she frowned. "You *think*? My cousin better be worth more to you than just *thinking* you're in a relationship with him. You're either in or out, and if you're out I'm gonna strangle you."

Jeez, what was with their family and ultimatums about relationship parameters? "I know he is. And yeah, I'm in." That was so frightening to think about.

Zoe raised both eyebrows. "But? I sense a but."

God, she didn't know if she had the energy for this conversation right now. Or ever. "No, just... It's a pretty big shift, going from barely seeing or talking to him to this. Lots to think about."

Zoe narrowed her eyes and took another sip of beer. "You know what'll happen if you hurt him, right?"

Celida snorted, having heard the threat before. "You'll smother me in my sleep, stuff me in your suitcase and take me back to Louisiana by bus where you'll feed my corpse to the gators."

Zoe tipped the neck of the bottle at her. "Exactly."

The thought of even inadvertently hurting Tuck

made her cringe. "God, Zo, I don't ever want to hurt him. I've just…never done this. Ever." And it was fucking scary, to be honest.

Zoe's face softened. "I know, *bébé*. But don't hold back from him just because you're afraid. He's not gonna hurt you or just up and walk out on you, I promise. He's not wired that way. You guys could make each other so happy if you'd only try."

She felt so stupid to be admitting her uncertainty to Zoe, who loved wholeheartedly and without reservation even after going through a bad marriage and less awful divorce. Celida was afraid to open herself up to a man that way—truly open up—even with Tuck, and she had none of Zoe's excuses. Just the loveless and rejection-filled example shown to her by her mother over and over until she'd been old enough to leave home. She could still hear the warning her mother had drilled into her after live-in boyfriend number four had up and left them when Celida was thirteen.

Never give a man your whole heart, Lida. If you give him that then he has all the power and he'll destroy you with it. Mark my words.

Oh, she'd marked them all right. Too well. Pretty pathetic, to still be holding onto that out of distrust, but for whatever reason she'd just never been able to move past it.

"Hello?" Zoe prompted, leaning farther forward. "You're gonna try, right?"

"Yeah," Celida answered. "I'll try." She owed it to herself as much as she owed it to Tuck. It was all still so new, the idea of being in a relationship with him, exhilarating yet scary.

"Anyway, with what happened this morning his work schedule's likely to be all over the place so I don't know when he'll be able to come over next. In the meantime, my boss called and told me I'm officially not allowed to come into work tomorrow." She rolled her eyes in annoyance and Zoe grinned. "So I've decided that tomorrow there's something important I need to do instead, if you're game." For Tuck. Though he'd never know about it. She just needed to do it.

Zoe's grin widened. "Sign me up, baby. Whatever you've got in mind, I'm totally on board."

Chapter Five

———————⟋⟍———————

That now familiar ball of dread settled hard in his stomach like a chunk of concrete as Tuck walked up to the care home's main entrance. The smell of the place hit him, a combination of old people and the remnants from whatever breakfast they'd served to the residents lingering in the stale air.

He nodded to the woman at the reception desk and continued down the hall to the elevator, trying to ignore the way his gut contracted at the sight of the residents positioned against the walls in the hallway.

One man sat slumped in his wheelchair, his frame withered and frail, eyes staring blindly down the hallway as he drooled onto the washcloth a care aid had placed between his chin and shoulder. A succession of strokes had rendered him little more than a vegetable. Barely anyone came to see him, Tuck knew, because he'd asked.

The cruellest and most horrifying part was, the man had once been a renowned neurologist. He'd spent most of his adult life treating stroke victims and now he'd wound up like this.

The way his father would likely wind up over the next few weeks.

Feeling ill at the thought, Tuck tore his gaze away and strode for the elevator, was just steps away when it opened and his cousin walked out of it. "Zoe."

Her head snapped upward, red and black-dyed pigtails swinging slightly, and her face lit up. "Hey, handsome." She reached for him, wound her arms around him and squeezed hard. "Good to see you."

"You too." He eased back to look down at her face. She'd gone a little lighter with the eye makeup today, maybe because she knew his dad preferred her without it. "What are you doing here?"

"Celida wanted to come, so I called and they told me Uncle Al was having a good day. We caught a cab and here we are." Her smile slipped a bit. "You look tired."

"Yeah." He was wiped. Had only gotten home at around four that morning and crashed for three hours before getting a text from the nurse saying what they'd told Zoe. Not wanting to miss out on visiting with his dad, he'd dragged his ass out of bed and driven over right away. "Celida wanted to come here?"

Zoe nodded. "She told me last night. Said she wanted to go see your dad and find out if he remembered her, so she could start coming by from time to time to give him more company. Thought it would be better if I was here with her, just in case."

A strange tightening sensation squeezed his throat. He swallowed. "She said that?"

Zoe gave him a soft smile. "Yeah. Now I love her even more."

He could relate. "She wasn't going to tell me, was she?"

"No," Zoe admitted. "She wanted to do this without

you knowing because she didn't want you to feel like you owed her or anything."

Hell. Tuck looked away, struggling with the knot of emotion lodged in his chest. He'd been handling all this alone up 'til now and having her volunteer to do this was way more than he'd ever expected.

He knew she cared, knew she wanted him but she was so closed off sometimes. Her self-protective instincts were strong, he knew some of it at least was because of her childhood, and it was rare for her to let him see behind the wall she held between herself and the rest of the world. Maybe she hadn't intended for him to know about her coming here, but it was definitely a glimpse behind that wall.

"Well, go on up and see them. I left them reading the paper together. I'm just gonna grab us some coffee and a few snacks then I'll be right up. Want anything?"

"Sure, whatever you guys are having." All the way up to the top floor he couldn't stop thinking about Celida. He rounded the corner and got his first look through the window of the activity room and what he saw made his heart twist.

Celida sat curled up next to his dad on the sofa beneath the window, her head bent close to his as she read something in the newspaper he held. Warm, yellow sunlight bathed them both, making golden highlights gleam in her dark hair. Her voice was muted through the glass but he could see the little smile on his father's face as she read to him.

Tuck paused with his hand on the doorknob, pulling in deep breaths to ease the sharp ache in his chest. When he stepped into the room Celida stopped talking, and she and his father both looked up at him. He caught the flash of surprise on her face before looking at his dad and braced himself.

The bright blue eyes staring back at him were

lively, filled with awareness, and when that familiar smile of welcome spread across his face, Tuck knew his dad recognized him. And Christ, it made him want to wrap his arms around those frail shoulders and cry like a baby out of sheer relief and gratitude.

He blinked away the sudden sting of tears and smiled back. "Hey, Dad."

"Morning, son. This pretty young thing tells me she's a friend of yours."

His father didn't remember her then. Tuck nodded, his gaze shifting to Celida. "Yeah, she is. A good friend."

Celida gave him a small smile, a bit hesitant as if she didn't know what his reaction would be to finding her here, and her lightly bronzed cheeks turned a pretty pink. God, he wanted to kiss her. "We were just catching up on the details of last night's Orioles win," she told him.

"Ah." She was so fucking pretty, and her being here like this out of the goodness of her heart just blew him away. She had so many layers to her. Tuck wanted to uncover the ones he hadn't seen yet.

"Not the same as when they had Cal Ripken," his father said to him with a sigh. "Remember how I took you to the game when he broke the record for most consecutive games played by any player?"

The lump in his throat was so huge he could barely speak. "I remember." Fuck, he was gonna lose it. He stared at his father, wanting to memorize every single second of this, every tiny nuance of his expression and the sound of his voice before it was all taken from him.

His father had been everything to him growing up, parent, mentor, asskicker. Since becoming an adult his father had backed off on the parental role and they'd become best friends. It was natural for a parent to go first, but dammit, not like this, with his mind and spirit and dignity stripped away first.

Tuck crossed to a chair beside his father and lowered his weight into it as Celida picked up reading from where she'd left off. They talked a bit more and a few minutes later Zoe came in with the coffee and pastries. His dad started talking about things Zoe had done as a kid, her pet tarantula Hairy, and made them all laugh. His long-term memory was still mostly intact, when he was able to access it. This was all so surreal, like a happy family gathering.

It was a miracle.

Tuck brought up things about his parents, things about his mom, and though his father's smile grew wistful as he thought about his dearly departed wife, he was a hundred percent present, both in the moment and in the memories. Celida asked him more about his service in the Army and his father's sunken chest seemed to puff out, pride radiating from every pore as he told her about his favorite memories.

Then his gaze shifted to Tuck, and the pride he saw in those eyes, the pride of a father for his son, just about did Tuck in. "Brad's the best son a man could ask for, and a helluva soldier. I couldn't be prouder. He's the best thing that ever happened to me, aside from his mother."

Fuck. A steel band constricted around his chest.

Celida looked over and met Tuck's gaze. Her understanding smile and the sheen of moisture in her eyes was the last straw. He stood, spoke to Zoe. "Will you excuse me for a minute? I need to talk to Celida."

Startled, Celida got up and followed him out of the room. He didn't look at her, didn't dare speak as he headed to the elevator for fear he'd break down. By the time they reached the lobby he was back in control and the cool, fresh air when they stepped outside loosened the bands locked around his chest.

Pulling in a deep breath, he walked to a private little courtyard around the side of the building. There was no one else out here, just the bubble of the fountain in the center and the chirping of birds.

Celida faced him with an almost wary expression on her face, watching him. "Are you mad? I didn't mean to intrude on you or your dad's privacy or anything, I just wanted to—"

"Quiet."

Her mouth snapped shut, eyes widening a fraction at the low command.

Tuck shook his head, at a loss for what to say. The woman had no freaking idea what her gesture meant to him, especially since she'd done it without the expectation of him ever knowing.

Unable to speak, he simply reached for her. He wrapped his arms around her back and pulled her to his chest, buried his face in the warm silk of her hair. "Thank you," he rasped out.

She relaxed at his words and nestled in close, her hands gliding gently up and down his back, over muscles strung so taut he knew they were quivering. "Don't thank me for it. I wanted to come."

Tuck squeezed his eyes shut and held on harder. Thankfully she seemed to guess how close he was to coming unglued and didn't say anything, didn't try to get him to talk. She just stood there pressed tight to him and rested her head on his shoulder, giving him the comfort of her embrace, the healing balm of her understanding and acceptance.

The emotions swirling inside him made it hard to breathe. He'd already been in deep with her but now his heart went into freefall. It should have scared the shit out of him but suddenly he didn't care about any of that. He only cared that this felt right. *They* felt right. And that was all that mattered.

He didn't know how much time passed while they stood holding each other, but it had to have been at least a few minutes before he lifted his head and put a hand on the side of her face to coax her eyes up to his. Her dark gray eyes were so clear and in them he could see a hint of vulnerability.

Cradling her face in his palm he lowered his lips to hers and kissed her tenderly, putting everything he felt into the caress of his lips and tongue. His reward was the little gasp she gave and the way her fingers curled into his shoulders as she pressed closer.

The sound of approaching voices reached him and he drew back, his thumb sweeping back and forth over the rise of her cheekbone. "Thank you," he said again.

Giving him a little smile, she nodded, still holding onto his shoulders. As she searched his face, her smile faded. "You look beat."

So did she, but he knew better than to ask her why she wasn't sleeping. "I am. Long night last night, but he hardly ever has days like this anymore," he said, nodding his chin toward the building. "When they call me to tell me he's having a good day, I show up."

"God I wish I could make this all go away for you," she murmured.

Ah, hell, sunshine, you're killing me. "You did more today than you realize."

She lowered her gaze as though uncomfortable and stepped back. "Will you stay here for a while then?"

"Another hour or so at least. He'll usually get tired pretty fast so when I see that I take him back to his room and sit with him until he falls asleep."

Her eyes met his once more and he caught the flash of pain there. "You don't know how lucky he is to have you."

"Well, I was pretty lucky to have him for a dad, so it's the least I can do." He knew she'd had it rough as a

76

kid, with a mother who wasn't exactly emotionally available a lot of the time. But it had forged her into the strong, determined woman she was today, and that strength was one of the things he loved most about her. "What about you?"

She sighed. "Travers told me I had to take the day off," she said with an annoyed expression that made him grin. "I talked to him this morning about the bombing. He told me there's still no one claiming responsibility and no known motive, let alone what or who the actual target was."

"We saw the security camera footage of the guy last night," he told her and her gaze sharpened with interest. "The car he drove onto base was stolen but he had a military sticker on the windshield and must've produced credible ID. Cops found the car right back where he'd taken it from, a housing project in Baltimore. No prints or anything left behind. Footage shows a guy in a ball cap and hoodie getting out of the car in the parking lot with a backpack in his hand. No clear shots of his face. It doesn't capture him planting the bomb but the EOD and forensics crews said the guy's an expert with explosives. He attached it to the engine block of DeLuca's truck, set the timer and left."

Celida frowned. "Well it wasn't a suicide bombing so we know he either doesn't want to die or he has more attacks planned. But was DeLuca's truck chosen at random?"

"They don't know. They don't know much of anything yet besides this guy being a serious ongoing threat until he's caught."

She exhaled. "Lovely."

He caught one of her hands, wrapped his fingers around it. "What about you?"

She blinked. "What about me?"

He gave her a bland look. "You were hit by a blast

wave yesterday," he reminded her. "How are you?"

"Fine," she answered with a stiff shrug. "Little sore, ears ringing a bit, but no big deal. And I had Zoe there last night."

Tuck immediately filled in what she hadn't said out loud. That Zoe's presence had made her feel better. He planned on being the one giving that comfort from now on, whenever he could. "I'm coming over later."

She ducked her head but he could tell from the little smile around the edges of her lips that she liked the idea. "Okay. We can eat dinner together."

"Sure. I'll call you then pick something up on my way over."

She looked up at him. "I told Zoe about us."

He grinned. "That didn't take long."

"No," she agreed with a smile. "She didn't seem that surprised. Actually, she threatened to kill me and feed me to the gators back home if I ever hurt you."

"She's pretty protective of me," he admitted, amused by the threat. Except yeah, Celida definitely had the power to hurt him.

"Sure, because you so obviously need it. I mean, just look at you. Only five-eleven and full of muscle." She punched him lightly in the shoulder, her fist hitting solid muscle, but a thrill shot through him at the way her gaze swept over the length of his body. He liked that interested, almost possessive light in her eyes. As if she loved knowing that he was hers. Although he doubted she realized just how far that went for him.

"I'll stay with you tonight."

Celida hesitated. "But Zoe's there."

"So?"

She seemed to flounder for a response and he wanted to laugh at the adorable blush that spread up her face. "So that's just way too awkward and weird. I mean, it's not that I don't want you to or anything, but—

"

"Why, are you really loud when you come?"

Her mouth fell open and she stared up at him with those wide, dark eyes as if he couldn't have shocked her more if he'd tried. "What?" she squeaked.

He bit back a smile, lifted a hand to stroke the side of her face. "Just wondering what kinds of sounds you make, that's all. I've been thinking about it a lot lately." Like, twenty times a night when he stroked himself and imagined what she'd feel like wrapped around his cock, what she'd taste like when he went down on her, what she'd sound like when he made her shatter.

She opened her mouth to respond, closed it and tried again, but nothing came out. It was pretty rare to see Agent Morales at a loss for words.

Taking pity on her, he chuckled and captured her lips in another lingering kiss that made her sigh and her lashes flutter. He didn't want Zoe or anyone else to hear what kinds of sounds she'd make for him.

For the first time ever, he couldn't wait until Zoe flew back home. "Guess we better get back inside before they wonder what happened to us," he whispered.

"Yeah," she whispered back, and he could tell she was thinking about what he'd said, about what it would be like when they finally got naked together.

Good, he thought as he led the way back inside. The anticipation would just make reality that much better for them both in the end.

Chapter Six

Alone in the dim hotel room, Ken tuned out the background noise of the cable news program he had on low and concentrated on his laptop screen. He'd been working on this for months and though he'd already revised the manifesto several times, he wanted to be absolutely sure each word was the right word. When the authorities read this he wanted them to know they were dealing with someone well educated and articulate, and very, very intelligent. He wasn't a raving lunatic.

He was far deadlier than that. A man who'd lost everything that mattered to him, and therefore had nothing to lose.

He reviewed the last five pages, played with a few word choices and finally saved and closed the document. After powering down his laptop he began pulling out all the supplies he'd need for tonight's op.

First, as always, he pulled out his wallet and opened it up before setting it on the bed where he could see the pictures that drove him. The smiling face of the most beautiful woman on earth. One shot of her in her wedding gown, glowing with promise and happiness. The other a shot of her with her hand placed protectively over the bump shielding the miracle they'd created together, glowing for an entirely different reason. He could see the difference in her eyes in the two pictures.

The first one brought back happy memories. The second filled him with a deep, unstoppable hatred.

He checked his equipment, measured out the lengths of the fuses and counted out the blasting caps. Once everything was packed away neatly into his backpack he tidied the room and hid everything in case anyone came into the room while he was gone despite the Do Not Disturb sign he'd hung on the knob, and took everything with him that could possibly implicate him in any of this before he was ready for them to find out.

Out in the cool night air he walked to the bus stop on the corner and took the bus to the closest Metro station in the heart of D.C. He rode it to the stop he needed, all the while doing last minute recon. There were too many cameras around here. He had to be careful to avoid those if he could and keep his face averted for the rest.

At his stop he ducked into the bathroom and changed into the uniform he'd packed. His heart rate picked up when he saw the security officers standing by when he emerged but they merely nodded at him in acknowledgement and he took the escalator to street level. From there it was only a short walk to his target.

Slipping into the back entry where he'd disabled the security system earlier, he made his way to the second floor of the government building. At this time of night there was no one else around, making his job easier. He got right to work placing the plastic explosives, adding the fuses and blasting caps. He intentionally used the same materials, configuration and timer that he had the day before at Quantico.

Ken wanted them to know something was coming. The Feds would quickly piece together the significance of this target, but they couldn't predict what he'd do next and he had a completely different setup planned.

Two days. Just two more days until he could put an end to everything and maybe find peace again.

He double checked everything, set the timer and left, careful not to leave prints. As he turned down the hallway to head for the stairs, he heard the faint sound of someone whistling behind him. He stopped, his pulse picking up. The bombs were set to go off in eight minutes. They were small, much smaller than what was coming, but still powerful enough to do significant damage to concrete and glass, let alone human flesh.

Though he'd convinced himself he didn't care about collateral damage, he couldn't make himself leave. Instead he hurried around the corner and saw a janitor mopping the linoleum hallway. A middle-aged man of Asian descent, whistling along to whatever was streaming through his earbuds. He stopped mopping when he saw Ken coming toward him. Pulled the earbuds out and seemed to brace himself, his face tensing.

"Building's closed due to a police investigation," he said to the man. "You need to leave immediately and not come back in until the building is cleared."

The janitor looked at him in surprise, but the police uniform Ken wore gave him all the credibility he needed because the man put his mop back in the bucket and followed Ken to the stairs. When the man was safely outside Ken turned the opposite way and hustled down the sidewalk away from the building, the nearly empty backpack bumping between his shoulder blades.

He stopped to grab something to eat before heading back to another Metro station. He'd go back to the hotel, go over the final plan again. He had only one shot at this.

Stepping off the curb to cross the street at a red light, he didn't even flinch when two loud booms echoed down the street behind him.

****

When the knock came at the door, Celida's heart began to pound. She drew her weapon and aimed it, her shoes silent against the carpet. An attack was coming, she could feel it. She had to protect the woman in the back room.

"Celida, who is it?"

She whirled to face Zoe, standing in the bedroom doorway. "Get in there and lock the door," she hissed in a whisper, waving for Zoe to hurry before she faced the door again. Those fuckers had gotten the drop on her once before, she wasn't letting them do it again.

Her grip was solid around her Glock, right index finger resting on the trigger.

It can't happen twice. Not this time, not when you're ready for them.

Backup was coming, but not in time. She'd kill the men on the other side of that door before they ever breached it.

She eased to the side, immediately feeling better with the wall between her and whoever was out there. All the while her gaze stayed glued to the wooden door. She had to stay away from it or she'd die.

The ball of her left foot had just touched the carpet when the shots rang out. Two rounds plowed through the wall this time. Twin impacts slammed into her chest, knocking her sideways. Pain exploded in a blinding haze as she toppled over, fighting to roll and bring her weapon up. The door. They would come through the door now.

Have to stop them. Zoe needs me.

Unable to move, barely able to breathe as the door flew inward, she struggled to bring her weapon up. Two men burst into the room. She squeezed the trigger, firing again and again until the magazine was empty but none of the shots hit them. She could see their faces now as they sneered down at her and the pool of blood she was lying in. The same men who'd been in that interrogation room at Quantico.

She opened her mouth to scream Zoe's name, needing to warn her, but nothing came out. One of the men raised his foot and struck out, kicking her in the side of the head.

"Celida!"

She jackknifed into a sitting position and glanced wildly around the room, hands blindly searching for the Glock that wasn't there. It took her a moment to realize where she was. In her own bed. She wasn't bleeding, wasn't dying. Her legs were trapped in the tangle of her covers, not paralyzed.

Violent tremors shook her as she focused on Zoe standing in the bedroom doorway. Her friend's face was grim, her eyes wide and a worried frown creased her brow. She stayed where she was, as though afraid to approach or make any sudden moves. "Are you all right?"

Her throat was squeezed off, her lungs desperately trying to drag in air as the adrenaline crashed through her. She nodded, ordered herself to calm down. It wasn't real. She was fine and Zoe was okay.

"You were thrashing around and moaning so I thought you were hurt…"

"No," she managed in a hoarse voice, fighting to get a grip on her out of control nervous system. Dammit, she was so tired of this. Tired of the nightmares, sick of feeling weak and constantly afraid that everyone else now saw her that way.

Zoe was quiet a long moment and Celida finally found her coordination and reached a trembling hand up to shove her hair off of her sweaty face. Her whole body was damp with it, suddenly making her cold. She shivered and pushed the covers off, got up and walked on unsteady legs to the master bathroom where she locked the door and sank down onto the seat of the closed toilet, burying her face in her hands.

God. They were always so real. So vivid. The pain was raw, the iron scent of her own blood still thick in her nostrils. Each time she failed to stop the attack. Each time they shot her even though she had her weapon aimed and ready to fire. Even her subconscious couldn't let her off the guilt hook. Constantly mocking her that she hadn't been fast enough, would never be good enough to stop it.

Her, a decorated former Marine.

Celida wiped a hand over her slick face and stood to reach over and run the water in the tub. When it started steaming she pulled up on the lever to activate the shower, stripped and climbed in, tugging the shower curtain shut behind her. Under the flow of hot water everything muted. The sickly thud of her heart vanished along with the voices in her head that said she was useless. That Rachel Granger had been taken and nearly killed because she'd failed to do her job.

By the time the water began to cool she felt like herself again. She got out, pulled on her robe and blew her hair dry. Emerging from the steamy bathroom, she stopped short when she saw Zoe sitting on the foot of her bed, watching her.

"They're not getting any better," her friend said in a flat tone.

Celida sighed. "It was just one dream. They don't happen all that often anymore."

"Define *all that often*. I've been here two nights and

you've barely slept at all. How long do you think you can function like that?"

No way was Celida touching that one. "Sorry I woke you."

At that Zoe made a disgusted noise in the back of her throat and shot to her feet. Folding her arms, she glared at Celida. "I don't care that you woke me, you stubborn-ass idiot. I care that you're still suffering like this."

"I'm not suffering." She wasn't a fucking *victim*.

Zoe shook her head in annoyance. "Does Tuck know?"

Celida blanched. "No, and if you say anything to him I'll never forgive you."

"Why? Because you're embarrassed?"

Yes. "No."

"Then why? Who else would understand better than him?"

"I don't want him to know, okay?" Jesus, it was humiliating enough that Zoe had seen her this way, let alone the man she'd just entered into a committed romantic relationship with and was rapidly falling in love with. "It's my stuff and I'll deal with it."

"Lida, he needs to know. You can't hide this from him, not when it's buried in you this deep."

Tuck had been over for dinner earlier but then had been called into work about something so she'd been spared the ordeal of having him stay the night and witness this drama. The thought of him seeing her in the throes of a night terror or panic attack made her skin prickle with shame. "No, Zoe." Her voice held a hard edge. "Just no."

Her friend shook her head, her expression one of disappointment, or maybe pity. The pity made it feel like her insides were being raked with thorns. "He'll understand. He'll help."

"He can't help, and even if he could, I wouldn't want him to."

Zoe stared back at her, her face incredulous. "You're ashamed."

"Hell yes, I'm ashamed," she snapped back, angry that they were even having this conversation and scared as hell that Tuck or another of her coworkers would eventually find out. "I screwed up, okay? *I* was the one left to guard Rachel that day. *I* was the one the agency trusted to keep her safe. How do you think it looks to everyone I work with? To Tuck, who's seen more shit than I ever will in this lifetime, let alone more combat, and still manages to function without any noticeable signs of PTSD?" Man, she fucking hated that catch-all term. Made her feel like a statistic.

"Maybe he hasn't been diagnosed with PTSD, but his military service changed him forever. He's not even close to the same happy-go-lucky guy he was before he enlisted. You need to talk to him about this. Let him help."

Celida threw her hands into the air. "What's he supposed to do, huh? Wave a magic wand and cure me?"

Zoe's stare hardened. "I never said you needed curing, Lida."

Whatever. "I got clearance from the agency shrinks, so I'm fine. It's probably just the bombing yesterday and me being back at work."

"You're lying to me. I bet the dreams have been consistent right since the day of the attack."

A few days later, actually, but she wasn't going to admit that to her. "It's just stress," she insisted, her insides quivering at the thought of Tuck and the others finding out. They'd see her as weak, unable to cut it in their world. She'd rather die than prove them right. "Sorry again that I woke you. Go back to bed, I'm fine now."

Without waiting for a response she turned on her heel and marched back into the bathroom to dress. There was no way she would sleep now. She was too wired from the dream and the fight with Zoe. Dressed in jeans and a T-shirt, she came back into the bedroom to find Zoe in the doorway.

"Your phone rang," her friend said in a cool tone, letting her know the fight wasn't forgotten, let alone forgiven as she held out her cell. "Someone left a text asking you to call them ASAP."

Celida walked over and took it from her, her stomach grabbing when she saw Travers's number. It was nearly one in the morning, so it had to be bad. "Hey, it's me. What's up?"

"Need you to meet me in D.C. as soon as you can get there. Another bomb just went off at a government building. All signs point to it being the same guy as yesterday."

Chapter Seven

The two bombs had done a hell of a lot of damage to the second floor, but not enough to take out the support structures and risk a collapse. From the setup and the expertise it would take to do this, let alone without being caught, Celida was ninety-nine percent sure the bomber had meant this as another warning.

Which could mean something even bigger was in the works.

"How many casualties?" Celida asked Travers as they surveyed the damage from inside the building.

"Just four, all passersby on the street when the bombs went off. None of them critical. We're interviewing a janitor who was on shift just prior to the explosions. He says a cop came in and told him to leave minutes before the bombing, but the cops say none of their members were here at that time. Janitor's working with a sketch artist now to see if we can get a decent composite of the guy."

A bomber that had no qualms with planting explosives or impersonating a cop, yet still had enough of a conscience to clear the building before he blew it up. Interesting. "What about CCTV and security footage?" They might be able to get a good enough view of the uniform to give them clues as to where he'd got it from. Could be a useful lead.

"Guy was careful to keep his head down. Can't get a good enough shot of him to be of any help yet."

"Any other attacks that match his M.O. besides this and Quantico?"

"Not that we know of."

This was the second in two days. Chances were good he'd try to strike again in the next day or two. The EOD guys had told them the bomber had used the same kind of device and setup as he had yesterday, but this time he'd set up two bombs. So next time there'd be three? They couldn't rule out the possibility that this guy was using the attacks as a kind of countdown clock.

"We've been lucky so far that he hasn't seemed to be targeting people," she said. "Yesterday and today the wounded were people in the wrong place at the wrong time. If the bomber had wanted to inflict significant collateral damage and casualties, he wouldn't have gone to the trouble of waiting until the parking lot was largely empty of pedestrians, and he wouldn't have made the janitor leave this morning."

"At least this new target makes things look a whole lot clearer," she added when Travers grunted in reply. The offices he'd destroyed were in a federal building, and these offices in particular were where certain reports from FBI investigations were processed. Hitting this one day after the attack at Quantico looked like enough of a pattern to start drawing conclusions from.

Travers's eyes turned glacial, his whole face stiffening. "He's targeting us."

She'd already guessed that, but hearing it confirmed by Travers still sent a chill up her spine. "You got any theories as to why?"

"Not yet, but all the evidence suggests he's a demolitions expert and I'd bet my retirement fund it's not because of stuff he learned on the internet. I want you to start gathering intel from our database. Call anyone you need and get them working on this. We're looking for a white male in his late twenties to early thirties, light brown hair, military or law enforcement background, maybe EOD. The janitor said the suspect left on foot, heading north."

"I'm on it." She turned away, threaded her way through the mass of agents, forensics and EOD teams inside the perimeter the cops had set up. Out in the hallway where it was quieter she went through her contacts list and started calling people she needed to begin working on the case: some to search, some to cross-reference and others to check CCTV footage in the area.

After that she drove to the D.C. office, helped herself to a giant mug of hot coffee, and delegated responsibilities to the agents trickling in. It was nearly three in the morning and within the hour all the domestic terrorism experts they needed would be working on this.

Celida sipped the hot coffee as she strode down a carpeted hallway to where she'd assembled a group of agents to gather intel, grateful for the jolt of caffeine to her tired system. This was gonna be a long few days, hopefully no more, until this asshole was caught, and the succession of sleepless nights was already catching up with her.

In the conference room she briefed everyone on what was happening, then divided the agents into groups to begin the search. She texted Travers to update him and told him she'd alert him once they found anything pertinent.

Though it was early all the news agencies and radio stations had already begun broadcasting about the bombing and a vague description of the suspect, urging everyone to consider him armed and dangerous and not to approach him. No other details of the case were given—yet—though she was sure some "expert" would be on TV before noon, talking about what the link between the targets meant.

Celida seated herself at the head of the table and opened her laptop to begin her own work. Within twenty minutes the first of the tips started coming in. Mostly from concerned members of the public who thought they'd seen him. But one in particular from Denver seemed to stand out from the others, and it was credible enough for her to move it to the top of the list to be checked out.

Her cell phone rang. Pulling it out, her heart did a weird little flutter when she saw Tuck's number on the display. She could feel her cheeks getting hot, which was stupid, because she had nothing to be embarrassed about. No one here knew that she and Tuck were together, and even if they did there was no breach in protocol because they didn't work together. "Hey."

"Hey. You on site?"

"Not anymore, I'm at the D.C. office. You still on shift?"

"Just got called back in, so I'm on my way there now. Since this is partly a business call, what's the latest?"

He had an even higher security clearance than she did so she told him what she knew, what she'd seen on site. Plus they both had encrypted phones so she wasn't worried about leaking classified information. "He's a demolitions expert, likely with military or law enforcement training in that area."

Tuck grunted. "Any theories yet on what his end game is?"

"No, but it looks like it has something to do with

the agency." Which didn't really narrow the field down any. A lot of people had a beef with the FBI, so it didn't make their job any easier to figure out who this guy was and what his agenda was.

He was silent a moment. "You be careful." That deep, concerned voice was so sexy, especially since that concern was meant solely for her, but his words made her snort.

"You're such a hypocrite," she said with a grin. His job was a thousand times more dangerous than hers and he loved it.

"Hey, I'm always careful. And I've got a team full of badasses to back me up."

She looked around the table. "My team's pretty badass too. Besides, I've already had my life-threatening incident recently. It's like being hit by lightning. Chances are it won't happen twice."

A low, rough chuckle answered her, stroking over her skin like a caress. "You're hardcore, Morales."

"Yeah, and you love that about me."

"Sometimes," he admitted, and his enigmatic response gave her pause.

"Only sometimes?"

"Yeah. Let me know when you're heading home."

It was sweet of him to check in on her. As long as it had nothing to do with Zoe saying something to him about what had happened earlier, but she didn't think it did and it was way too early for Zoe to be calling him anyway. "Sure. Text me if you're off before then."

"Okay. Hope you find the bastard, sunshine."

Those two words were so incongruous in the same sentence, it made her smile. "We will. Take care."

"You too. I'll see you later."

The promise in his words sent a pang of yearning through her. Ending the call, she blew out a breath and shoved all thoughts of Tuck aside so she could deal with what mattered most at the moment. There was a terrorist loose in the city. She was going to bring him down before he could strike again.

****

As he headed to his truck in the team parking lot just after one p.m., Tuck's heart sank when he listened to the message from the care home on his cell. His father wasn't doing well at all today and they'd had to restrain him during an outburst of rage.

He deleted the message and put the phone to his ear to call them back just as a text came in. It was Celida, telling him she'd gotten a call about his dad and was at the care home now for a few minutes during a quick lunch break. He'd had the care home add her name to the emergency contact list after she'd volunteered, since his job made it tough to drop everything and run over there if something happened. Celida's schedule was tight too, but a bit more flexible than his and he was grateful for the backup.

Meet you there, he texted back, his heart swelling with emotion. His father was the least violent man he'd ever known, so if the staff had had to restrain him he must have really lost it. Another one of those episodes where the confusion and panic took over and he turned on the staff, roaring at them in his NCO voice, honed to perfection by decades of service to his country. *Who the hell are you? Where is my wife? What have you done with my son?*

When he got like that he literally didn't know where he was, why he was there or even *who* he was. Had to be terrifying.

Tuck ran a hand over his face, the stubble scratching at his callused palm. While he didn't want Celida to see it or have to deal with any of this shit in the middle of a critical investigation, he was so damn grateful for her help. Once again, she'd just stepped up without him even having to ask. Damn he loved that woman.

He drove straight to the home and stopped at the reception desk where a nurse was waiting for him. Celida must have told them he was coming. "Your father's up in his room with a Ms. Morales," the woman informed him with a sympathetic smile.

His stomach muscles grabbed. "Is she safe?" Not that Celida couldn't handle herself, but she didn't know what his father was like in one of his rages and she'd be too worried about not hurting him instead of defending herself.

"Oh, yes. As soon as we got him back to his room he settled down. He's eating lunch right now."

Still worried, Tuck hustled up the stairs because the elevator took too damn long, and jogged down the hall to his father's room. The door was partially open, probably for security reasons. He halted in the doorway. Celida was in a chair next to his father's bed, patiently holding a spoon to his lips. She glanced at him there in the doorway, and the tentative smile she offered made his stomach cramp.

"Al, look who came to see you," she said softly.

His father turned his head to follow her gaze, and the absolute emptiness in his eyes as he stared at him made it feel like a giant hand was crushing his chest cavity.

Tuck stayed in the doorway, unable to move.

Celida glanced from his father to him and back. "This is my friend Brad," she told him, spooning up another bite of soup.

His father said nothing, his expression eerily blank, and docilely opened his mouth for the soup. Celida fed him a few more spoonfuls, paused to wipe at some that had dribbled down to his whiskered chin. "Soup's all done." Her quiet voice was gratingly cheerful in the awful silence.

Tuck forced himself to enter the room. As though drawn by the movement, his father's eyes landed on him once more, without a hint of recognition or even interest. He was merely observing. Existing.

"Did they sedate him?" Tuck asked, his voice sounding rusty.

Her eyes were full of sympathy. "No."

The hand around his lungs squeezed harder, until it hurt to breathe. This wasn't the first time his father hadn't recognized him. It shouldn't hurt this much by now, at least not every time.

But it did.

He cleared his throat and crossed to her. "Thanks for coming. I'll take it from here." He didn't meet her eyes as he switched places with her and picked up a clean spoon to offer his father some applesauce. His dad opened his mouth when the spoon touched his lip, responding by sheer reflex. It reminded Tuck of a baby bird. His throat clenched.

Celida stood close behind him, settled one hand on his shoulder. His muscles bunched beneath it, almost a flinch, but she didn't withdraw. "How's the investigation going?" he asked as he fed his dad another mouthful, hating this goddamn disease and everything it had taken from the man he'd worshipped his entire life.

"Lots of tips coming in. We're following up on a few promising leads right now but we don't have any big breaks yet."

He nodded, tried to keep the conversation going when his mind was in chaos. "Not sure if I'll get called back in later, but I'm gonna stay with him a while. Maybe after that I'll head to your place, hang with Zoe until you get home." She had to get back to the office and who knew when she'd be able to go home.

The hand on his shoulder squeezed, conveying her empathy and support. "Whatever you want. You just let us know what you need."

I need *you*, he wanted to say. He wasn't sure what held the words back. His father was so out of it it's not like they really had an audience. Instead he nodded.

"I'll text you when I'm off." Her hand fell away and her soft footfalls started across the carpet. Then they stopped.

He looked up as she came back to him, met her eyes for a moment before she bent and wrapped her arms around him from behind, squeezed once then kissed the top of his head. "Hang in there," she whispered.

Jaw tight, he nodded, the back of his throat burning when she withdrew. His father continued to stare across the room with that sickeningly blank expression.

As the door shut softly behind her, Tuck had never felt so alone in his life.

Chapter Eight

———————⟲———————

Ken looked up from his laptop when the newscaster said something about a composite sketch. Curious, he set the computer aside and looked at the TV. A sketch popped up on screen as the anchor once again described him as an unknown suspect, a Caucasian male with medium brown hair and short beard, six feet tall with a muscular build. It didn't really look like him but there was enough of a resemblance that he couldn't take the chance of not altering his appearance.

"...officials warn that the suspect may be impersonating a police officer in order to infiltrate his targets..."

There was such bitter irony in that statement that a smirk twisted his lips.

The screen flashed again to the federal building he'd attacked, outlining the damage and that officials didn't yet know why he was carrying out the bombings but that it was almost certain he had either military or law enforcement background.

All well and good, but if everything went as

planned they wouldn't put the breadcrumbs together until he'd released his manifesto. Which was ready.

He closed the document and turned off the laptop, then shut off the TV as well. In the bathroom he opened his shaving kit and set everything on the counter: razor, shaving cream, hair clippers.

As he pulled the last item out, his wedding ring tumbled out of the bag onto the chipped counter next to the sink. He stilled, staring at it, a muscle flexing in his jaw. He never wore it but couldn't bring himself to leave it back home for this, so he'd packed it in his shaving kit.

For just a moment he saw Carla's face; her cap of blonde hair framing her oval face, wide blue eyes smiling up at him. He knew what she'd think of this, knew she wouldn't understand. But she wasn't here and if he ever got to see her again in whatever came after this life, he'd beg for her forgiveness then.

After burying the reminder of his old life at the bottom of the shaving kit, he leaned over the sink, turned on the clippers and gave himself a short skull trim. Then he filled the sink and covered his beard with shaving cream. He waited a minute or two for the cream to soften the whiskers then took a deep breath, released it and raised his gaze to the mirror, studiously ignoring his eyes.

His hands were steady as he scraped the long whiskers off his face, even though seeing that ring had rattled him. It reminded him of all the times she'd watched him quietly as he'd done exactly this in their master bathroom before each shift. She'd have that secret little smile on her face as she watched him shave and get ready for work.

He'd meet her eyes in the mirror and smile at her fascinated expression. *"What?"*

"It's so sexy."

"Me shaving?"

"Yeah." She stood and crossed over to him, pressed her lithe body up against his back as she wound her arms around his waist, added a little rub of her breasts along his spine that made him go hard. *"Think we have time?"*

"Oh yeah," he answered, wiping the last of the shaving cream away so he could turn and reach for her.

And he'd thought they would have time. All the time in the world to repeat countless little moments like that one, tiny pieces of a life together as husband and wife. It had taken him more than a year to convince her to marry him, and another eight months before the wedding itself.

She'd died four days shy of their eighth wedding anniversary.

Sucking in a deep breath and letting it out slowly, he consciously forced the painful memories away and resolutely finished shaving. He set the razor down, rinsed his face clean and wiped it dry with a towel. Steeling himself, he glanced up once more to confront the man in the mirror.

It was a shock to see himself like this again, and though Carla's death had changed him irrevocably forever, he could still see a little of his old self in the reflection staring back at him. And he'd seen that same man again last night, when he'd sent the janitor to safety before the bombs went off. It had been a knee-jerk, instinctive reaction, one so ingrained in him that he hadn't been able to stop it.

But he had to stop it next time. Collateral damage was an unfortunate but necessary part of this operation. And he needed as many civilian lives hanging in the balance as possible to pull it off. Without enough of them, his target would never be called in.

Tearing his gaze away from the mirror, he got busy

cleaning up, making sure to flush the hair clippings that had fallen onto the floor and counter, and left the bathroom. He turned off the light and climbed under the sheet, ready to face one last sleepless night spent wrestling his inner demons.

****

Celida dragged herself out of the car and started up the walkway to the back door of her townhouse. She was so tired she didn't even remember the drive home and her mind was in a kind of fog.

It was after eleven p.m. already, and Travers had sent her home forty-five minutes ago with a brusque, "Get out of here and go home before you drop". She'd left, but only because she was no good to anyone there and Travers had promised to alert her if something more came in.

On the way to the door she glanced across the yard to the visitor parking and spied Tuck's truck there. Smiling, suddenly much more alert, she unlocked the door and stepped inside. The scent of something spicy and delicious welcomed her. Zoe must have cooked, which made her the best house guest of all time.

After putting away her computer, shoes and coat she headed through the foyer and kitchen on her way to the living room. Tuck appeared in the archway that led into the living room, his rugged face breaking into a welcoming smile when he saw her. There were shadows under his eyes and she knew he was probably as tired as she was but he appeared to be every bit as glad to see her as she was to see him.

"Hey," he said. "Long day?"

She nodded, fought a smile, but didn't fight her instinct to go to him. Without pause she closed the distance between them and reached up to wind her arms around his neck. His strong arms wrapped around her and pulled her tight against his hard, warm body.

She closed her eyes and sighed, her heart thumping like a teenager's with a crush, enjoying the feel of him holding her. "How are you holding up?" she asked softly, keeping her voice down so Zoe wouldn't hear.

"Good." He didn't let her go, nuzzled the top of her head as he hugged her.

"Any change with your dad?" She wasn't in any hurry to leave his embrace either.

"No. I stayed with him for about an hour after he finished eating, then he got really tired and fell asleep. I took a walk, came back a bit later but he was still out so I headed here. Zoe made you dinner."

"It smells awesome, Zo," Celida called out.

"Tastes pretty good too," she called back. "Chicken enchiladas."

"I'll grab you a plate," Tuck said to her. "Go sit down and I'll bring it to you."

"I could get used to that," she murmured, rubbing her cheek against the solid slab of one pec.

"Go on," he said, easing back and giving her a little nudge toward the living room. She went, finding Zoe ensconced on one end of the chocolate brown, tufted leather sofa watching a movie.

"Thanks for cooking," Celida said as she sank down beside her. "I'm starved."

"Figured you would be." Zoe lifted an arm in silent command and Celida leaned against her friend's side with a grin. "You look beat, *bébé*."

Celida grunted. "Thanks."

Zoe huffed out a laugh. "Just an observation."

Tuck appeared with a plate of enchiladas and a glass of ice water. Celida thanked him and scooted over to make room for him. He settled his big frame beside her as she dug in and though the meal was flavorful and delicious, she barely tasted it because she was too preoccupied with Tuck's nearness. He smelled of soap and laundry detergent and she could feel his body heat radiating against her side.

"Really great," she muttered to Zoe, suddenly wishing she and Tuck were alone. But it wasn't very polite to ask her house guest to get lost just so she could make out with her new boyfriend. And man, did that word feel so weird when it came to Tuck.

All this time he'd been unattainable, and now he was here, hers—for the moment at least—and she couldn't do any of the dirty, filthy things she'd dreamed about doing to him. Not without making Tuck uncomfortable and sending Zoe into therapy.

"So no new developments, huh?" he asked her.

"Nothing useful yet, no," she answered in between bites.

Everyone was frustrated that no solid leads had come in yet, but she didn't want to think about work anymore. Tuck's nearness was making her nerve endings hypersensitive. Her whole body was alive with tingles and the only thing he was touching her with were his eyes.

What the hell would happen when he put those big hands and his mouth all over her naked skin? She'd probably spontaneously combust from a combination of repressed longing and sexual frustration.

"It's so scary," Zoe muttered. "I feel like there's some mass shooting or terror attack in the States every week now."

Yeah, it seemed like that to her, too. Their department's tempo had definitely increased since she'd started there almost a year and a half ago. "The heat's really on this guy. If he's still in the area—and we're pretty sure he is—we'll get him." She prayed that happened before he was able to unleash whatever attack he had planned next.

Tuck took the empty plate from her and went into the kitchen with it, she presumed to put it in the dishwasher. Sure enough, a few seconds later she heard water running in the sink and then the sound of the dishwasher door opening and closing. She grinned at Zoe. "I feel spoiled."

Zoe laughed. "Feels pretty good, doesn't it?"

"I'm not hating it." She sipped at her water, knowing she was dehydrated, which combined with her fatigue level explained the dull pounding in her skull.

Tuck returned to his seat and this time wrapped an arm around her shoulders. The move had a possessive vibe to it that Celida found she really liked. In the past when guys had gotten possessive with her she'd been quick to put them in their place, but with Tuck it was different. Everything female in her got all soft and melty when he touched her like that, whether it was in front of anyone or not. She liked knowing he thought of her as his.

For now, a little voice reminded her. So far she hadn't been very good at the whole long-term thing. She was taking this one day at a time with Tuck.

"Well," Zoe announced, pushing to her feet. "I'm gonna be on my way now. You guys have a good night."

Celida assumed she meant she was heading to bed, but then she noticed the carryon suitcase set beside the sofa. She blinked at Zoe. "Where are you going?"

"Tuck's place," her friend answered, already wheeling the suitcase toward the back door.

"What? Why?" She scrambled to her feet. Was Zoe that uncomfortable with her and Tuck being together?

Zoe stopped and gave her a knowing smile. "Sweetie, you guys need some time alone together. I honestly don't mind, and this way I get to bug Bauer a bit more, so win-win."

Celida started to go after her but Tuck grabbed her hand to still her. "How are you getting there?" Celida asked.

"Cab, and it should be waiting outside already. Look, don't worry, okay? I'll see you tomorrow." With that she was gone.

Celida sat back on the sofa and looked at Tuck. The sound of the door locking behind Zoe reached her. "Was this her idea, or yours?"

"Hers." He reached one hand out to brush the hair back from her cheek with his fingers, stirring shivers across her skin. His hand was so large, so strong, yet he touched her with a gentleness that bordered on reverence. It made something low in her abdomen do a little flip.

"I feel bad."

"Don't. She's perfectly comfortable at my place, and it's only for a night." Those warm brown eyes ran over her face, assessing her. "You need some peace and quiet anyway, because you're exhausted."

That put a slight damper on her building arousal. "Wow, you and Zoe are both great with the compliments tonight."

He didn't apologize. "You know what I mean. I'm gonna make sure you get a good night's sleep."

"Not tired." Not now, when they were finally alone and had the place to themselves for the whole night. He'd told her he wanted her to think about them getting naked and she'd taken the challenge to heart. She had a whole slew of her favorite fantasies about him to try. Oh, the possibilities…

He grunted, the frustration in his expression taking her by surprise. "Because you're afraid to go to sleep."

She stilled inside as his words registered, all traces of arousal and anticipation evaporating. Suspicion and unease took root in their place. "Who told you that?"

"No one."

Bullshit. "That's why you're staying?"

"Partly," he allowed with a nod.

Celida sat back, pulling away from him as a chill slid through her. "Did someone say something to you?"

"Travers texted me when you were on your way home," he said evenly. "He said you needed to sleep before you crashed."

Well that was insulting. She was more than freaking capable of taking care of herself. "I need babysitting now?"

Tuck's gaze cooled. Hardened. And suddenly he was the experienced operator staring back at her. "If you keep ignoring what's going on, yeah, maybe."

Her stomach seized. "Zoe told you." The betrayal sliced deep. A humiliated flush crept up her face, settled in her cheeks as she stared at him in accusation.

Tuck exhaled and leaned back, never taking his eyes off her. "About the nightmares? Yeah."

Celida glanced toward the door, part of her wanting to storm out there, go after Zoe and tear into her for this. She folded her arms. "What else did she tell you?"

"She's worried about you. And so am I."

Her gaze snapped to his. "I'm fine."

He kept looking at her in that calm, resolute way of his, making the ripples of panic in her gut stronger. "Do you have them when you're awake too?"

She shot off the couch and re-crossed her arms. "I said I'm *fine*."

He wouldn't let it go. "How often?"

Celida forced herself to take a deep breath, knowing that if she got defensive he'd use it to his advantage. "Not often, and I'm handling it, okay? Just leave it alone."

"PTSD isn't something to screw around with or ignore. I've seen way too many guys destroyed that way.

I don't want to see it happen to you too."

God, she *hated* that acronym. She held out a hand in warning, palm out. "Tuck, *leave* it." Before she exploded and took the anger and hurt bubbling inside her out on him. She understood he thought he was trying to help, but all it was doing was making things worse.

He raised a dark golden eyebrow. "Are you still getting help?"

It was humiliating enough that he knew she'd been seeing a therapist after the attack. "I don't need help anymore. It's normal, the agency shrink told me to expect things like this when I came back to work. It'll just take me a while to get back into my routine."

"So this has just started since you went back?"

No. She gave a humorless laugh. "This is so not how I pictured this night going when I saw your truck out front." She'd been looking forward to going to bed all right, with Tuck, and not for sleeping. At least not until they were both sated and too exhausted to move. That definitely wasn't happening now. At the moment she was way more likely to punch him than let him touch her.

A muscle in his jaw flexed. "I'm saying all this because I care."

"And I appreciate that, really, but we need to change the subject now." She kept her voice even, her tone civil despite the way her heart was pounding against her breastbone, but then that muscle in his jaw jumped again, the deep gold stubble catching the light streaming in from the kitchen.

"So that's it?"

Something about his tone set off a warning buzz in the pit of her stomach.

She frowned at him, the headache gathering in power in her temples and the back of her skull as the exhaustion tugged at her, a relentless weight pulling her down. His earlier words hurt because they were true.

She *was* afraid to fall asleep. She was afraid of waking in the middle of another night terror, soaked with sweat and the sheets tangled around her, heart pounding so hard and fast it felt like she was on the verge of a heart attack. And she definitely didn't want him to see any of that.

But that flat tone he'd just used bothered her. "What do you mean?"

He stood up and faced her, hands on hips, his aura of sheer masculine authority seeming to suck all the air out of the room. "You're seriously going to shut me out, even after everything you've seen going on in my life?"

She drew her head back in shock, baffled why he'd think that. "What?"

He shook his head once, his frustration and yes, hurt, showing through that tough exterior. That she might have hurt him pierced her. "I let you in. You've seen me at my worst, at my weakest, in a way no one else has, and you're still going to shut me out?" His voice rang with disbelief. And hurt.

The hurt bothered her, but didn't take the edge off her temper. "I'm not shutting you out!" She didn't even care that she was shouting at him. A mass of emotions roiled inside her: hurt, anxiety, anger, but mostly, fear. Fear that she was losing her grip on her sanity, and that he wouldn't want her anymore if he saw her come unglued. That her career might be affected if word got out that she had to seek treatment just because she couldn't get over the attack. She'd seen guys lose their security clearances over exactly this same issue, both in the military and the FBI.

"I'm not," she insisted when he didn't say anything, trying to make him understand.

"Then fucking talk to me!"

She blinked in shock. He'd never raised his voice at

her before. Not once, not even in the two years when they'd been partnered together. She threw her hands up in frustration a weariness taking over. "What the hell do you want me to say?"

A taut, brittle silence filled the room as he stared at her, and the disappointment she read in his eyes made it feel like someone had punched a hand through her ribs and crushed her heart. "Nothing. Forget it." His voice was cold, clipped, and then he turned on his heel and headed for the door.

She stayed where she was, locked there in indecision, part of her refusing to believe he was actually going to leave. But then the front door opened and shut and she heard his footsteps on the concrete path outside.

Panic flared, hot and acidic. She had a terrible, bone-deep certainty that if she let him walk away now she'd lose him. For good.

Despite all her self-preservation instincts screaming at her to stop, to hold her ground, she couldn't. She ran to the door, flooded with the overwhelming fear that it was already too late. A hot knot of tears lodged hard in her throat. Flinging the door open, she cast a wild glance around outside but didn't see him.

"Tuck!"

No answer. He was already gone.

Pain stabbed through her, stealing her breath. She lunged out the door, left it wide open behind her as she ran up the pathway, her bare feet slapping against the concrete.

Rounding the corner, she jerked to a halt when she saw him paused in the act of climbing into his truck. Her heart seized for a second, then settled slightly.

Tuck looked at her for a long moment, then stepped out of the truck's cab, shut the door and walked back to her. Slowly.

He halted a step or two away, watching her with a

guarded expression that tore her up inside. He was right, she hadn't been fair. He'd let her in, let her see private, emotionally devastating things in his life and in return she'd shut him out. Consciously and unconsciously, but not for the reasons he probably thought. She *did* trust him, did want this to work, but it was so hard to let go of this awful, crawling feeling of vulnerability that scared her so much.

She was a goddamn hypocrite, expecting that of him and not giving it back.

Tuck didn't say anything, simply stared at her as the endless seconds of silence stretched out. Celida swallowed, the lump in her throat so huge she was afraid to open her mouth and say anything because she was terrified a sob would come out instead. But the thought of losing him over this was so completely devastating that her walls crumbled.

Don't leave. She felt her face crumple, felt her mouth and eyes scrunch up as she stared up at him.

His expression instantly softened. He sighed and reached out for her, used both hands to brush the hair back from her forehead in a gesture so tender it broke her heart.

She hitched in an unsteady breath, blinked fast so she could see him through the blur of tears and locked a hand around one of his thick wrists. "I'm not okay," she croaked, something shattering inside her at the admission. "I'm not."

Chapter Nine

The look on her face damn near shredded him. She was totally laid bare before him, more vulnerable than he'd ever seen her, and her choked admission made his heart roll over in his chest.

Tuck sighed, all his anger draining away in the face of her devastation at the thought of him walking away. "C'mere." He tugged her close and wrapped his arms around her tight. She shuddered and burrowed into him, her face pressed hard against his chest as though trying to hide as she gasped in deep, ragged breaths, clearly fighting back sobs.

"I'm not okay," she repeated, her voice shaky, and he heard the edge of her fear there.

"I know you're not right now, baby, but you're gonna be." He knew she'd come out the other side of this stronger than ever, and he'd do whatever he could to help. But she had to be willing to *let* him, or they would never work.

Celida shook in response, the tremors ripping through her and reverberating through his own body. "D-don't go."

Aw, fuck. He'd hurt her by walking out. More than he'd realized or meant to. "Shh, I won't. It's okay." He buried his face in her hair and held her close. Eyes closed, he focused on surrounding as much of her as he could with his body, driven to protect his woman, to comfort her.

He hadn't been bluffing about leaving earlier. He'd had every intention of climbing into his truck and driving back to his place and rethinking this whole thing with Celida in the morning. He knew all about the way she conducted her personal life, and how she liked her flings to be short, and how she liked to be the one to break it off before things got messy emotionally.

Tuck wouldn't allow that. Not with her. It was why he'd never made a move before now.

And there was no way he could be in a relationship where he was emotionally wide open and she wasn't. That's not how it worked. Part of him had known when he'd told her that he wanted all or nothing that she hadn't really believed him, or maybe hadn't understood.

He was going to make that crystal clear tonight.

"Come on, let's go back inside," he murmured against her hair. She took a deep breath, drew back and kept her face averted as he wrapped an arm around her shoulders and walked back up the path to her front door. She'd left it wide open in her haste to get to him.

In the kitchen she moved away from him and rubbed a hand over the nape of her neck, closing her eyes as she rolled her head around.

"Headache?" he asked quietly.

She nodded, still refusing to look at him, and went to the cupboard next to the sink to grab some pain relievers. Tuck filled a glass with water and handed it to her. Her hand was steady as she took the meds but he knew exactly how shaken she was. That uncharacteristic show of emotion from her earlier told him just how much she trusted and wanted him. He was both humbled and relieved by that.

When she set the glass in the sink but still wouldn't look at him, Tuck eased a hand around her nape and squeezed. She winced a bit but stood still and let him knead the tense muscles at the back of her neck. "Wanna go sit down?" he murmured.

Again she shook her head, then turned and leaned into him, her forehead resting in the hollow of his shoulder. She felt so perfect in his embrace, those hourglass curves molding into him. While he massaged her neck with one hand he smoothed the other up and down her spine. It was so rare that she let anyone help her with anything; he was grateful she was letting him.

He didn't know how long they stayed that way, but after a long while she slid her hands up to the back of his neck and trailed her fingers through the back of his hair. She nuzzled his pec, the move making every muscle in his whole body tighten. Her warm breath seeped through the cotton of his shirt as she began pressing a string of kisses along his chest to the base of his throat.

The feel of her parted lips against his skin sent a bolt of heat through him. His blood pumped hard and hot through his veins, making his cock swell. Her fingers clenched in his hair as she skimmed her open mouth up his throat, pausing to nip his earlobe before she drew it between her lips and sucked.

A burst of heat exploded inside him at the unexpected move.

Jesus.

He cupped the back of her head and pulled her tight to him just as she turned her head to drop little biting kisses across his jaw to the corner of his mouth. His hand contracted in her hair, tipping her head back to meet that full, lush mouth. A low moan shivered through her and she opened for him, sliding her tongue along his, the firm press of her breasts against his chest a sweet torture.

But there was something off. He'd always known they'd burn hot and fast together, but he could feel the desperation in her kisses, the frantic energy thrumming through her.

He drew back just far enough to give him room to speak. "I'm not goin' anywhere, darlin'."

She didn't seem to hear the words, or if she did they didn't calm her because she grabbed him and kept on kissing the hell out of him, apparently determined to drive him out of his fucking skull. Both her hands clenched in his hair and she pushed up on tiptoe to explore his mouth with her tongue. Wild, needy kisses, rubbing that delectable body against him.

But the desperation set off a warning buzz at the back of his brain. He didn't want her to worry that he'd stop and walk out, leaving her to deal with this emotional aftermath alone.

Tuck tore his mouth free and held her head steady, resisting when she whined and tried to come back for more so he could look into her eyes. He read the desperation, the plea there, but there were also the things he needed to see. They were dark, glazed with need and a longing he would kill to satisfy.

There was no way in hell he could just put her to bed and hold her like he'd originally intended.

Any reservations he'd had went up in smoke. "Okay," he muttered, decision made. He shocked a gasp out of her by grabbing her by the hips and spinning her around so her back was facing the wall, backing her up against the closest counter.

Holding her there with his pelvis pressed against her, he watched the flare of lust burn hotter as she felt every inch of his erection digging into her abdomen. Before she could drag him down into another kiss he hoisted her up onto the granite countertop, shoved her skirt up her thighs and pushed them apart to make room for his hips. He rolled his hips and kissed her, swallowing her moan at the feel of his covered cock rubbing against her.

Celida twisted in his grip, her hands trailing over his back to grab his T-shirt and start pulling it upward. He moved back just enough to give her room, separating their mouths for the split second it took for him to wrench the thing off and fling it over his shoulder. She murmured in pleasure and stroked her soft hands all over his naked torso, her tongue dancing wickedly in his mouth.

Tuck gripped her left hip to haul her snug against his groin, absorbed the little mewl she made, then reached for the buttons on that clingy silver blouse. She clung to his shoulders and arched her back to hurry him along, pulling the fabric taut as he plucked at the buttons. They fell away one by one, revealing the deep valley of her cleavage displayed by a cream lace bra.

His gaze stuck on her dusky brown nipples displayed through the lace, his hands finally freeing the last button. She shrugged off the shirt and reached back to undo the bra, and he groaned when her breasts spilled free. Full and round, the nipples taut little peaks he couldn't wait to taste.

He cradled the mounds in his hands and lowered his head, placing little nipping kisses down her throat and to her collarbone while he drew his thumbs across her hard nipples. Celida let out a throaty moan and grabbed his head, pushing him down. But he didn't need the encouragement. He had no intention of stopping now, not until he had her panting and begging and then sobbing with release.

Squeezing the soft flesh he'd fantasized about more times than he could remember, he opened his lips and drew one hard center into his mouth. She cried out, her fingers digging hard into his shoulders, her breathing already shallow and unsteady as she rocked her center against his cock. He licked and sucked one peak before switching to the other, one hand splayed across the center of her back to hold her. She tasted so good and smelled even better, all warm fragrant skin and aroused woman.

When she was twisting and panting he released her long enough to reach down and yank her skirt up higher, to the tops of her thighs, revealing the lace bands of her thigh-high stockings and the lacy cream thong covering her sex. His gaze stuck there as he trailed his fingertips over the tops of those sexy as hell stockings, making her shiver and squirm. Fucking hell, the woman was the most erotic sight he'd ever seen in his life.

Impatient, she raised her hips when he hooked his fingers in the waistband of her thong and began to draw it down. He couldn't hold back a groan when the fabric lowered enough for him to see the flushed, glistening folds exposed to his gaze.

In one rough sweep he pulled her panties down and off, and looked up to savor the view. Her cheeks were flushed, lips swollen from his kisses, eyes molten with desire, blouse wide open to expose the naked glory of her breasts, the nipples still damp from his mouth. And below, the skirt hiked up to expose her pussy, long legs wrapped in those stockings.

With a dark, hungry sound that came from his gut, he grabbed hold of her hips and dragged her a few more inches toward him, then placed one hand on her sternum and pushed. "Lie back for me." His voice was deep, guttural, the command clear.

Celida licked her lips and eased back onto her elbows until her head met the tiled backsplash, eyes glowing with arousal, those amazing breasts heaving with each shallow breath. Then she drew her legs up to wind around his ribs and parted her thighs more, offering him everything.

Tuck groaned and gripped her hips hard as he leaned down to lay a line of teasing kisses across the top of the tiny, neat triangle of dark hair between her thighs. The muscles there trembled, her legs squeezing around him, one of her hands easing into his hair in a clear demand. He obliged, closing his eyes to better savor the moment as he opened his mouth and kissed her open sex.

Her high, tight cry echoed around the kitchen. Her legs jerked and the pressure of her hand in his hair increased.

"Easy," he murmured against her aroused flesh. He trailed his tongue over her damp center, enjoying her desperation and the tangy-sweet flavor of her arousal, then delved inside her to stroke the hot, needy spot within.

She mewled and pressed against his mouth, clearly wanting more. Tuck raised his eyes to look up the length of her body and met her smoldering gaze.

Slowly, so slowly it killed him, he licked softly from her opening, up the flushed folds to the swollen nub at the top of her sex. He flattened his tongue against her and circled it, flicked gently, watching her gaze grow hazy and heavy-lidded with passion. The muscles in her thighs and belly began to quiver the more he teased her, her breaths coming in short little pants.

Gauging her reaction, he closed his lips around her clit and sucked.

"*Brad.*"

Everything inside him lit up at the sound of his name. Oh, fuck. She'd never called him by his first name, not once since they'd first been introduced. Hearing it now from her lips in that breathy, needy voice almost made him come in his jeans.

With a low growl of approval, he released one of her hips to bring his hand between her legs and ease a finger into her. Her head fell back on a soft cry, her mouth parting, eyes squeezing shut. Still sucking her clit, rubbing his tongue against it, he added a second finger and curved them, stroking over her inner sweet spot. A loud whimper escaped and she began pumping her hips against him, riding his fingers and tongue in a way that made his already aching cock pound for relief.

"Give it to me," he growled against her heated flesh. Licking her, fucking her with his fingers, he listened to the insanely hot sounds she made as her inner walls began to flutter around him.

Three more strokes with his fingers, another caress of his tongue and she shattered, her hand clenching frantically in his hair. He felt her delicate muscles ripple and pulse around his fingers, kept licking while she writhed in his grip and came for him.

When her body stilled and she groaned in completion, he withdrew his hand and gently stroked her hips, thigh and belly, pressing slow, firm kisses over her mound while she came back down. Finally the hand in his hair eased, her fingers now stroking through his hair, the nails scraping erotically over his scalp, making goose bumps break out over his body.

Raising his head, he looked up at her. She was staring down at him with a sated expression on her face, a little smile curving her full mouth, and her eyes were still smoldering at him.

"That was good," she whispered, moving her hand to glide the pad of her thumb across his damp lips. He kissed it, let his tongue caress it and his blood heated even more when a look of pure hunger flashed through her eyes. "But I still want more." As if to prove it, she rolled her hips a bit, her body splayed and open for him in an erotic display he'd only ever dreamed about.

Her low, husky words were like dumping accelerant on a fire.

They also challenged him. She was obviously used to calling the shots in bed. But so was he. And he was determined to strip away all that iron control she encased herself in, make her give her everything, no holding back.

Something dark and possessive expanded in his gut. She was his, and he wanted her to know it. He vowed that she would after tonight.

He nipped the pad of her thumb and straightened, his hands once again gripping the full curves of her hips, fingers flexing there in a silent show of power. Her eyes flared, a hint of uncertainty in their depths, as though she understood there was far more at stake here than hot, intense sex and a couple of orgasms.

Oh yeah, he was going to strip her bare in a way she'd never been with another man, burn every moment of this into her memory in such a tactile way she'd never be able to forget his touch, his taste, the feel of his cock inside her.

His gaze held a clear warning as he stared at her. "If you want more, it's gonna be my way. And you should know that I like control and I like it a little rough." She shivered in reaction, the banked heat in her eyes suddenly bursting back into flame at his words. *Jesus Christ.* "If you say yes, I'm gonna make you give me everything."

Her answering smile was feline, and pure sex. "Yes."

Chapter Ten

Celida caught her breath as Tuck hoisted her off the counter. She clung to his broad shoulders as he whirled her around and walked to the closest flat surface to place her on—her pine farmhouse-style kitchen table. The wood was cool against her overheated skin, causing her to gasp as he laid her back on it.

Tuck loomed over her, backlit by the warm yellow tones of the kitchen light. His face was tense, every muscle in that rock hard torso taut, his eyes ablaze. Usually she liked to be in charge in the bedroom, but she couldn't deny that the thought of handing over the reins to Tuck made her insanely hot.

Still, she wasn't prepared for him to catch her wrist when she went to touch his face, or for him to grab the other and pull them over her head. She resisted, just to test him, watching his face the whole time. He stared right back at her and firmly, inexorably pushed her arms up and back until the backs of her hands touched the cool, hard wood.

"Don't move them," he growled, nostrils flaring as though he was already hanging onto the edge of his control.

She licked her lips and obeyed—for now—and lay there like an offering, spread out before him on her table. Never again would she be able to sit down and have a meal without remembering this, which was likely exactly what he intended. There was something so primal about knowing how much he wanted her it sent another shiver through her.

Tuck slid a hand beneath the small of her back and made short work of her skirt's fastenings. With a quick jerk he tugged it down and over her hips, down her legs and off to drop on the floor, leaving her in nothing but her open blouse and stockings. The muscles in his arms and chest flexed as he turned back to her, reaching into the pocket of his cargo pants for his wallet to take out a condom.

Her gaze dropped to the bulge at the front of his pants and her inner muscles squeezed in anticipation. Cool air washed over her as she lay there, watched him undo his pants and shove them down along with his black boxer briefs. His cock sprang free, thick and flushed. Squirming a little, she tore her gaze away and looked up into his face.

"Hold on." The gruff order sent another wave of heat through her even as he reached up for one of her hands and turned it so that she could hold onto the edge of the table. She did as he said and curled her fingers around the edge, the way he made her wait making this a thousand times hotter than she'd ever imagined.

And she'd imagined a *lot*. Though usually it was of her doing bad, bad things to him while he writhed in helpless agony. Things that involved scarves or soft rope to tie him to the bed and drive him insane with her mouth while he could do nothing but lie there and take it. Maybe she'd do that later tonight.

Her thoughts scattered when he tore open the packet

and rolled the condom down his length. Without pause he took hold of her hips and pulled until they were near the edge of the table, then reached down to take her feet and place the soles on the very edge. Her toes curled at the feel of those large, hard hands on her inner thighs, the silky material of the stockings somehow heightening the sensation as he stroked his palms up to the juncture of her thighs.

With one hand on her hip he stepped into her body and positioned the blunt head of his cock against her opening. He was hot, hard, and she couldn't wait to feel him inside her. Finally, after all this time wanting him.

Tuck's grip tightened around her hip as he eased forward, pushing the swollen crown into her. Celida groaned at the delicious stretching sensation and tried to wriggle closer but his fingers bit deep into her flesh, holding her still. "I said, don't move."

"No, you said not to move my hands."

The hint of a smile played at the edge of his lips for a split second, then was gone, extinguished by the heat in his gaze. "Don't. Move," he repeated. "Or I'll tie you down so you can't."

A shocking burst of arousal shot through her. With his advanced experience in subduing enemy combatants, she knew he could immobilize her without much difficulty, and knew knots she'd never even heard of. And holy hell that was hot. Forget the fantasy of tying him up, she was totally on board with handing over the rope into his capable hands. Body humming with anticipation, she did as he said and lay still, dying to find out what he'd do next.

As though he read her acquiescence, he held her in place with his strong hand and his will. Staring down into her eyes, he began a slow entry and withdrawal. Slow, shallow strokes that teased and seduced with the promise of what was coming.

She squirmed, she couldn't help it, but got nowhere. The proof of his control over her only made her hotter, wetter. "Tuck." It didn't even sound like her voice, all breathy and pleading. Her fingers curled around the table edge.

"Shh." He didn't change his pace, didn't bury himself in her body the way she wanted him to; only continued with that maddening shallow rhythm while he skimmed a hand up her belly to torment her nipples.

Celida hummed and arched her back, trying to take him deeper, but he wouldn't allow it. In and out, in and out, he teased her, pulling all the way out every few strokes to glide the slick head of his cock up to rub against her tingling clit. She was wet from her earlier release but he was making her even wetter and she wasn't going to be able to withstand the burn much longer.

The muscles in her arms, thighs and belly pulled taut as his cock caressed her most sensitive place, then slid back down to press inside.

This time he pushed deeper, slowly burying himself inside her inch by torturous inch. She gasped at the slight burn of the penetration, that heavy stretch that increased the ache inside her. Her hips rolled uncontrollably, her range of motion restricted by the iron hold on her hip. There would be marks there later on, and for some reason that knowledge only drove her arousal higher.

Tuck gave a low, rumbling groan as he pushed in the last inch or two, only stopping when he was buried deep inside her. "So goddamn good," he muttered, and withdrew. She made an inarticulate sound of protest and his gaze sharpened on hers as he sank into her once more.

Celida's eyes closed, her head rolling back on the table. Then he slipped a hand between her legs to stroke her clit and the pleasure suddenly increased tenfold. Her pleading cry echoed around them, her eyes too heavy to open as he continued those slow, full strokes in and out of her as his fingers caressed her most sensitive spot.

Tension gathered inside her, the hot ache melding into something deeper, stronger. She tried rolling her hips again, frustrated by the slow pace that wouldn't give her the friction she needed to come. "I want to touch you," she blurted.

His low, rough chuckle vibrated against her skin as he bent to nibble on the side of her neck, right where it joined her shoulder. Right where it felt the best. Oh yeah, he'd definitely been paying attention, and now the man was using it against her. "No."

"Why?" she demanded.

"I like knowing you're helpless right now."

Oh, shit, that deep drawl made it sound even dirtier. Needing more, everything he could give her, Celida uncurled her fingers from around the edge of the table and reached for his shoulders.

"*No*." Tuck caught her hands and muscled them back into place above her head, this time locking her wrists in one strong hand while the other went back to her hip to hold her steady.

Pinned, helpless, Celida had no choice but to lie there and take what he gave her. She panted and flexed in his grip but he held her there easily as he fucked her slow and deep, his mouth finding one straining nipple as his hand released her hip and slipped between her legs to find her swollen nub.

The building orgasm swelled inside her, teasing her with the promise of ecstasy. But he wouldn't speed up.

She growled in protest and dug her fingers into the back of his hand, her entire body drawn taut. "*Brad.* "

At his name he growled against her breast and raised his head. She could see the strain of ecstasy on his face, the glint of triumph and arousal in his eyes, nearly black with desire. He loved having her at his mercy, and dammit, she did too.

"You love taking it like this," he said, his voice laced with heavy male satisfaction.

Heart pounding, helpless to deny it, she could only nod and hope he would let her come soon.

Still stroking her clit gently as he took her slow and deep, he moved up the length of her body and brought his mouth down on hers. The slick, erotic glide of his tongue against hers, the feel of that powerful body moving over, in her, was too much. She gripped his hand hard and cried out into his mouth as pleasure took her, the orgasm pulsing through her in endless shockwaves.

When it began to fade he eased into a standing position, cock still buried deep inside her. She gasped as the motion stroked sensitive nerve endings, but before she could move he slid both arms beneath her and lifted her into a sitting position.

Celida automatically wound her arms and legs around him, her cheek resting over his pounding heart. He was still so hard inside her, so hot.

Tuck straightened for a second, lifting her, then lowered himself into the wooden kitchen chair closest to him. She set her feet on the bottom rungs and sighed, the pleasure still ebbing gently.

His hands swept into her hair as he gently raised her head and swept his thumbs across her hot cheeks. He gazed deep into her eyes, his expression a mixture of pure male satisfaction and unsatisfied arousal as he set both hands on her waist and began to move her on him.

Somewhat surprised that he'd let her be on top, especially when he'd just illustrated how much he loved being in control, Celida seized the opportunity to take charge. Her weakened thigh muscles protested with a quiver as she fell into the slow, languid rhythm he set.

She felt strong and sexy, having this powerful man at her mercy.

Her hands contracted on his broad shoulders, reveling in the heat and strength beneath her fingertips. His eyes were heavy-lidded with desire as he stared at where they were joined for a few seconds, then up to watch the way her breasts moved with each movement. Finally he looked into her face and laid his head back against the top rung, his features pinched with need.

A low groan rumbled up from his chest as he raised one hand to tangle in her hair and bring her mouth to his. He kissed her deep and hard, his thrusts growing stronger, faster. Celida hummed in enjoyment and met each caress of his tongue, clamping her inner muscles around him.

He tugged her head back, let her see the molten lust in his eyes. "Finish me," he grated out.

A little thrill shot through her. Steadying her hands on his shoulders, she settled more of her weight onto the balls of her feet and began to ride him. Slow and easy at first, as he'd tortured her, but soon faster, harder, loving the way his face tightened and the way his hands gripped harder.

His breathing grew harsh, the flush of arousal on his cheeks darkening as he neared the edge. The powerful muscles in his arms and shoulders trembled as she worked him. He was the most insanely gorgeous man she'd ever seen and she wanted to see his face when he exploded inside her.

She kissed his jaw, his whiskered face, the tip of his nose, then pulled back to watch him, a strange and slightly scary possessive tenderness flooding her. She'd never felt this way before.

Ignoring it, focusing on him and what she was making him feel, she clamped down on the hard length inside her and rocked, adding a little twist at the end that made his breath catch and his grip tighten on her hair and waist.

"Lida, fuck... Ride me." The plea buried in the demand made her shiver with longing and feminine power.

Three more strokes, four and he lost it, teeth bared in a primal expression of ecstasy, an agonized moan ripping free. She slowed her movements, taking his face between her hands to drop gentle kisses there. He groaned and turned her mouth to his, treating her to the most intimate kiss she'd ever experienced, deep and languid with pleasure, his tongue stroking and caressing with a tenderness that turned her inside out.

Pulling free to gather herself, she tucked her face into the hollow of his shoulder and breathed him in. Shit, she'd always known her heart would be in danger with him. She'd just never expected to lose it to him completely.

Her thoughts scattered once more when Tuck's arms came around her, enveloping her in a heart-melting hug as he buried his face in the curve of her neck. "Time for bed, sunshine."

She didn't protest as he gathered her close and stood, merely tightened her arms and legs around him as he carried her into her bedroom and pulled the covers down her bed where she curled onto her side.

After dealing with the condom in the bathroom he came back and slid in beside her, reaching for her even as she turned and rolled into the solid warmth of his body. He wrapped one muscled arm around her waist and buried a hand in her hair, stroking gently.

Lulled by his heat and the unbelievable tenderness he evoked in her, she drifted for a while.

"Ready to get some shuteye now?" he whispered against her temple, his breath soft and warm against her skin.

"Soon," she whispered back. This feeling inside her was so new and powerful, she wanted to savor it a while longer. She could wrestle with her emotions all she wanted, it wasn't going to change anything. She was in love with him, and it was both scary and exhilarating. But something held her back from saying it. She didn't want him to ever think she was saying it just because of the amazing sex they'd just had.

But she could give him something else right now instead. Something that she would never consider giving to anyone else, not even Zoe.

She ran a hand over his bare chest, mapping the contours and hollows, the slightly rough texture of hair beneath her palm, little nicks and dents he'd taken over the years in the line of duty. One day she'd kiss each and every one of them, showing him how much she adored him and his readiness to serve his country.

"I keep dreaming about them getting the edge on me," she said, her voice quiet. "That's what bothers me most, that I didn't put it together fast enough, and that they got the first shots off."

He kissed her temple, hand stilling in her hair. "What else?"

She swallowed, grateful that he wasn't judging her. "I always dream about the door. Every time I'm waiting for the bullets to come through and even though I've got my weapon drawn I never react quick enough. I see the shots come through the door, feel them hitting me."

Tuck made a low, rough sound somewhere between a groan and a growl, as though her words bothered him. "I saw the room when the EMTs were getting ready to transport you. And I've seen how good you are in action, so if they could get a jump on you then it could have happened to any other agent."

She hoped that was true. That was the only thought that made any of it bearable for her. Tuck had taken her to the range many times when they'd first been partnered together, and she'd been thrilled to get one-on-one coaching from a former Delta operator. Her shooting had been pretty good to begin with when she'd become an agent, but with his tutorage it had improved tenfold. Yet even that hadn't been enough to stop her attackers.

She struggled with her next words, shame threatening to drown her. "I wasn't strong enough."

At that Tuck eased her away from him, put two fingers beneath her chin to tip her face up. "Hey."

Celida reluctantly looked up and met his gaze.

"It had nothing to do with you not being strong enough. It was one of those freak things that no one saw coming, and they should have had someone else with you up in the room."

Maybe. "I just don't want anyone in the agency to think I don't have what it takes."

His eyes softened. "Darlin', any of them who think that need a punch in the throat. You're good. Damn good, and you don't have anything to prove to anyone."

"Not even you?"

Her question seemed to take him aback. His brows drew together. "Why would you say that?"

"Because you were in SF then Delta for years and years and never screwed up like I did." How could he *not* think less of her after all he'd seen and done throughout his career? It was one of the reasons she'd held back from him until tonight.

He shook his head. "We screwed up plenty, believe me. We lost guys on missions, a few on training ops, and we lost allies and civilians because things went sideways out in the field."

She blinked. He'd never mentioned any of that before. "But you never buckled under any of that stress."

"You haven't buckled either," he reminded her. "It took me leaving to make you admit to any of it, and I'm not sorry I did it. And I never faced an attack alone, fighting off two armed tangos while wounded and being held at gunpoint. Shit, just thinking about you facing all that scares the hell out of me, but here you are. Back to work, getting the job done and doing the best you can to move past it. That's all anyone can ask, as long as you don't bottle it all up until that shit eats you from the inside out."

He pulled her close again, resumed stroking her hair and back. "I want you to talk to me. I understand you wanting to keep it quiet with people at work, but dammit, at least come to me. Let me be there for you."

His words, his touch, completely melted her. She settled against him with a sigh, snuggling in close. It was a huge relief to have him to talk to. Fighting this battle on her own was exhausting and she was done with it. "I will."

"Promise?"

She heard the skepticism in his tone and smiled. "Yeah, I promise."

He grunted. "Good. Now let's get some sleep."

Celida couldn't ever remember having someone to rely on before Tuck came into her life. Even as work partners she'd recognized that he had her back no matter what, as she did his. Now he was her lover and it was even better.

And yet, exhausted as she was, she was still nervous to fall asleep in case she had another nightmare. She knew he wouldn't judge her if she did, it was just that she didn't want him to see her that way. He definitely cared, but she didn't know how far it went for him. There was a part of her that desperately wanted him to love her back.

One day at a time, stupid. Enjoy the moment.

Forcing the thoughts away, she allowed his warmth and presence to lull her to sleep.

Chapter Eleven

C lay lifted his head from the rim of the hot tub when he heard the hum of the lifting garage door through the open sliders up on the deck that led into the kitchen. A few seconds later he heard the door to the mudroom close and quiet footsteps on the tile floor.

"Hey, can you grab me another beer?" he called out, not too loud since it was the middle of the night and he was outside.

No answer, but he heard Tuck head toward the fridge so he leaned his head back and closed his eyes, enjoying the feel of the jets and the hot water all over his body. His pre-existing lower back injury—slightly bulging discs in his lumbar spine that he'd been going to physio for relief for months now—had started bugging him again a few days ago and he had a bunch of new bumps and bruises after all the rappelling and entry work they'd done today. This form of hydrotherapy felt awesome and it helped loosen up all his muscles after a long day.

Footsteps crossed the wooden deck above and started down the steps to the patio where the hot tub was.

Clay lifted his head and reached out an arm for the beer. "Thanks—"

He jumped and jerked his arm back when he saw Zoe standing there instead of his roommate. *Shit!* He blinked at her, then looked down at his lap to make sure the swirling water covered all of him before looking back at her.

"How'd you get here?" he blurted, totally caught off guard.

Her soft, husky laugh drifted over him, sounding like pure sex to his sex-deprived system, with predicable results. The woman definitely wasn't shy. He shifted on the built-in seat, thankful his lower half was hidden by the water. "I took a cab. And Tuck gave me the code to the garage last time I was in town."

His brows came together, his brain having trouble catching up. "Yes, but *why* are you here?" Tuck wasn't here. Why else would she be here?

Her mouth curved in amusement. "Tuck and Celida needed some time alone together, so I made myself scarce." Her lips twitched, drawing attention to the sheer red gloss she wore. He could fantasize for a long time about the things he'd like to see that full red mouth doing to him. "I can't believe I snuck up on a SEAL and scared the crap out of him."

He snorted. "Not. You just caught me off guard."

"Whatever, I saw you jump."

"I was *startled*," he clarified. "And only because I'm out here in my yard all relaxed with my guard down."

"Okay, whatever you say." She held out the beer and raised her eyebrows. "Don't you want it?"

He was worried he wanted *it* a helluva lot more than he should, and he wasn't thinking about the beer. "Thanks," he said, reaching out a hand to take it from her, unable to stop his gaze from roaming over the length of her.

The woman was walking sex. She was wearing a black dress with a shredded-looking hem, the long pieces coming to below her knees but exposing little peeks of bare, toned thigh whenever the breeze moved them. The top of the dress was snug and low cut enough to expose the tops of her firm breasts, which peeked over the bodice or whatever the hell that part was called. She had her hair wound up into a knot at the top of her head but some shorter pieces had fallen out, framing her face and neck, and her makeup was way more subdued today, enhancing her natural beauty rather than covering it.

He'd never seen her look hotter.

Not liking the direction of his thoughts or his inability to control them, he took a sip of the beer to give himself a few seconds to think. "So...you're staying here tonight?" The thought actually made his pulse thud in his throat.

He'd never admit it, but for some reason Zoe intimidated the shit out of him. Not that he'd ever let her or anyone else know that, of course. She was just so different from any other woman he'd ever met, and she had a disconcerting way of making him feel off balance. That she did so naturally and without any seeming effort on her part made it all worse.

Her eyes tracked the movement of his arm as he lowered the beer, trailing from there across his chest and shoulders before moving back to his face. Her tongue came out to wet her lips, the unconscious move telling him she liked what she saw. He flexed the muscles in his arm as he raised the bottle to his lips to take another sip, and yep, her gaze shot to his arm and stayed there until he lowered the bottle again.

Hell, he liked her reaction a lot more than he should, too.

"Yeah, if you don't mind," she said, dragging her

gaze back to his and folding her arms across her chest. Which only pushed her breasts up farther.

Tuck's cousin, asshole, remember? He looked back up at her face to see whether the move was intentional, and saw nothing to make him think she was playing with him.

Not that he trusted his instincts about someone's character anymore, especially women. His ex's manipulation had taught him how lousy his intuition had been about that.

Still, there was something honest and open and guileless about Zoe—at least, if she was faking it, he sure couldn't tell—and a deeply buried part of him wanted it to be real.

"'Course I don't mind," he answered, not wanting her to think he cared one way or another. He'd learned a lot from his clusterfuck of a marriage, including the all important lesson to protect himself more, even when people didn't seem like a threat at first. He was harder now, way more cynical, and he wasn't sure it was always a bad thing. Tuck said he was bitter, but Clay disagreed.

What he was, was stronger. Wiser. Battle tested and not about to be fooled like that again, by anyone.

"You gonna crash in Tuck's room then?" he asked her.

She tucked a wisp of fire hydrant-red hair behind one ear. "Maybe, but I was thinking of just sleeping on the couch. Feel like watching a movie with me?"

A movie? He'd been up since oh-four-hundred, it was past midnight, and he had to be up again at five. For some reason, staying up a while longer with her seemed like a much more appealing idea than sleeping right now.

"Sure." He set the beer down on the edge of the tub. "Better turn away now or I might embarrass you."

Her golden eyes widened a fraction as his meaning set in. "Oh." She turned around but didn't walk away, which he found interesting.

Reaching down to snag the towel he'd put on the step leading up to the tub, he stood and climbed out. Water sluiced down his legs in rivulets as he wrapped the thick terrycloth around his waist. He was half hard already and it wouldn't take much to put him at full mast. While part of him wanted her to notice, he didn't want her to think she could lead him around by his dick, either.

"You decent?" she asked a moment later.

"Yeah."

She turned around, seemed to falter a moment at the sight of him standing there in nothing but a towel, her attention zeroing in on his naked torso. He'd knotted the front so the folds gave him extra volume to hide his semi-erection, but he wasn't sure if he was successful. And at the way her eyes moved over him, sliding languidly over him from neck to feet and back, a slight flush on her cheekbones, he decided he didn't much care if she could tell he was aroused.

"What movie do you have in mind?"

Her eyes flashed up to his, blinked once, then she seemed to shake herself. "Oh. Nothing too heavy. But whatever you want, I'm easy."

No, she wasn't, and that was one of the things he liked most about her. For all her in-your-face attitude and her Goth persona, both a statement of confidence and a metaphorical middle finger to the rest of the world, from what he knew of Zoe she was very selective about her hookups with guys. That made her all the more appealing, which added yet another complication to his interest in her. It'd been over four months since he'd last had sex, with some girl he'd picked up at a bar. He'd taken her home, fucked her hard and fast, then left. He didn't even remember her name and could barely remember what she'd looked like.

Zoe was here and she was clearly interested. If he was a dick, he'd seduce her tonight while they were here alone. Take her to his bed, fuck her while Tuck was away and get her out of his system.

But even he knew that was way out of line and that Zoe deserved better.

Huh, he thought with a frown. Guess that meant he wasn't as much of a dick as he'd thought.

Besides, she was Tuck's cousin, so that would be just messy and awkward, and he didn't want to do anything that would make her feel cheap and used later on. Plus, since sex was all he had to offer her right now and he wasn't even sure why she got to him so much, they were both better off keeping things platonic. Too bad, though. He had the feeling Zoe would be just as direct and edgy in bed as she was in person. It'd been way too long since he'd relaxed his guard enough to have fun.

"We'll find something. Come on." He led the way up the wooden steps to the deck, crossed it to the sliding glass doors. He paused to let her go inside first.

She flicked a quick look down the length of his body and back up as though she couldn't help herself, then smiled at him, her golden eyes luminous in the light coming from the kitchen. He knew he was big, knew his own strength and that his size intimidated some women but when she looked up at him like that and smiled as though she truly enjoyed being in his company, he felt fucking bulletproof.

As he followed her inside it occurred to him for the first time just how big a fucking shame it was that he no longer knew how to let a woman in.

****

136

Celida dreamed she was in a garden surrounded by a swarm of bees. They flew around her gathering pollen and nectar from the roses and other flowers, their buzzing getting louder and louder in her consciousness.

It was starting to irritate the shit out of her because it was so peaceful and warm out here. She'd been feeling more relaxed than she had in forever until the damn buzzing had suddenly increased in volume.

Someone put a hand on her shoulder, startling her. "Celida. Hey."

She frowned, reached a hand back to bat them away and grumbled something, not appreciating the interruption.

"Sunshine, wake up."

Her eyes opened. It took a moment for the dream to recede, to realize that she was in her bed, naked, and that Tuck was sitting on the edge of it, his warm hand curved around her shoulder. He was already dressed, wearing cargo pants and the T-shirt he'd been wearing last night.

Oh, God, last night…

Blinking, she pulled the sheet up to modestly cover her breasts and pushed up onto one elbow as warmth stole through her. "What?" she murmured. Jeez, she'd been deep under. It was hard to shake the cobwebs out of her brain.

He withdrew his hand, eased back into a sitting position and brought his other hand around. Her phone was in it. "Travers just called."

She doubted it was to check on her. "What time is it?" she asked as she took it.

"Just after six."

She'd slept through for a solid six hours? Holy awesome.

Just as she began to check her voicemail, a text came through from him saying it was urgent and to call

137

him. She sat up, sheet still wrapped around her, and tried not to notice how Tuck's gaze went all hot and focused as he stared at the bare skin exposed above the sheet. She wasn't shy about her body, but after the way she'd been last night the idea of being naked while he was dressed made her feel too vulnerable. "Sorry, I was sleeping," she said when Travers answered. "What's up?"

"You better get into the D.C. office, now."

Her fingers curled harder around the sheet at his grim tone. "Why?"

A hard, frustrated sigh filled the line. "We just received a manifesto via e-mail."

"From the bomber?" All traces of sleep were gone now, vaporized by the surge of pure adrenaline that shot through her. She met Tuck's gaze, found him no longer staring at the sheet as though he could see through it, but watching her face, his shoulders tense.

"Looks like. How soon can you be here?"

She dragged a hand through her hair. "Half an hour."

"Hurry."

"I will." She set the phone on her nightstand and got up, hesitating for a split second with the sheet clutched against her breasts, then decided the hell with it and let it drop.

"Bomber sent in a manifesto," she explained to Tuck on her way to the bathroom and it was an indication of how serious the situation was that he merely gave her naked body a cursory glance as she passed by. The bathroom was steamy and damp, the shower walls wet so she knew Tuck must have already showered. She couldn't believe she hadn't woken up, she was normally a really light sleeper.

"I'll put some coffee on," he said as she started the shower, and the thought of hot, fresh coffee made her love him even more.

She wasn't sure when she'd be ready to tell him though.

After showering she dressed in black slacks, a black T-shirt, and slipped on her shoulder holster before pulling an FBI-issue windbreaker over her head. She brushed her teeth, blew her hair semi-dry and put it up in a no-nonsense ponytail, ran a mascara wand over her lashes and slicked some gloss on her lips before leaving the bathroom.

Tuck was in the kitchen, already holding a steaming travel mug for her when she came in. "Call me later if you can," he said as he handed it to her, the muscles in his roped arms shifting with the movement. "I'm on shift today, will probably be working late if we're put on standby."

The likelihood of another attack seemed high. She nodded. "I will." He was so incredibly good looking. He'd not only reduced her to a puddle of bliss last night, he'd soothed her worst fears later in bed, and now he'd made her coffee. Damn, the man made it impossible not to love him. "Thanks for this," she said, nodding at the travel mug. This felt nice. Having him at her place, making himself at home, doing thoughtful little things that couples did for each other. She could easily get used to having him around. "And for last night."

"You're welcome. And I was gonna thank *you* for last night." His eyes were warm, but they held a predatory gleam as he gazed down at her.

She loved that look in his eyes. "We're pretty amazing together."

At that he gave her a slow, sexy smile that made her heart thump and her belly flutter. "Yeah, we are." He raised a hand, cupped the side of her face as he leaned down to kiss her, his thumb stroking over the scar on her cheek in a gentle caress. "Take care of yourself out there, sunshine."

His concern was like a warm blanket, chasing away the last hint of unease that she didn't have what it took on the job. "I will. You too." She pulled him down for a slightly longer kiss, letting her mouth meld with his before easing away.

God, she loved this man, didn't see how she could be happy without him in her life from now on. Not after the way they'd given themselves to one another last night. "Bye."

"Bye."

They climbed into their vehicles at the same time, and she couldn't help but imagine them doing this every workday from now on. At the entrance to her townhouse complex, they turned in separate directions. She waved, caught his answering one in her rearview mirror as she sped down the street. If not for the ongoing investigation and the increased threat of another attack, she'd be downright giddy right now, thinking about Tuck and the way the last few hours had played out.

Traffic was light enough at this time of the morning that she made it to the office with three minutes to spare from the timeline she'd given Travers. He was in the main conference room reading through a printed document with a team of other agents.

His normally perfectly-styled graying hair was all mussed as though he'd either been dragging his fingers through it or had been woken from a dead sleep and had rushed in without so much as running a comb through it. Or both.

When he looked up at her, his pale blue, bloodshot eyes held a look she'd never seen from him before. Alarm.

Her stomach fisted in reaction. "Is this it?" she asked as she stepped up to the table to look at the document. It was thicker than she'd expected.

"Yeah, we've already got it divided up into sections. You take this one, it's from the middle." He shoved a handful of papers into her hands. She immediately started leafing through it, saw that it was twenty-one pages long.

"Anything else?"

"Yeah," he said in a flat tone.

When he paused she stopped and looked up at him, the knot in her stomach expanding when she saw the look on his face. "You know something new about him?"

Travers nodded. "That tip from the cop back in Colorado matches exactly what we've already found in the manifesto. Name's Ken Spivey. He's former Army, and an ex-cop."

Oh, shit. That upped the threat level for everyone involved, and explained both why he'd managed to evade detection so far, and why he'd been able to successfully pose as a cop before.

"Know what unit he served in?"

Celida lowered the pages, aware of her heartbeat pounding in her ears. Whatever else there was, it was bad. Very bad. "Combat engineer?" she guessed.

Travers's jaw clenched before he answered. "EOD. After he got out of the Army he served on the Denver bomb squad for six years."

Celida digested that with a sinking sensation and rushed to the nearest chair to begin reading in earnest. She could feel the seconds ticking past as she read the surprisingly well-crafted and articulate prose. What was his next target? Whatever it was, they were dealing with a man whose training and expertise would help him avoid detection and use devices that were likely more sophisticated than anything they'd seen in a long time. He'd also know the majority of their protocols.

Dread clawed at her insides like sharp fingernails.

He had the advantage right now. They had to find this sonofabitch and take him down before he capitalized on it.

Chapter Twelve

Ken pulled out of the museum parking lot and turned west, heading for his final destination. Even though he was still free and clear, his heart rate was elevated, his muscles tense as he drove through traffic across town. They had to have found his manifesto by now. He'd posted it on one of his social media accounts about fifteen minutes before leaving the first clue this morning at around oh-eight-hundred.

A few minutes ago he'd left his second clue. It would take the Feds a while to figure it all out and connect the dots, so to speak, but he needed the time. Even though he'd spent the past few days prepping everything for today, he still needed the head start to make sure everything was ready.

At the next traffic light he turned left and got into the right hand lane to enter onto the highway. Everything he needed was in the trunk, or in the backpack on the seat beside him. In it was another visual reminder of why he was doing this.

His son's favorite toy, his giraffe stuffy, stuck partway out, the nose and soft little horns on top of the head worn from use. Like his wedding band, this was the one piece of his son's life he hadn't been able to leave behind.

Every night he'd tucked Eli into bed with his giraffe, and his son's little arms would hug it to his chest, holding it close even while asleep. He'd dragged it with him everywhere, including into the bank that fateful October morning three years ago. The cops had found it lying next to Eli's body, just out of reach of his outstretched fingertips, as though he'd been trying to touch Raffi for comfort.

He'd never found it.

Sucking in a deep breath as the pain welled up, Ken pushed the razor sharp images away and shoved the giraffe back into the pack where he couldn't see it. Reminding himself about the reasons why he'd undertaken this mission were one thing; sinking into the ocean of grief and rage that existed in the depths of his withered soul was quite another. In order to do this he needed to keep a clear head.

The pain had to drive him, not control him. In a few hours it would all be over. He'd have his revenge, make his statement, and with any luck, he'd get to see Carla and Eli again. One way or another, he'd be dead and his earthly suffering would be over.

The lingering tension in the pit of his stomach had nothing to do with having second thoughts or doubts about this mission. He'd set his course, now there was no going back. He'd done everything he could think of to prepare for this, carefully outlining the most probable contingencies, and a few improbable ones.

He was acting on his own because it had to be that way. It meant full control, full responsibility, and fewer chances that someone else would screw everything up. And no sane person was likely to work with him on this. He wasn't a terrorist—though some would no doubt accuse him of being just that—and the last thing he wanted was to get mixed up with some jihadi or fundamentalist asshole.

This was personal.

His hands tightened on the steering wheel as he merged onto the freeway. This next test was going to be the hardest of all though. Not because he knew it was the final one, or because he already knew he likely wouldn't live to see another sunrise. But because it went against everything he'd once stood for, everything he'd been trained to do.

The price for righting an unforgiveable wrong and meting out justice on his terms.

No parent should have to bury a child. No parent should ever have to stand by and watch helplessly as the coroner wheeled a little sheet-draped body out to one of the waiting ambulances, the sheet soaked through with blood because they hadn't had time to even wrap him properly before removing him from the rubble.

They hadn't let him see Eli. Wouldn't let him touch or hold his baby or let him ride with him to the hospital where he'd been placed into a refrigerated drawer in the county morgue.

Ken had withstood all that, then been forced to suffer the sight of his wife's body wheeled out a few minutes after that. Agonizing hours later he'd had to stand there in the morgue and stare down at his little boy's body and the two dark, blue-tinged bullet holes marring the perfect skin of his little chest, including the fatal shot through his left lung.

Carla's death had been more merciful, a shot through the neck that had clipped her spinal cord and her carotid artery. She'd been dead within minutes, whereas Eli had suffered for close to eight minutes, bleeding profusely the entire time before finally suffocating.

First responders had found Carla wrapped around

Eli, her last act to transform herself into a human shield in a futile effort to protect their son. The fatal bullet—a ricochet, they'd told him—had struck her first, then changed direction and buried itself in Eli's chest. But he'd learned the hardest truth of all weeks later after the forensics reports had been released.

Both had been killed by the very men sent in to save them.

It had taken years to do his own investigative work, off grid and making sure to stay under the radar so as not to arouse suspicion, merely existing one day to the next until he'd found the intel he needed. Today Ken was going to ensure the man responsible for everything would never go home to his family again.

****

The worst part about this entire investigation so far was that no matter what they did, they always seemed to remain a few steps behind this guy at every turn.

Celida raked a hand through her hair and blew out a breath as she leaned back in her chair, the open manifesto on the desk before her. "We're still missing something. What the hell are we missing?"

From all the reports they'd read so far, Ken Spivey had been a model soldier and a good cop. Nobody they'd talked to had a bad thing to say about him, and all of them were shocked that he might be at the center of an FBI investigation, let alone one involving terrorist activity.

Loss could twist people into someone beyond recognition.

Still sorting through various passages that other agents had highlighted for further analysis, Travers grunted and shifted from his stance bent over his desk. "Tell me about it."

The team going through the hotel room Ken had stayed at under an alias hadn't reported anything of use yet, since he'd cleaned the place out before leaving. All they had were fingerprints and some of his hairs for DNA analysis later. They needed to know what the first *clue* he talked about at the end of the manifesto was, and what it meant.

Celida stood and rounded the desk to look at what Travers was reading. He'd sorted all the segments into color coded rows. Green for agenda, yellow for motive, orange for intel they might find useful.

Travers tapped one section marked in yellow. "Got someone digging into this bit about the op in Denver. Should know more shortly."

That was one of the biggest things to come out of the manifesto. They'd learned that Ken was motivated by devastating loss. He'd been at work on the morning his wife and son had been taken hostage at a bank in Denver. The suspects had barricaded themselves in the bank with all the hostages and no negotiator had been able to talk them down. Things had deteriorated and so much media attention gained that the FBI HRT had been called in two days after the standoff had begun.

Ken had been standing outside the perimeter, helpless, when the assault team went in. Apparently his wife and young son had been killed in the crossfire. The report he'd found stated that ballistics had proved the bullets had come from an HRT member's weapon. Whose, they weren't sure yet because the agency had buried it, but Travers had a call into the HRT commanding officer to get some answers. Until they talked to him the only thing left was to go through the paperwork in the reports, and that was going to take the team of analysts at least a few hours, if not longer.

Celida pulled up another database, cross referencing the names of guys on the team back then and the nearly one hundred current members. She flagged the duplicates for further analysis, but was secretly glad that Tuck had joined the team after the Denver incident that had killed Ken's wife and son.

"You get hold of DeLuca yet?" she asked Travers. DeLuca would no doubt know who had fired the fatal shots.

"They're out training someplace. I've tried his work and personal cell a couple times. He'll call me when he gets a chance."

Before she could say anything else, Travers's phone rang. He checked the number, answered, and his whole body went taut, his gaze pinned on the far wall as he listened. Was he talking to DeLuca?

"I'm on my way," Travers said in a clipped tone, then looked at her as he lowered the phone. "Seems we got our clue. Team at the hotel found a note in a garbage bag claiming there's a bomb inside a local mall trashcan. Security's being dispatched to the area and the cops are on scene. Our bomb techs are on the way," he finished, already striding for the door and motioning for two other agents to follow.

Celida was right beside him. They jumped into Travers's vehicle and took off for the mall. Hundreds of people were already standing outside the perimeter as the cops attempted to keep the area secure. Once they got inside, another agent met them at the entrance.

"Found what looks like an inert bomb planted inside one of the trashcans in the food court," the man told them. "Bomb squad's working on retrieving it, but in the meantime, here's a shot of the note attached to it."

Celida leaned over to see the photo on the man's phone. Hand written in neat block letter print.

Newseum. Second floor. Northwest corner. One hour. Don't be late.

"What's he got up his sleeve now?" she muttered,

pulling out her phone to call the Newseum while Travers spoke to the other agent. In a few minutes she had her answer. "It's a new exhibit," she told Travers, "featuring the FBI."

His lips thinned. "Fucker's playing with us."

He ordered the other agent to keep him apprised of the ongoing situation, then got on the phone and motioned for her to follow him out of the mall. On the way to his vehicle he got everything in motion for teams to descend on the Newseum. They were nearing the end of the school year and with the nice weather it was prime field trip season for schools all over the city.

By the time they reached the Newseum the cops had the building locked down. A few school buses full of kids were parked beyond the secured perimeter, curious and frightened faces staring out of the windows. The entire area was swarming with cops and agents. The D.C. police's own bomb squad was on scene.

Celida and Travers worked with the other law enforcement officials there while they waited for an update from the bomb squad. News vans and their crews dotted the scene just beyond the perimeter. Celida could just imagine the kind of stories the reporters were broadcasting.

She gritted her teeth. Had someone leaked the perp's name already? The initial psych eval they'd been briefed on this morning said that Ken was on a crusade and wanted public support in addition to revenge. Broadcasting his name and picture would no doubt give him the notoriety he was hungry for.

Celida sympathized about his wife and kid, but in her books, carrying out a string of bombings just made him another terrorist asshole.

After helping coordinate various teams at both scenes, Celida put her phone back on her belt and walked up to Travers, who was talking with a SWAT officer. Travers raised his eyebrows. "Anything?"

"Bomb at the mall was a dud. Spivey planted a dummy to act as a diversion." And it had worked. What was it a diversion for, though? The first two targets had clearly been aimed at the FBI. Was the next target going to do the same, or would it be different?

So far they hadn't found any other clear connections to what happened in Denver. That made Celida edgy as hell. There *had* to be something more to this. Something significant.

Travers grunted. "Bomb squad reports finding explosives in a trashcan by the FBI exhibit."

"Probably a dud too." Because why the hell would someone with as much experience as Spivey go to all this trouble just to blow up a museum exhibit after the building was evacuated?

"Fucker's having a grand old time watching us chase our tails."

Yup, and they were letting him do it too.

She continued to run interference for Travers until the bomb squad finally reported back that it looked like the explosives they'd found were also duds. "I wanna see it," Celida said and Travers walked with her into the building. The bomb squad was at the exhibit with their robot, a little camera attached to it to peek inside the trash can.

"Video shows him walking right up to it with a backpack, then dumping it inside," Travers told her as they waited for the team leader to approach them.

The balding man was somewhere in his early forties if she had to guess. He showed them a handheld monitor displaying what the camera was looking at in the trash. "Standard C4," he said. "No blasting caps, no wires. You say this guy's former EOD?"

"That's right," Travers said.

The guy blinked at them in surprise. "Why the hell

is he going around planting duds like this then?"

Exactly. He was either toying with them, amusing himself at their expense, or successfully drawing their attention elsewhere while he hit his real target. Whatever his plan so far and the relative lack of casualties, Celida knew in her bones there was something far worse coming in the next few hours.

Rather than answer, Travers changed the topic. "Anything else in there? Anything attached to it?"

Using a toggle on the handheld device, the tech manipulated the camera to a different angle, showing a lighter color material attached to the fake bomb. "Something right here."

"Looks like the same kind of paper he used on the other one," Celida remarked.

It took another critical fifteen minutes for the techs to assert the bomb was inert and remove it from the trashcan. One of them carried it over, note side up. The name of the bank jumped out at Celida.

A federal bank here in the capitol. She looked at Travers. "Just like the one his wife and kid were at."

The answering flash of concern on Travers's face, the certainty that this was Spivey's true target, was like a punch to the gut. "Get everybody over there now and evacuate that bank," he growled, then spun on his heel to run down the hallway to the stairs.

Heart pounding, Celida chased after him, the slap of their shoes echoing off the empty stairwell as they raced for the lobby. With every running step the sickening feeling in the pit of her stomach got worse.

While they'd been running around town chasing the trail of breadcrumbs Spivey had left them, he'd had ample time to set up whatever attack he'd been planning all along.

Chapter Thirteen

———— ⌇ ————

When he finally arrived at the target, Ken's heart nearly stopped when he saw the two bright yellow school buses parked in the bank parking lot. A fucking *field trip*? Today?

You gotta be kidding me.

His heart rate doubled, sweat gathering under his arms and across his lower lip. He'd planned this so carefully, taken great pains to set things up bit by bit so as not to draw attention to himself, only to come up flat against a brick wall. There was no way he was taking children hostage for this. Just none.

A sick feeling took hold as he continued driving past the bank. It was almost ten. The Feds didn't appear to have figured out yet that this was his target, but he couldn't afford to give them any lead time. He pulled over at a playground a few blocks away and shut off the engine, mind working frantically. Everything hinged on him taking *this* bank. There was no going back now. He either executed the plan as he'd envisioned it, or he walked right now.

And go where?

Shit. Shit, shit, shit. He hadn't considered a field trip at this point in time. Most schools were already out for the summer, so it must be either a camp or some kind of child care group that had organized it.

He pulled off his ball cap and ran a hand across his skull trim. Fuck, was this a sign? Were Carla and Eli trying to tell him something? He'd already get one hell of a federal sentence for the things he'd done. He wasn't going to jail. He wanted this to end and for his suffering to be over. To finally join his wife and son.

For nearly half an hour he sat and watched the kids playing on the playground, then couldn't stand it anymore and drove back to the bank. The restrictive band around his chest loosened when he saw the line of kids crossing the lot to board the buses.

Thank God.

A strange feeling of peace settled inside him. The op was still a go.

Circling the block once, twice, he saw the first bus pull out of the lot, and the second one pull away from the curb. *All clear.*

He parked a half block north of the bank and got out of the vehicle he'd stolen from another run-down neighborhood an hour earlier. He paused for just a moment to peer through the window at Eli's toy giraffe where he'd left it on the passenger seat. Raffi wasn't coming along this time. He called Eli's face to mind, the tumble of dark hair and the brilliant blue eyes so like his own.

I'll see you soon, buddy.

"I hope," he muttered under his breath and turned away.

His backpack was heavy, filled with the last few items he needed. Beneath the vest he'd hidden under his black hoodie, he was already soaked with sweat. His shoes were quiet against the sidewalk, his feet moving without conscious thought, body already on autopilot as he mentally reviewed what he was about to do.

Enter the bank. Take stock. Lock it down. Secure the perimeter. Trap the hostages.

Then it was out of his hands. He'd done everything he could to ensure the plan would bring his target to him, but in all honesty he couldn't guarantee it. His best hope now lay with whichever FBI negotiator they sent in.

As he headed up the sidewalk the June sunshine seemed overly bright despite the brim of the ball cap and the shades he wore. Maybe because it was the last time he would ever see the sun. The air smelled sweeter too. In fact, all his senses were heightened, as if they were starved for sensory input since his body knew his time was running out.

The bank loomed ahead of him, an imposing structure made of stone built back in the mid-eighteen hundreds. It had been upgraded slightly over the years, but had very few windows and a solid door. That and the fact it was a federal bank were the reasons he'd chosen it.

His pulse drummed in his ears as he approached the front door. Were his wires still in place? Had anyone reported that they'd found something suspicious? He'd worked as a janitor here on and off for the past few weeks using an extremely well-made fake ID, allowing him ample time to come in after hours and not only case the building, but work out his ideal setup.

At the door he paused to let an elderly woman exit. She faltered slightly when she saw him and Ken guessed she could see the way he was sweating. But she merely gave him a hesitant smile and hurried away from the building. His hand curled around the metal edge of the door for a moment. He didn't doubt his decision to go through with this, only felt anxiety that it wouldn't work out the way he'd planned or that his target wouldn't show up in the end.

Go. Get it over with. Carla and Eli are waiting.

Taking a deep breath, he let it out and forced himself to enter the bank. Immediately his gaze swept the room. Nine customers and two tellers, probably a few more staff in the back. Around fifteen hostages total. Good.

The moment he cleared the threshold, he reached one hand into the kangaroo pocket on his hoodie and activated the dead man's switch with his thumb. No way out now, for any of them. Only forward.

As the door swung shut behind him he reached up for the dead bolt and locked it. Then he armed the security system using the keypad beside the door and the combination he'd used as a janitor, which automatically activated all the locks on the exterior doors and windows. The blackout blinds began to slide down, blotting out the sun. A fitting metaphor for the sunset of his life.

People stopped to look at him, one or two taking a step back in alarm. The two bank tellers at the front desk stood frozen, staring at him in uncertainty. The lower halves of their bodies were hidden by the granite-topped counter but he knew they wouldn't be armed.

Ken pulled the Glock from his waistband, aimed it at the chest of the teller on the right. "Everyone move toward the counter. *Now.*"

His voice held enough menace that, even though he only held one pistol, people gasped and instantly began backing away. He kept his line of sight clear, his attention on the tellers, who would have hit the silent alarm by now.

Didn't matter. He was ready.

To drive the seriousness of the threat home and to prevent anyone from trying something stupid, he pulled out the dead man's switch, held it up. "Nobody try anything. I'm wearing a suicide vest and I've got all the doors and windows rigged. Anyone tampers with anything and this whole place will go up. Try to take me and this failsafe will detonate the vest, then all the other bombs with it."

The hostages started grabbing onto each other, cowering as they backed away from him. At movement in his peripheral vision he caught sight of the security agent creeping into the doorway that led to the back offices.

Without pause Ken raised the pistol and fired one round into the wall right where the officer was hidden. Gasps and cries of fear echoed in the resounding silence.

"Slide your weapons to me," he commanded the man. A moment later a service pistol slid across the polished marble floor. Ken stepped forward to take it. "Your backup too," he snarled.

A curse answered him, then the second pistol slid his way. After putting it in his pocket he motioned at the man to come out. "Hands up. Against the far wall with the others."

The guard emerged from behind the wall, hands up, his expression a mixture of fear and hatred. Ken didn't blame him one bit. But he had to make it clear he wasn't fucking around. "I was bomb squad for over six years, so believe me when I tell you there's no way out of here. Stay by the wall and be quiet."

One of the hostages, a middle-aged woman with graying hair, glared at him balefully. "Why are you doing this?" she demanded, voice shaking.

"That's none of your business," he snarled, thumb pressed tight to the trigger on the switch. He really didn't want to have to use it. Not yet, not until he'd eliminated his target. But he would if he had to avoid being taken alive. He'd made his mind up about that months ago.

He stalked forward toward the front desk, ready to take his final position to endure the wait when he saw more movement from the back of the bank. Automatically he twisted and aimed his weapon in the doorway.

He froze, his heart stuttering in his chest when he saw the young woman standing there, her dark eyes wide with terror, her body half-turned away to shield the little girl she had her arms wrapped around.

For a few endless heartbeats all Ken could hear was the roaring of his own blood in his ears. Denial slammed into him like a sucker punch to the gut.

No. Goddamn, it, no!

The young woman stayed frozen in place, staring back at him in absolute terror while the little girl huddled in her arms. She had to be no older than five or so, her long, dark hair tied into pigtails that trailed down to her shoulders.

The look in her big blue eyes seared him bone-deep. The naked fear on her face, the way her little mouth trembled as she looked at him made his resolve waver.

But he couldn't. Besides the dead man's switch in his right hand, disabling the wiring around the door would screw with his timeline.

Steeling his resolve, he lowered the weapon slightly and waved it impatiently from the woman toward where the others were gathered along the wall. "Get over there and wait. Go," he snapped when she hesitated.

The woman's throat moved visibly as she swallowed, her steps jerky as she towed the little girl toward the wall.

"Mommy, no," the girl cried, burrowing into the woman's hold. "Please, take me away from the bad man!"

Ken's heart slammed sickeningly against his sternum. *The bad man.*

A man appeared in the doorway where the woman and child had been. Late thirties if Ken had to guess, hands raised, face pale. A younger woman stood behind him, her hands also in the air.

"I'm the manager," the man told him, voice surprisingly calm as he gestured to the woman. "This is my assistant manager. Please don't hurt anyone. Just tell me what you want and I'll help you."

"I want you to get your ass over against the wall with the others," he growled, raising the pistol as an added threat.

The manager waved his hands slightly. "I'm going, I'm going. Don't shoot anyone."

"Shut up and move. Both of you."

He kept an eye on the managers as they joined the others. When they were safely against the wall with everyone else, he set the backpack down and opened it, taking out a handful of flex cuffs.

"Everyone slide your phones over to me. I'm starting at the front of the line over there," he said, jerking his chin at the elderly woman on the far right of the wall. Once he had them all subdued with their hands behind their backs, he could breathe a little easier. Then he had other things to take care of.

Refusing to let himself look back at the mother and child, Ken got to work securing his collateral.

****

Celida ended the call to the D.C. police commissioner and threw a hand out to brace herself against the passenger door when Travers took a hard right, tires squealing and skidding as the back end of the SUV fishtailed around the corner. They'd only gotten the call about the hostage taking fifteen minutes ago.

"Cops are already on scene, our bomb techs are en

route but I still can't get hold of DeLuca or Tuck, though I assume DeLuca's already on his way here," she said.

Travers's direct boss had alerted the HRT commanding officer about the situation just prior to her and Travers leaving the office. Right now the team was assembling at Quantico and gearing up.

They needed to speak directly to DeLuca about the Denver op where Spivey's wife and son had been killed. Since she and Travers were going to be the ones heading up the situation on the ground at the bank, they were responsible for keeping DeLuca apprised of what was happening while he was en route and once he arrived on scene.

Only they couldn't get through to him because his fucking phone was continually busy.

As they raced to the bank she thought of Tuck, imagined him getting his team ready, maybe hauling ass back to base to review intel and grab their equipment. He hadn't told her if they were training off base today and she hadn't thought to ask because she'd been in such a rush to get into the office once the manifesto was discovered.

Now she wished she'd taken those extra few seconds to tell him how she felt, hug him hard to back it up. Though she was pretty sure he knew just how hard she'd fallen for him, given how she'd dropped her guard for him completely last night. She'd never done that for a man before.

Tuck was definitely worth it.

Travers accelerated faster, keeping his eyes on the road. The engine revved higher and higher as they tore down the highway, FBI and police escorts clearing their way on the route to the bank. "DeLuca's probably on the line to the deputy director right now. Keep trying."

Well, duh. Scowling, she tried Tuck again. It went straight to voicemail. This time she left a message. "Hey, it's me. Our bomber upped the stakes and has over a dozen hostages at a federal bank in D.C. Travers and I will be acting as DeLuca's liaisons on scene." *And therefore by extension, yours too.*

She paused, then added, "Be careful." She didn't care that Travers overheard her and didn't give a damn what conclusions he drew about her and Tuck or what he thought of it. Because she was ninety-nine percent certain Tuck and the HRT guys would have to respond to this incident.

Just as she was now certain that he and his teammates were Spivey's real target and had been all along.

They didn't know who on the team specifically yet, if anyone, since the paperwork for the subsequent investigation after the Denver incident had been buried deep and analysts had only started looking at it just before the call about the bank had come in. But the manifesto had said he was targeting a specific individual he blamed for his family's deaths.

The earlier bombings and now this had ensured his case had gotten the agency's full attention, and the number of hostages combined with the bank's proximity to Quantico—less than a thirty minute drive—pretty much guaranteed them responding to the incident.

Spivey had planned this carefully. Celida was going to make sure she ruined all his plans today.

Knowing that Tuck and his teammates were almost certainly going into harm's way today against an expert and motivated suspect made her feel sick with fear but she didn't dare let it show. "I've got people tracking down Spivey's friends and relatives right now," she said to Travers. "We might be able to use one of them to talk him down."

"Maybe," he muttered, but he didn't sound hopeful about that and she wasn't either.

In a way she and Travers were going to be Tuck's team's lifeline, relaying critical intel to DeLuca and the rest of the HRT's logistics and comms personnel. She had to stay calm, professional. Tuck was a seasoned, experienced operator and so were the guys on his team, everyone from command right down to the newest guys like Jake Evers.

She tried DeLuca again and got his voicemail once more. After leaving him an urgent message she lowered the phone into her lap and forced herself to relax. They were less than ten minutes from the bank now. Travers had gotten the call from the police that one of the tellers had triggered a silent alarm.

Apparently Spivey had already barricaded himself in there and initial reports from cops arriving on scene said there were no visuals inside the building because Spivey had activated all the blackout blinds. Knowing they were dealing with an explosives and demolitions expert who also had insider knowledge of law enforcement protocols upped the stakes for everyone involved.

Local cops had already blocked off the area around the bank by the time she and Travers arrived, and a dozen or so Feds were assisting in establishing the secure interior perimeter. Jumping out of the vehicle, they jogged to the large truck serving as a mobile command unit.

Sniffer dogs were already working the perimeter of the building. As she watched, one of the dogs stopped sniffing and sat with its ears perked, looking at its handler. A clear signal that it had found explosives.

"How much do you think we're dealing with here?" she asked Travers, following him into the command truck.

"A whole shitload," he muttered, stepping inside.

Seven agents seated before computers all looked up

at them. Another senior agent from the D.C. counterterrorism unit Celida recognized, Dave Abbott, nodded at them and spoke to Travers. "Right now we think there are fifteen hostages. Bank manager, assistant manager, four tellers, security agent and eight customers, according to the surveillance video we got before he shut it down."

"Tell me about the security agent," Travers said.

"Two years in the Army before being discharged for medical reasons. Depression, apparently. After that he worked for three years as a deputy for a sheriff's office in a small town in Oregon before moving to D.C. ten months ago and got hired on by the security firm the bank uses." He paused to draw a breath and adjust his glasses.

"So far four of the five K-9 units have indicated explosives in or around the building. At this point we're assuming he has all the doors and windows wired. Nobody has been able to get eyes or ears inside yet. We're pretty sure Spivey must have complete control over everyone inside already because there have been no phone calls from anyone in there."

One of the agency hostage negotiators she'd worked with before was seated at a desk near the front of the truck with a phone to her ear. "He hasn't answered the landline in there yet?" Celida asked, switching her gaze out the window as the K-9 units continued their inspection around the building.

"Nope. Two of our techs are trying to figure out a way to get a fiber optic camera in somewhere, maybe through the ventilation system."

"He'll have thought of that and be ready for it," Celida said. They couldn't do anything that might jeopardize triggering the explosives he'd set.

"Well, we need eyes in there somehow," Abbott argued, his expression and tone slightly belligerent.

"Not if he's got the place rigged to blow with all those hostages inside," Travers said, a hard edge to his voice.

Celida doubted Spivey would blow the place if he could help it—not until his real target arrived, anyway. "We can't risk it." She turned to Travers. "SWAT's out for sure?" If they could take this guy down with a conventional team then Tuck and the others wouldn't be called in. The agency had some of the best SWAT teams in the business.

Face grim, Travers shook his head. "Not with this high profile a case, and not with that many hostages in there. In this case, unfortunately we might have to give the fucker exactly what he wants."

The HRT, including Tuck.

Celida shoved back the fear clawing its way up her spine. The sudden blare of her cell phone made her heart rate spike. She grabbed it, hit with a simultaneous blast of relief and disappointment that it wasn't Tuck's number on screen. "It's DeLuca," she said to Travers. "He's ten minutes out."

Chapter Fourteen

P istol gripped firmly in his left hand, Ken wiped his forearm across his damp forehead. All the hostages were now in flex cuffs, hands secured behind their backs, all seated against the far wall with no doors or windows in it.

All except for the little girl and her mother, who he hadn't tied up. They were sitting with the others, the girl in the woman's lap. In wiring all the doors and windows he'd forced the HRT to attempt either a ceiling or a wall entry, and they wouldn't risk blowing through the wall if there might be hostages lined up against it. Without eyes or ears inside the bank, they would have to play it safe.

That is, if they'd even been called in yet.

He'd given the Feds and cops outside more than ample time to get into position. There would be snipers in place on surrounding rooftops, staring through scopes at the blacked out windows, looking in vain for a shot. His only worry for now was one of the hostages trying something stupid out of desperation as the hours dragged by, or an assault team coming through the ceiling.

Or that the HRT wouldn't show at all.

No, they had to. Everything hinged on that, otherwise all of this would have been for nothing. He refused to even allow that possibility.

Raising his arm to swipe the sleeve of his hoodie across his face, he assessed his hostages. Everyone was silent, staring either at him or the floor. The mother and child he considered to be the lowest probability for a threat, which was why he hadn't cuffed them. He was banking on her protective maternal instinct to guard her child rather than try to make an attempt to disarm him.

Not that she looked like she was the type who would have a clue about hand to hand combat. He'd hate like hell to shoot her, let alone in front of her daughter, but he would if he had to.

Reality had no doubt sunk in for all the hostages now, except for the child, he hoped. By this point they realized they weren't going anywhere and that he meant business.

They were all sweating now. Whoever was running the show out there—he presumed it was the FBI—had cut power to the air conditioning unit. All it did was make them all more uncomfortable and him cranky as shit. The heat reminded him of his tours in the Middle East.

"We're going to need some water soon," the old lady on the far right said, having taken on the role of spokesperson for the group. Ken had expected the security guard or bank manager to assume the responsibility, but neither had stepped up.

"I'll take care of it later." This phase could drag on for hours while they tried to talk him down and look for a weakness in his defenses for an entry point. They'd find out soon enough neither one was going to happen.

Ken checked his watch. Nearly eighty minutes since he'd taken the bank. With the amount of sweat they were already producing though, he'd have to ensure the hostages were hydrated within the next couple of hours. That would require him picking up the phone, and he hadn't been willing to do that yet.

He'd wanted to make it clear that he wasn't interested in establishing communication, that he wasn't going to be talked down. By now that had to be pretty clear to everyone involved in the investigation.

Before he addressed the water issue, he had something more critical to take care of first. It had taken some mental recalculating, but circumstances demanded he alter his plans slightly and he'd figured out a way to make it work, mostly to his benefit.

Time to make some lemonade out of this lemon.

He shifted his weight from one foot to the other as he leaned against the front counter. His right thumb was numb from holding down the button on the switch. Every so often he changed hands, careful to maintain pressure on the button the entire time. Each time he did, several of the hostages watched him with tense faces, seeming to hold their breath until they saw he had control. That was one thing to their advantage, though he doubted they'd appreciate it.

He was extremely careful and conscientious in his work, two reasons why he'd excelled at his job in the Army and on the force. Nothing in this bank was going to detonate without him allowing it to.

The landline on the desk behind the counter rang again. They'd tried contacting him twice already, and both times he'd ignored it. His original plan had been to ignore all their calls. Now he was going to use the situation to his advantage. A certain amount of give and take was unavoidable now, at least in the initial stages.

He picked up the receiver. "Yeah."

"Is this Ken?"

"Yep." Man, did it feel fucking surreal to be on this end of the call.

"This is Special Agent Donna Gunderson. I'm an FBI negotiator, here to make sure we resolve this peacefully without anyone getting hurt. Is it okay for me to call you Ken, or would you prefer Mr. Spivey?"

Knowing the Feds were already here eased a little of the tension thrumming inside him. Unlike most hostage takers, however, he wasn't interested in talking. Not about him, his dead wife and son, or about this operation. "Ken."

Agent Gunderson and every other Fed gathered outside right now had no doubt already been well briefed about his situation. So if Gunderson was hoping to establish some semblance of a connection with him, she was in for a huge disappointment. He wasn't going to engage in the dialogue she'd been trained to pull hostage takers into.

"Great, Ken. How many hostages are in there, and are they all alive?"

"Fifteen. Affirmative."

"Is anyone hurt?"

"Negative."

"What about you, are you injured?"

"Negative."

"That's great news, Ken, it's important that we get everyone out of there safely, including you. We've got a lot of concerned people out here."

He was sorry for the hostages and their loved ones but it couldn't be helped because it was necessary to his plan. With this many innocent lives at stake, he was counting on the Feds calling in their best. And he didn't care to continue this conversation with the usual negotiations protocol bullshit—*Is the electricity on, Ken? No? Well I'll work on getting it back up for you, but first I need you to do something for me…*

"Is DeLuca here yet?" he demanded.

A pause, as though the abrupt change in topic had

taken her off guard. "Who?"

"Special Agent Matt DeLuca. The commanding officer of your Hostage Rescue Team." If she'd been assigned as the hostage negotiator for this case then Ken knew she'd have to be somewhat familiar with him and the manifesto he'd written. He wasn't sure if she didn't recognize the name or if she was playing dumb, and he didn't much care either way.

"Stand by." The line went quiet. He imagined Agent Gunderson hitting the mute button and asking for intel from everyone in the command truck. She came back on a few seconds later. "He's not here, Ken."

"Is he on his way?"

"I'll find out for you."

In other words, she had no clue, but wouldn't dare say no to him in case it escalated things. "You do that." He injected a steely edge to his voice.

"I will. In the meantime, I need you to do something for me, okay? Keep this phone line open so we can keep talking."

The negotiations game was starting to wear thin on him already. Next she was going to try to get him to talk about why he was doing this, what he wanted, then offer ways to help him, all in a series of open-ended questions designed to keep him talking. Stalling for more time.

The HRT could deploy within four hours and head anywhere in the world. So they could definitely make the thirty minute trip here from Quantico in far less than that.

It was way too late for anyone to help him, and he wasn't giving away anything more until he knew DeLuca was on scene. "Call me back when he gets here," he said in a hard voice. "And not until." He slammed the receiver into its cradle and stalked out from behind the counter toward his hostages.

****

The tension inside the command truck was so thick Celida could feel it pressing against her chest whenever she took a breath. She and Travers both wore headsets and they'd both heard the conversation between Agent Gunderson and Spivey.

Gunderson looked back at them and let out a low whistle. "I get the feeling he knows what I'm going to ask before I ask it, and I can tell me trying to get him to talk is already pissing him off. And it was only a two minute conversation."

Yeah, her gut already told her that he wasn't going to crack through negotiations. They were going to have to find another way to get him to surrender, otherwise a full breach was imminent, as were the deaths of all the hostages and likely several of the assault team.

No goddamn way she was letting that happen on her watch.

Celida folded her arms and looked at Travers, who was finally speaking to DeLuca, briefing him on what they knew so far. Was Spivey's end game DeLuca? Was *he* the target?

The manifesto hadn't mentioned anyone specific on the HRT, only that Spivey was out to take an eye for an eye and kill whoever's bullet killed his wife and son. DeLuca had been the team CO that day in Denver, so it made sense, and he'd gone to great pains to try to emulate the same scenario.

Travers ended the call. "He's here."

Relief washed through her and the tension in the room eased. She busied herself reading everything they had on Spivey to pick apart his life, figure out what they could do to take him out before he blew the building or launched an attack on the HRT assault team if they were called in to make a breach.

She tried not to think about Tuck, what would happen here if his team had to make the assault, but it was impossible. He meant more to her than anyone, in some ways more than Zoe. She had to find a way to end this before the HRT got involved, protect Tuck and his teammates.

Heavy boots on the steel trailer steps sounded. An agent threw open the back door of the mobile command unit and Matt DeLuca strode up the steps leading into the trailer, dressed in a gray T-shirt and cargo pants, a San Diego Chargers ball cap on his head.

In his mid-forties, broad shouldered and with a minimal amount of gray in his light brown hair, he was an imposing man. There was no mistaking the aura of authority he wore, or the confidence in his movements and body language that spoke of a man who'd spent his entire adult life in uniform in the service of his country.

His bright green gaze swept around the group, then landed on Travers. "My sniper teams still don't have any eyes in there yet and right now it's zero visibility. You guys got anything?"

"Nothing," Travers answered in frustration. "He's still waiting for us to say you're here. You two know each other personally?"

DeLuca shook his head. "I only know his name and face from the investigation after the Denver incident."

"Any other reason why you'd be his personal target in this?" Celida asked.

DeLuca turned his gaze on her. "I was in command that day. I made the call to order the assault. I was responsible for my guys and everything they did, including the casualties they inflicted. He likely blames me for his wife and kid dying."

Certainly appeared that way. "I started looking into the paperwork from the investigation before we were called here but I didn't get through it all. I've got someone on it right now but mostly we're focused on doing more background research on Spivey," Celida said. "In his manifesto Spivey mentions a ballistics report proving who killed his family, and he accuses the agency of a cover up during the investigation. Who fired that fatal shot, and could Spivey know it?" Some of the investigation was public record but this hadn't yet been released.

"He could, but it would've taken some serious digging because even though the ballistics report tells us which round killed those two hostages, the eye witness accounts and testimony make things murky."

"Who was it, and are they still on the team?"

"The agent in question was cleared of all charges a year after the incident. He left the agency shortly thereafter and died on a contract job in Afghanistan about eight months ago." He held her gaze for a tense moment. "There's something more going on here."

Before she could say anything else DeLuca strode to the back where Agent Gunderson sat at her station near the rear of the trailer. "Call him."

The female agent didn't ask questions, just got back on the phone as someone handed DeLuca a headset. A now familiar male voice answered. "He's here?"

"Just arriving now," Gunderson lied to buy them time, her well-modulated voice soft and calm, befitting her role.

"I want to talk to him."

The negotiator shot a questioning glance at Travers, who shook his head in a flat-out *no way*. "I'll see what I can do about that. In the meantime, can you tell me more about the condition of the hostages? With the electricity turned off it has to be hot in there."

"I want food and water for them."

"Okay, I'll get to work on that right away, Ken."

"I want twenty bottles of water and fifty protein

bars. No wires, no bullshit like that in the boxes or bags they're packed in or I kill a hostage."

"I'm not going to do anything to jeopardize the safety of the hostages, Ken. I'll get you the food and water."

"I want something else too."

"Okay, tell me."

"Put DeLuca on the phone, and I'll give you two hostages. A woman and her young daughter."

Catherine and Marlee Bancroft, Celida thought, her attention riveted on Gunderson. Relatives had confirmed their identities from the surveillance feed prior to Spivey taking the bank. Apparently Spivey couldn't stomach the thought of another child getting killed. If they came out it would be less of a burden on his conscience and he could be even more likely to set off his explosives. She glanced at Travers to see his reaction.

Travers shook his head again while DeLuca looked on, his eyebrows drawn together in a tight frown as he listened in. They couldn't risk putting DeLuca on the phone yet—even if DeLuca was his intended target, letting Spivey talk to someone he blamed for all this might set him off. It could destabilize an already perilous situation and push him to act now, give him no reason to keep the hostages alive.

"Before I can let you speak to Agent DeLuca, I need something from you in return, in a show of good faith," Gunderson said.

"I'll give you the woman and the girl. No weapons, hands up as you approach. I want you and another female agent to bring the supplies and do the exchange. East door."

Why another female? Celida wondered. Did he not think she or Gunderson had the skills or the guts to take him out if possible? *Screw you, asshole.*

Gunderson blinked and looked up at Travers for

confirmation. A muscle flexed in his jaw, but he nodded and turned his gaze on Celida. "You go with her."

It felt like someone had cranked a vise around her ribcage. *Me?* Celida nearly blurted, but didn't argue. She was the only other female agent handy and Travers clearly trusted her to handle herself in this situation.

Gunderson's expression said she was less than thrilled by the order to make the exchange, but she took the special receiver off mute and spoke to Spivey. "All right, Ken, Agent Morales and I will bring you the supplies and take the hostages back with us. Give us twenty minutes to get everything ready."

"Ten minutes. East door. Both of you come unarmed, hands up where everyone can see them. Don't try to be heroes. The kid's scared enough as it is without anything blowing up." The line went dead again. Instantly the command vehicle erupted into a mass of noise and movement as everybody started talking at once.

Travers stuck two fingers in his mouth and let out a shrill whistle that froze everyone. "Listen up! Everybody at your posts to await further instructions." His pale blue gaze landed on her. "You up for this?"

Now he asked her? He'd already committed her so she wasn't backing out, especially when she felt like she had something to prove to the rest of her fellow agents after the hotel attack. "Yeah." She was afraid of being shot or blown up, but would never let him or the others know it.

"Get as much intel as you can when he opens the door. HRT's gonna need everything we can give them. Somebody wire her up," he added in a raised voice as he turned away to continue coordinating everything.

Feeling off balance, Celida took off her headset and raised her shirt while a fellow agent taped a wire up her bare stomach, securing the little microphone to the underwire where the cups of her bra met in the center.

DeLuca was on the phone, to his superior or maybe Tuck, she guessed as she shrugged into a Kevlar vest. Someone handed both her and Gunderson a backpack full of water and protein bars.

Ignoring the wild thump of her heart, she put the pack on, a little surprised that her hands were so steady as she fastened the Velcro straps around her torso. The weight of the vest was reassuring but it didn't take away the awful grinding dread in her stomach.

"One minute," Travers called out, lowering his phone as he met her gaze. He gave her a nod she guessed was supposed to be reassuring. "Snipers are all in position. We've got you covered the whole way there and back."

Pulling in a deep breath, she faced Gunderson. "You ready?"

The woman gave a short nod. "Guess so."

Travers all but herded them outside. Stepping out of the dim, air conditioned trailer into the bright midday sunshine, the heat and humidity was like a slap in the face.

Celida glanced around, noted the news vans parked around the exterior perimeter and all the cops and Feds lining the interior one. She rounded the back of the command trailer, her gaze darting from the metal side door of the bank to the rooftops of the surrounding buildings where sniper teams were already positioned.

It still didn't make her feel any less secure about this exchange. But if she could free two hostages and maybe save the lives of the HRT members with some intel she could pick up with a look inside... Her fear meant piss-all in the face of that.

"You ready for this?" Gunderson asked her, as though she couldn't quite believe they were doing this.

"Yes," she answered with a hell of a lot more

conviction than she felt. The plan was to follow Spivey's directions exactly, but if shit went sideways Celida was to immediately get her and Gunderson as far away from the building as possible, or, if not, hit the deck and do what they could to shield themselves against a possible blast.

Hopefully with the woman and little girl in tow.

"Just get as much of a visual as you can inside so we can get it to the tactical team." Spivey was a pro. If the HRT really was his target, Tuck and the boys were gonna need as much help as they could give them for this one.

The anxiety in her gut congealed into what felt like a hard ball of concrete as they crossed the empty parking lot together, their shoes sounding loud on the hot, cracked pavement. High above them, a police helicopter circled the area.

A trickle of sweat rolled down Celida's side. When the exchange happened, and hopefully Spivey was right about being able to disarm the door he was about to open, she had to do her recon carefully. If she made it too obvious that she was gathering intel, who knew how Spivey would react.

She kept her head held high as she walked beside Gunderson, breathing steady, raising her hands once they came closer to the building. No one else needed to know about the panic she was fighting.

The steel door on the east side of the bank loomed before them. Despite her resolve to stay mentally strong, her vision tunneled, her mind instantly yanking her back to that day in Rachel's hotel room. Taking another deep breath to combat the fear clawing at her, she kept her eyes pinned to the metal doorknob.

He's going to shoot you, just like they did, her mind whispered. *The same as before, right through the door before you're ready, and this time you have nothing to fire back with.*

Stop it, she ordered herself sternly.

More sweat trickled down her sides, down her temples. She could see the dents in the steel door now, the rough, rusted patches around the edges of it. When they were a dozen yards from the door, the knob began to turn.

Celida faltered, fear turning her legs wooden. She felt naked and vulnerable out here with her hands up and no weapon, even with the vest. As she stared at the knob part of her cringed, bracing for either the impact of a bullet or the concussion of a blast. But the seconds ticked past and there was only silence.

"Step forward and knock twice," Spivey called from somewhere inside, his muffled voice telling her how thick the reinforcement was in the walls and that door.

Forcing her feet forward, Celida cautiously walked with Gunderson over the remaining distance. At the door she paused. If the perimeter of it really was wired, Spivey had hidden them well. She glanced at Gunderson, who met her gaze for a moment and nodded once.

Go time.

Raising her hand, Celida knocked twice, the sound seeming to echo around them.

A second later the door cracked open. Celida took a hasty step back, her right hand twitching, wanting to reach for the weapon that wasn't there. Her heartbeat was loud in her ears over the expanding silence.

A pale, slim hand emerged, palm out, wide-spread fingers trembling slightly. A slender arm followed, then a little face topped by dark brown pigtails appeared beneath it. The little girl stared up at them, blue eyes huge in her pale face. Her gaze locked on Celida, so wary and full of hope that it made Celida's heart ache.

"It's all right, Marlee," Celida coaxed. "Come on

out and I'll take you someplace safe with your mom."

Still uncertain, the girl slid out of the small space the slightly cracked open door allowed, then stopped and reached back. "Mommy…"

"It's okay, baby, I'm right behind you." Catherine squeezed out slowly, both hands up, and focused on Celida, blinking against the bright sunshine.

"Get the supplies," Spivey ordered from inside. Celida still didn't have a visual on him yet. He obviously knew there were snipers in position. The woman and child took a few steps toward them, still clearly afraid.

Celida tensed and waved for the hostages to come out fully, watching the black slice of space between the edge of the door and the stone wall. If she'd had a weapon maybe she could have rammed the door open enough to get a clear shot on Spivey and end this all now, before anyone else got hurt.

"I'm supposed to check the bags first before I hand them over," Catherine said in a small voice. She sounded both apologetic and as though she was on the verge of bursting into tears. Her daughter stood a few steps away, her back pressed against the stone wall as she watched her mother with anxious eyes.

Shit. Being taken out of the transfer would take away Celida's opportunity to get a good look inside. "That's fine, Catherine," she answered, her voice calm even though her heart was pounding against her ribs. Spivey was *right there,* somewhere behind the door, just out of view. Did any of the sniper teams have a decent visual now?

Slowly, Celida shrugged out of the backpack and handed it to Catherine. "It's gonna be fine," she said to the woman, whose eyes were welling with tears. "As soon as you hand over the supplies we're gonna get you and Marlee to safety, okay?"

The woman nodded, lips trembling. "Ok-kay."

Gunderson took off her backpack and set it on the ground. Catherine edged forward to take both bags and when she bent to unzip one, Celida seized her opportunity to try and get a look inside. Tuck and the others needed *something*. She had to find a way to help them. Catherine had been inside for a while. Surely she'd know or have heard or seen something of use to them.

While Catherine rummaged through the contents Celida stepped as close to the door as she dared, peering into the dimness beyond. From what she could see, only a few emergency lights were on at the very back.

She caught a faint glimpse of the hostages at the opposite end of the bank, all seated on the floor, appearing to have their hands tied behind them. She could see the door for the first office in the back, but couldn't get a visual on anything else. All the blinds on the windows and front doors were fully in place, barely any hint of daylight seeping around the blackout blinds. There were two large vents in the ceiling an entry team might be able to make use of. No obvious explosives of any kind around the windows or—

"Get back, *now*."

Shit!

Her breath caught in her throat and she took a hasty step back as her gaze swung to her left. Ken Spivey stared back at her, not five feet from the door, his expression filled with menace. He held a pistol aimed at her head—and a dead man's switch in his other.

He took a threatening step toward her, face set in a cold mask, and Celida automatically reached for Catherine's shoulder, grabbing and shoving her back out of range.

"Ken, we've brought you the supplies I promised," Gunderson said, her calm voice doing nothing to slow Celida's racing pulse. "Let Catherine hand them over

178

and let us take her and Marlee back with us."

The pistol never wavered from Celida's head and it was like facing her nightmare all over again. Her blood iced over in her veins, her gaze welded to the black hole at the end of the muzzle.

The weapon was nearly at point blank range. If he fired there was no way he could miss. And if he decided he wanted her for another hostage he could easily grab her. All the self defense skills in the world wouldn't help her against a man his size with that kind of training, and a struggle only increased the likelihood that he lost his grip on the dead man's switch.

"Quickly," he snapped, his order a low growl.

Standing still, barely daring to breathe, Celida kept her hands raised and avoided Spivey's gaze as Catherine checked the second bag. "There's only water and protein bars," Catherine told him as she straightened. "No microphones or cameras or anything."

He never looked away from Celida as he spoke to Catherine. "Take everything out and throw it along the floor, away from the door. Then leave."

Catherine did as she was told, emptying the bags and tossing everything inside away from the door. When she was finished, Spivey spoke again to Celida. "Step back slowly."

She did.

"Keep going."

She slid her right foot back, then her left, all the while watching that pistol, aimed dead center on her face. Gunderson was behind her, scooping the little girl into her arms.

"Gunderson."

The negotiator froze, looked back at the door, into the blackness beyond it where Spivey stood hidden in the shadows.

"I've held up my end of the bargain so far. I want

DeLuca on the phone in the next fifteen minutes, or I'll start making this ugly. If he doesn't call I'll kill a hostage at sixteen minutes." He switched his gaze to Catherine, jerked his chin at her. "Shut the door and go."

Not needing to be told twice, Catherine reached for the door handle and slammed it shut. Celida flinched at the sudden bang, but thankfully there was no explosion. It took a moment for that to sink in.

Safe. You're safe.

She exhaled the deep breath she'd been holding. Though her knees felt weak she lunged for Catherine, seized her by the upper arm and took off at a dead run away from the building, back toward the command trailer. Gunderson was a few yards ahead of them, carrying Marlee, the little girl's pigtails flying behind her.

They reached the interior perimeter. Other agents rushed forward to take the hostages. Celida followed Gunderson on rubbery legs, fighting the flood of adrenaline lashing her system.

Travers was at the command trailer waiting for her with DeLuca, her boss's shrewd blue eyes sweeping over her once. "You okay?"

No. She nodded and proceeded to rip the Kevlar vest off, then sat down on the curb. The rush of cool air over her sweaty skin, the relief of the weight taken off her chest, helped a bit. Her hands were shaky as hell as she peeled the wire away from her damp skin, her breathing choppy.

"You're okay. Just take a minute," Travers said, his voice surprisingly gentle, setting a hand on the back of her head and pushing down a bit.

Celida shook him off and closed her eyes, gritting her teeth as her jaw trembled, hating that both he and DeLuca were seeing her like this. Hell, her entire body was shaking in the aftermath, her mind still telling her what could have happened. She wanted to call Tuck, hear his voice on the other end and personally warn him about what he would be walking into.

Thankfully Travers didn't say anything more, just went about his business, issuing orders until she got herself under control a minute later. "He's got a dead man's switch," she blurted when she got her breath back, drawing Travers's attention back to her.

His eyebrows drew together. "Figured he might. What else?"

She wiped a hand over her sweaty face. "All the other hostages seem okay. Did the sniper teams see anything?"

DeLuca shook his head, his mouth a thin, flat line.

Damn. "I couldn't see any wiring on the windows and doors but there are a couple of vents in the ceiling. Might be the only option, but as of right now the snipers or even a breach are out."

"Not necessarily," DeLuca said, drawing her and Travers's gazes.

As though they had some sort of unspoken code, Travers nodded at him. Then he took her hand, helping her to her feet. "This asshole's counting on a breach," he said, stating what she was already thinking.

The manifesto made it clear that he wanted retribution and was prepared to die here today. His demands and lack of willingness to negotiate merely solidified it. Whatever he was planning, he wanted DeLuca specifically to know about it.

Anticipate it. Witness it.

That last part made Celida's blood run cold, because it meant Tuck and the others would be in direct danger.

"If we don't give it to him, he'll force our hand by killing hostages," Travers said.

Releasing her, he turned away. "We've got some

time before the deadline. Let's go talk to Catherine and put everything we can together so DeLuca can brief his boys with something useful after."

Chapter Fifteen

A s his phone's work ringtone went off Tuck straightened and grabbed it from his pocket. He'd been expecting this call for a while now.

When he saw Celida's number instead of DeLuca's, however, his heart rate kicked up a notch. His sniper teams had been in position for the past hour. He'd known the moment when Celida and the other agent had approached the bank to make the exchange. What he'd seen in the video from one of the spotters had made his blood run cold.

"Hey."

"I've got an update," she blurted. "DeLuca's finishing up interviewing a hostage we just retrieved—"

"The woman?"

"Yes, and her young daughter," she added, her voice calm even though he detected the hint of a tremor in it.

From what he'd learned about Spivey so far, the man wasn't just your ordinary psychotic asshole. However twisted his reasoning about this situation and however fucked up his mind was, his conscience was still alive in there somewhere. In some ways that made him even more dangerous because they couldn't predict what he'd do.

"DeLuca's getting you all the inside intel he can, but he's got to call Spivey within the next seven minutes or he's threatened to kill a hostage."

Ah, shit, that shortened their timeline by a whole bunch, and it also explained why he hadn't heard from his CO in nearly twenty minutes.

"He's asked me to update you and your team in the meantime," Celida continued. "Can you put me on speaker?"

Her voice sounded a little shaky, and it was no wonder why. "Are you okay?" Going into that situation blind, unarmed, would have shaken any agent, but her especially, considering what she'd just gone through a few weeks ago.

As he awaited her answer he was aware of his teammates gathered around the table all watching him and he didn't care. He needed to know she was truly all right before they moved onto the briefing.

"Yes. Put me on speaker," she insisted in an impatient tone that made him smile. In spite of everything she was in full operational mode, ready to take this fucker down. His girl had brass.

Whatever she had to say was obviously vital to the team's preparations, so everything else would have to wait, but he was definitely continuing this conversation with her in private later. He set the phone down on the table strewn with maps and blueprints and put her on speaker. "Okay, go ahead."

"This is Agent Celida Morales. I'm updating you on behalf of DeLuca, who's questioning a female hostage we just retrieved from the bank."

Tuck could hear other agents talking in the background, heard phones ringing and guessed she must be inside the command trailer.

"Spivey's trying to replicate the Denver op. He's wearing a suicide vest and holding a dead man's switch. He had a Glock on him but I'm unsure what other weapons he's got in there. We know the security guard he took hostage had a Beretta that Spivey must have taken as well. The female hostage didn't see any other weapons but she said he's got a backpack and we don't know what's in there. Based on his background and training it could be anything from a submachine gun to grenades to more explosives."

He hated knowing that she'd been confronted once again by a man holding a weapon on her. Tuck's jaw clenched as he remembered her walking up to the bank to retrieve the hostage and coming face-to-face with Spivey and his weapon.

His frown turned into a scowl. *Hell.* Without pause he mentally locked his emotions down. He had to focus on the job now, nothing else.

"I couldn't see any wiring around the doors or windows but we have to assume they're all rigged as that's what Spivey told the hostages. Entry through any of those are out, and given the dead man's switch, so is a sniper shot."

"Okay, we'll work around it," Tuck said. Their specialized equipment meant they still had a few options open to them at least. "Anything else?"

"So far all the hostages are in good shape and they now have food and water. DeLuca's call will hopefully stave off an execution in the next few minutes but it's pretty clear this guy's not going to be talked down. He only let the woman and child go because they reminded him too much of his own dead family."

So from here on out things were likely to escalate. They'd been prepping for an assault since they'd gotten word about the hostage incident, but the way things were going Tuck didn't think they'd have a lot of time to pull a plan together. "What's Spivey's interest in DeLuca?"

Celida blew out a harsh breath. "He was CO the day of the op in Denver that killed Spivey's wife and son."

"I know. What else?" None of the men standing in the room with him right now had been on that op, but they all knew about the woman and little boy being killed in the crossfire to bring down the hostage-taker after he'd killed two others, forcing the assault team to act.

"We won't know for sure until DeLuca calls him but right now it's pretty clear Spivey holds him responsible for what happened to his family. He's gotta know we'd never allow DeLuca to exchange himself for more hostages, even if Spivey demands that, so right now the thinking is that *you* guys are his target. He wants to make a statement, force a breach so he can attack the team."

Unease settled in Tuck's gut. This was unlike any situation they'd dealt with before. Sure they were at risk on every op because a lot of perps wanted to take advantage of the opportunity to shoot the Feds trying to take them down. They'd never before faced making an assault with someone like Spivey in there waiting for them, his entire operation planned for the moment they entered the building so he could kill them.

Even though Tuck and the others had suspected they might be the target since hearing about the crisis, hearing it confirmed by Celida made it hit home hard.

Tuck glanced around the table, met his teammate's eyes one by one. Bauer. Farmboy. Schroder. Blackwell. Cruz. Vance. Seven of them on the primary assault team, and Grant, the leader of the other assault element acting as backup for this op.

Every one of them knew the dangers facing them on this op, and every one of them stood ready and willing to meet them head on in order to get those remaining hostages out and bring Spivey down. Subdue him and take him into custody if possible. Kill him if necessary.

One way or the other, they were bringing him out of that bank.

"We copy," Tuck said to Celida. He turned his attention back to the schematics on the table in front of him. "We've got blueprints of the bank but it underwent renos two years ago and some of them aren't shown on here. Were you able to see any vents, any other access points anywhere in the interior?"

"I went to the east door and only got a quick look around so I couldn't see past the front counter or back to where the offices and vault are. I saw two vents in the ceiling, one on the east side and one on the west. All the hostages were cuffed and seated along the west wall."

So coming through the one wall without any windows or doors that were probably rigged to explode wasn't an option. Spivey had planned this well.

Tuck and his guys would plan better. "Anything else?"

"Sorry, that's all I've got. Believe me, I wish I had more."

What she'd given them was better than nothing, and he was proud that she'd managed to get that much considering she'd been staring down the barrel of a Glock. "It's all right."

He wanted to say so much more, something personal that reminded her how much she meant to him, but he wouldn't in front of an audience. Not that he minded a little ribbing from the guys but Celida would kill him for what she'd no doubt consider embarrassing her in front of his teammates.

"I gotta go—DeLuca's gonna make the phone call now," she said. "You guys take care of yourselves out there. DeLuca will be in touch ASAP."

"All right, thanks for the intel. Talk to you later." *Sunshine*, he added to himself.

"Yeah." She paused a moment, as though she wanted to say more too and couldn't. "Bye."

He ended the call and looked up at his guys. "So we're left with ceiling or sub-floor entry."

Both would make their lives difficult, but ceiling entries were pretty much always a last resort and a total fucking nightmare to execute. There were so many things that could go wrong; wires and piping and insulation for them and their gear to get hung up on.

Getting stuck at the critical moment of coming through the ceiling would delay their entry and leave them perfect sitting ducks for any shooter within range, let alone for someone with Spivey's training. Not to mention their entry could trigger any and all the explosives Spivey had wired into the place. They were considering him to be suicidal, so without a doubt he'd use them.

Tuck's first priority was to make sure all of his guys went home in one piece tonight. Everything else was secondary.

He rubbed a hand over his jaw, the whiskers scraping his palm. "Since it's our best option at the moment, let's take another look at the underground approach."

He pulled the street map from the bottom of the pile and set it on top, tapped on the faint markings that showed an old tunnel first used during the Civil War by Union troops charged with fortifying the capitol's defenses. It traveled directly beneath the bank, three meters below ground.

City crews had used it over the years since as a means to access various parts of the sewer or electrical systems. That didn't mean it was still accessible.

"Bauer, your contact at City Hall still on hold for

TARGETED

us?"

"Yeah, I'll call him now."

"Good. Find out if anyone's been in this tunnel recently and whether we can access the bank from it. In the meantime, let's grab our gear and load up so we can get rolling." Because he had a feeling they were gonna get the call soon anyway, and the order to assault shortly after.

"You got it," his roomie replied, pulling out his phone on the way to the loadout room.

After everyone had their gear the team loaded into two of their trucks. Schroder drove the one Tuck was in while he and the others held a pow-wow in the back.

Bauer verified over the phone that the tunnel did have direct access to the bank, through an old trap door in the floor of one of the back offices. It had been used by counterfeiters after the Civil War, and had long since been welded shut. Luckily they had the tools to fix that.

Tuck pulled out the map once more so everyone could see the access tunnel beneath the bank. "All right, let's go over this," Tuck said, and they began discussing their strategy, including backup plans for all conceivable contingencies. As he visualized the entry, a foreign sense of foreboding settled over him. He'd only felt this way a handful of times throughout his career and it always meant bad shit was going to happen.

Shoving it aside, he glanced at his watch, noting the time. They were about ten minutes from their destination, the closest access point to the tunnel from the bank. They'd wait there, prep as much as they could and stand by for further orders. If DeLuca's call to Spivey didn't go well, they could be given the order to assault immediately.

Didn't matter when the order came, Tuck wouldn't take his team into this blind.

No matter what happened in the minutes or hours

ahead, he was going to make sure they were ready.

****

Every passing minute dragged by with agonizing slowness. He'd been planning this for so long. The constant overload of adrenaline was takings its toll because he could already feel the exhaustion starting to drag him down. Now, more than anything, he just wanted this over with.

Ken wiped his upper arm against the side of his face to catch the trickle of sweat that ran down his temple. It was sweltering in the bank now.

Since releasing the woman and child, he'd given each of the remaining thirteen hostages some water and a few mouthfuls of protein bar. They'd accepted him hand feeding them without looking at him, except the old lady, who'd glared a hole through his face the entire time he'd fed her.

The security guard had finally shown some backbone too, refusing either food or water with a mute shake of his head. The buried rage in his eyes and his watchfulness told Ken the guy was looking for an opportunity to act.

He wouldn't find one.

In the dimness he checked his watch. Six minutes until the deadline. He was sure DeLuca cared enough about safeguarding the hostages to make a simple phone call.

When he looked back at the hostages, the old lady was wiping her face against her shoulder again, the fourth time in as many minutes. The polyester material of her shirt was dark with sweat from repeated wiping. He only needed one hostage for this next step, and his choice was a no-brainer.

He stalked out from behind the counter. "Everyone

on their feet." They all stared at him for a moment. "Up, now. Except you," he said, turning the pistol on the security guard. "You stay right there where I can see you, and don't move."

The man's jaw flexed and his nostrils flared but he didn't move, just stared back at Ken with utter loathing. "Come on, move it," Ken snapped at the others, ushering them around the counter toward the back.

At the doorway that led to the vault, he paused and looked back at the security guard. "Every single door and window in here is wired. You try to open any of them, you kill us all."

Another baleful glare was the only reply.

Turning his back on the man for a few seconds, Ken herded the other twelve hostages to the vault. There was a small air vent inside, mostly used to control the humidity. They'd have plenty of air.

After demanding the vault code from the manager at gunpoint, he opened it and forced them inside. Some resisted, but quickly got moving when he put his Glock to the back of the bank manager's head and threatened to shoot him here and now if they didn't get their asses inside.

The air felt at least twenty degrees cooler in here, so there was less risk of them dehydrating or succumbing to heat exhaustion. With their hands secured behind them there was no way the manager or anyone else could access the keypad beside the door or enter the code to open the vault door, and they wouldn't be able to see anything in the darkness once he closed the door anyway.

Leaving them there in the dark, knowing they wouldn't be able to do anything to cause him trouble at this point, he shut the vault door behind him and hurried back to the front of the bank. The guard was exactly where Ken had left him, which wasn't a surprise. There was nothing the man could do to disarm the trigger on Ken's explosives vest, even if his hands were free.

Ignoring him, Ken walked to the desk and waited. The phone rang moments later. Holding the trigger switch hard in his left hand, he lowered the pistol in his right to the desk and answered.

"This is Special Agent Matt DeLuca, commanding officer of the HRT. I understand you wanted to talk to me?"

Even though he'd expected this call, had anticipated it for months and practiced exactly what he'd say, Ken couldn't control the sudden leap in his pulse at the sound of the other man's voice. He sucked in a calming breath, tightened his hand around the receiver. "Are you on site?"

"I am."

The sonofabitch sounded every bit as arrogant as Ken had expected. "Are you interested in being the hero today? Because I might be willing to make a deal with you."

"What kind of deal?"

"You for nine of the hostages." All the females, because he didn't want any women dying here today if he could help it.

DeLuca grunted. "We both know that's not an option."

"Then their deaths will be on you."

"They'll be on *you*," DeLuca corrected, a bite to his voice, "unless you do the right thing by letting them go and giving yourself up. You haven't hurt anyone yet. It's not too late to end this before things escalate."

"We both know that's not an option either," Ken sneered, echoing the earlier reply. He was too invested now and had passed the point of no return the moment he'd taken these hostages.

Killing the agent responsible for his wife and son's

deaths wasn't possible because the man was already dead. He would have gone after the original HRT if possible, but it had proven impossible to find the names of the members, and it had taken him years to plan and put all this together. In hindsight maybe he could have more easily hunted DeLuca down and killed him before all of this.

But that wasn't what Ken was after. He wanted to deal the hardest blow possible and that's why he'd gone to the lengths he had to ensure the HRT would respond to this hostage taking.

A few seconds of taut silence followed. "What did you want to talk to me about?"

"About how you can sleep at night after what you did."

"What did I do?"

The rage he'd been suppressing for the past few hours suddenly flared to life. Hot. Searing his insides. His breathing increased, pulse thudding in his ears. "You killed my wife and son, you son of a bitch."

"No, I didn't. You're misinformed. I wasn't even inside the bank."

Ken's lips curled into a sneer. "You gave the order for the assault. It'd only been three hours since you guys showed up on site. Your negotiator hadn't even begun to try to de-escalate things and the hostage-taker was a strung-out amateur bank robber. You rushed the assault and people died because of it. That's on you."

"I take full responsibility for my decisions that day. The hostage-taker had already killed two people, Ken, and he was about to kill another. I had no choice but to order the assault, and as a cop and former soldier you must know that."

"What I *know* is that you ordered that breach prematurely and my wife and son died as a result. Killed by one of *your men*, even though your unit's fucking

motto is *Servare Vitas*." To Save Lives. The bitter irony
of it burned like battery acid inside him.

"It was a ricochet, Ken. A terrible accident. I know
you read the reports."

"Yeah, and that's why I know it's bullshit. What I
also know is that you covered for your guy. You made
sure the truth got buried during the investigation. That
the witnesses conveniently forgot or were confused
about who fired first so you could claim rightful
authorization of lethal force." His voice was raised now,
the anger pushing at him hard.

"Ballistics and physics don't lie. You read the
report on those too."

"They do if there's a cover up." That was the part
that enraged him more than anything else. How could
DeLuca have done it? His hand shook around the phone,
his thumb twitching on the vest trigger. "You know
goddamn well it wasn't a ricochet that killed my family.
It wasn't a fucking magic bullet that took them both
out—it was one of your guys lacking discipline, being a
trigger happy cowboy, dying for the opportunity to take
the perp out and not caring who got in his way."

"You're wrong, Ken. The man who fired that round
was one of the best operators I've ever worked with, and
a good friend. He'd never take that shot unless he had no
other option. And he'd certainly never have endangered
your wife's and son's lives on purpose."

Ken wasn't stupid. He realized that Special Agent
Jason Holland hadn't gone into the bank intending to
hurt Carla and Eli that day, let alone kill them, but there
was no fucking way someone with his training,
experience and expertise should have *ever* taken that
shot. Not when innocent hostages were in the line of fire.

Yet he'd done it anyway. Ken's nostrils flared. "I
think you ordered him to take that shot."

"I didn't, I promise you. But even so, I take full

responsibility for what happened that day. I'm sorry for your loss."

The lame apology meant less than nothing to Ken at this point. "Bullshit. And afterward you lied through your fucking teeth during the investigation so you and the other federal assholes could cover the truth up, to save his ass—and your own," he spat, vaguely aware that he was shaking all over now. DeLuca's part in the cover up was unforgivable. "You made sure the charges were dropped against him and that he was cleared to return to duty so you could put him on a security detail you were forming overseas." Where he'd died. At least there was some karmic justice in that.

Still wasn't enough. He wanted DeLuca to pay for everything Ken had endured. All of it. DeLuca's wife had died a few years ago and he didn't have any kids. His men, his career, were his life now. Ken wanted him to watch his men die, as he'd been forced to stand by while Carla and Eli had died, and for DeLuca to be helpless to save them.

"Look. What happened that day was a terrible tragedy and I'm sorry for all of it. All of us are. But this—this isn't going to make it better. The folks you've taken hostage had nothing to do with what happened. They're innocent and have families of their own."

It wouldn't make the situation better, no, Ken agreed, but it would make it better for *him*. Knowing he would die today was the only thing that gave him the strength to go through with this. He was so tired. Tired of the anger and the pain and the loneliness, the anxiety of the last few days. Only a few hours more remained at most. He would see this through.

"Let me put Agent Gunderson back on the line," DeLuca said, his tone softer now, trying to sound reasonable. "She wants me to tell you she's been on the phone with your parents. They're worried about you and want to talk to you."

Ken had nothing to say to either of them. He'd said everything he needed to when he'd visited them back at Christmas. The Feds were still stalling, wanting to try to defuse the situation, still thinking he could be talked down. Or they were hoping he could be.

Not. Fucking. Happening.

"Don't bother, I'm done talking," Ken snapped, his voice ringing with finality. He looked up, over the top of the counter. Met the security guard's gaze. The man stared back at him, wary and tense.

This was it. The moment of truth. He had to make them act. Maybe he couldn't kill DeLuca directly or take his family from him, but he could still inflict plenty of pain and grief on the man. Before he left this earth, Ken needed to know DeLuca would suffer for what he'd done.

His fingers clenched around the phone. "This time you're gonna be the one standing on the perimeter, watching. Helpless to protect the people you care about."

"Ken, hey—"

He dropped the receiver to the counter with a clatter and grabbed the Glock, leaving the line open so DeLuca could hear what was happening, and stalked around the end of the counter.

Still against the west wall, the guard scrambled to his feet, his face tight with fear as Ken came at him. He raised the pistol and the man's eyes widened with terror. "Tell them your name," he growled. "Tell them!" he yelled when the man didn't comply right away.

"Mike Ippoliti," he said.

"Louder, so they can hear you."

"Mike Ippoliti!" he shouted.

Ken stalked toward him, pistol aimed center mass at the guy's chest.

"No," the guard rasped, shaking his head. "No,

don't." Arms still secured behind his back, he was unable to do anything to protect himself except twist away. "Don't do this—please!"

Ken kept coming, resolved in his course of action. There was no other way to make everything else happen.

The guard whirled and tried to run, his scream ripping through the hot, still air. "For God's sake, *no!*" He took a single lunging step, a futile step toward escape.

Ken halted, took aim as he drew a steadying breath, and squeezed the trigger twice.

Chapter Sixteen

As the sounds of those gunshots echoed in her ears, everyone in the command trailer went totally, eerily still.

The victim's final scream for mercy was cut off and a moment later the phone connection was severed. As if Spivey had yanked the line out of the wall.

Celida's heart lodged in her throat in the sudden silence that enveloped the command trailer. Before anyone could move or speak, the radio on DeLuca's hip squawked and the voice of someone on one of the sniper teams came through in the awful stillness. "Shots fired, shots fired."

DeLuca pounded a fist on the table, shattering the silence. "Fuck!" He threw the now useless phone receiver onto the desk with so much force it bounced and hit the window beside Gunderson.

Without pause he whirled and stalked toward the rear doors, his boots thudding on the steel floor. He and Travers shared a long look. Then Travers gave a nod and Celida's stomach sank like a lead weight because she knew exactly what it meant. Tuck and his boys were about to get the call. Mike Ippoliti had been the security guard on duty at the bank today. He had a wife and infant daughter. Now he was dead.

As DeLuca exited the trailer into the brilliant sunshine, Travers turned to Gunderson. "Keep trying. See if you can still reach him on one of the other phones in there."

Celida didn't say anything. They all knew it would be futile, but they had to try. Without eyes or ears inside, at least one hostage likely dead and no way to communicate with the suspect, they were rapidly running out of options to end this thing peacefully.

Every cop and federal agent on scene knew what that meant.

At this point there was jack shit Celida or anyone else in here could do to stop the situation from continuing its downward spiral. There was no point looking up more friends or relatives of Spivey's to see if they'd make the difference in forcing him to reconsider and stand down, and they couldn't communicate with Spivey anyhow.

She curled her hands into fists as she awaited Travers's next order. As the officer in charge on scene, what happened now was his call. He was already on the phone, presumably talking to the assistant director of the FBI or maybe the director himself.

As he ended the call his gaze landed on Celida, his face set in grim lines. "Move everyone back. Secure a new perimeter fifteen yards further out."

Even though she'd known it would come to this, she couldn't shake the terrible dread expanding inside her. She wished she'd come clean last night and told him how she really felt about him, rather than just show him. "I'm on it." She dumped her headset on the desk and rose.

Tuck's face swam through her mind. Tense,

focused and full of possessiveness as he'd taken her on the kitchen table last night. Soft with tenderness and affection this morning when he'd seen her off to work. A lump settled in her throat. She couldn't lose him. She'd just found him again, wanted him to be a big part of her life.

As she headed out the doors to start coordinating everything, she saw DeLuca standing near the rear of the trailer with two other heavily armed agents, big men dressed in cargo pants and FBI windbreakers. Two more members of the HRT.

DeLuca was on his phone. When she stepped off the bottom step of the trailer he ended one call, then dialed someone else. She passed by him, close enough to catch him say "That's affirm, the director's okayed it. You've got a green light", there was no doubt who he was talking to.

Feeling sick to her stomach Celida quickly walked away, her phone to her ear to call the chief of police and get everything in motion. Moving this many people and vehicles back that far, and fast, was going to take a combined effort of every law enforcement agency here.

While she waited for the call to connect she called out to the people closest to her—clusters of federal agents and uniformed cops standing at edge of the marked perimeter. "All right, listen up—I need everyone to move back fifty feet, now. Spread the word. Everyone report to your superiors once you're in position."

People started moving immediately. Celida hustled to get the word out all along the perimeter, struggling to focus on the task at hand when her attention kept straying back to the bank behind her.

Unless a miracle occurred in the immediate future, an assault was imminent, but few people here would know when it was about to happen. Whether Tuck and his men were on their way here or already in place, they would be going in at any time and there was nothing she or anyone else here could do to help from the outside now.

Other than securing the area right now, all she could do at the moment was pray that whatever plan they'd come up with would keep them safe from the asshole barricaded in that bank.

****

Crouched in the darkness of the tunnel beneath the bank's floor, Tuck aimed his Maglite at the steel roof above him and studied the weld marks around the edge of the two-by-three foot rectangle in it, a sense of urgency driving him. Ten feet above them right now, things were critical.

Spivey had fired another two rounds twelve minutes ago, presumably meaning he'd killed another hostage in addition to the security guard. With the way things were deteriorating, the chances of saving the remaining hostages were dwindling with every passing minute. They had to find a way inside the bank, and fast.

Tuck double checked the coordinates on the map he'd pulled from his pocket and the pedometer they'd used to calculate the distance they'd traveled underground. Their vehicles were almost a quarter mile behind them and they'd had to carry all their weapons and equipment on their backs. Not an easy feat, considering how narrow the ancient tunnel was in spots and all the refuse they'd had to scramble through. A few sections must have caved in over the years because even though crews had obviously patched them up and cleaned it out somewhat, piles of brick and stone still littered the tunnel.

He tapped his earpiece, wiped at the sweat that beaded his face. Beneath all his gear, he was soaked with it. By comparison it was much cooler underground than it was on street level but it had been a hell of a trek getting everything here through the confined space. His beat-up, already twice-scoped knees were aching; they'd likely be flared up for a few days after this op. "Grant, you copy? We're in position."

"Loud and clear," the backup team leader responded. "We're in position as well, standing by."

The other assault team was in place near the newly defined interior perimeter, sequestered from everyone else, and would act if necessary. "Roger."

Tuck looked over his shoulder. Bauer crouched behind him, his huge frame filling the tunnel. Evers was next, then Schroder, the team medic and former PJ. Blackwell and Cruz were behind them, and Vance brought up the rear. Each man carried a different piece of equipment for the op, on top of their regular load of tools, weapons and ammo. "You guys ready?" he asked them.

Every team member answered in the affirmative. Tuck tapped his earpiece again, this time contacting DeLuca, who would have received his orders on the assault from the director by now. "Dagger one's in place, standing by for your order."

"We've got you on GPS, Dagger one, everything looks good. No change up here. Still no viz, no comms with the suspect," DeLuca said. "Op's a go. Execute at your discretion."

"Roger that. Dagger one actual, out." He tapped the earpiece again, looked back down the line of men to Blackwell. "Give me the ladder."

The men passed the extendable aluminum assault ladder up the line. Tuck and Bauer got it in position, wedged between the low ceiling and the uneven floor. Bauer braced it and Tuck slung his MP5 across his chest, pulling the most critical weapon out of one of the pockets on his web gear. The hand-held EMP device was around the same size as a pistol and fit in his hand easily. Its range was debatable, but supposedly effective up to about thirty feet. The pulse it emitted wasn't especially powerful but it was precise, and it was all they had to take care of the dead man's switch.

If Spivey didn't just blow the whole building in response to the breach, and *if* Tuck could get within range to fire the thing.

He wiped at his upper lip with the back of one hand, focused on the welded trap door above him. There were so many unknowns about this op—more than they usually had to contend with—and the chances of everything turning to shit were too damn high. No one knew whether Spivey was even aware of the trap door in the manager's office, or whether he'd booby trapped it.

Even if the team managed to cut through the welding without Spivey hearing and coming to investigate, there was no telling what they'd find above it. More steel, concrete, marble, no one they'd talked to was sure. Could be they'd have to blow a charge to open up a hole in the floor for entry, and that risked Spivey blowing the entire building to hell, along with everyone in it.

Their job was to get everyone out of that bank alive—including Spivey. Based on what he'd done so far, there was no way he was going to give himself up willingly.

Tuck didn't plan on dying today, and he sure as hell wasn't losing any of his men on this op.

He stepped back and nodded at Evers, who'd carried the blowtorch and tanks. Not only was Tuck team leader, he was also the smallest guy here, so there was no question that he'd be the first one through whatever hole they made. Bauer would hold the ladder for everyone and come up last, but his big frame put him at a definite disadvantage for this one.

Evers climbed the ladder while Cruz slid past Tuck to balance the tanks. "Here's hoping Spivey doesn't have microphones in this room," Evers muttered, and lit the torch. The brilliant, hot flame shot out and Evers got busy cutting through the hundred and fifty year old steel. It was slow, painstaking work to cut all the way through the half inch thick steel, the torch throwing sparks as it cut a molten orange line in the roof.

Tuck stayed at the base of the ladder with the EMP device clutched tight in his right hand, mentally rehearsing his movements. By the time they'd actually made a hole in the floor, Spivey would likely either be right on top of him with that explosives vest, or he'd blow the perimeter windows and doors.

There was nothing he could do about the second, so his only shot was to prevent the vest from going off. Assuming Spivey didn't hear them coming and blow the explosives wired to the doors and windows, the moment Tuck's head and shoulders cleared the hole he'd have to locate Spivey, aim at the trigger in his hand and fire the EMP device to render the vest useless.

And then hope to hell the thing worked so he could take the fucker down without dying in the process.

It weighed heavy on him that Celida was up there, watching and waiting. She'd be worried, and he didn't want to think about what would happen if he didn't make it. All he knew was, if he made it through this one, he wasn't going to hold anything back from her anymore. He couldn't. She was too important to him.

And he loved her. The first chance he got, he was saying everything he needed to say, get her to promise she was in this for the long haul along with him.

Shut the hell up and focus. You've done undercover snatch-and-grab ops on warlords in broad daylight in freaking Somalia, for God's sake. You're going to make it.

A few minutes later, DeLuca's voice came through Tuck's earpiece, tense and grim. "How long?"

"Another six or seven minutes to cut through the roof. Why, what's happening?"

"Spivey just fired another two shots. Still no visual or any other info."

Another hostage dead. Tuck's jaw flexed. "Understood. Will update you once we've cut through this steel." Then he'd have more of an idea what they were dealing with in terms of their entry possibilities.

Evers kept making steady progress with the torch and finally moved onto the last, short side of the rectangular cut. When he finished the last few inches, he handed down the torch and pulled off his goggles, wiping his sleeve over his sweaty face to mop up the moisture. Cruz climbed down with the torch and tanks, the ladder creaking and bowing with his every step.

Evers pressed his gloved palm to the cut panel and pushed to test it, then added his other hand, his face tightening from the strain on his muscles. "It's giving a bit," he said in a quiet voice that barely carried to the base of the ladder. "Bauer, gimme a hand."

Tuck steadied the ladder while Bauer climbed up, lending his considerable size and muscle to the effort. A shrill groan sliced through the tunnel as the metal began to give way. Both men froze, everyone waiting to see if Spivey had heard anything and was going to act. Tense seconds ticked past, all eyes pinned to the rectangular panel.

When nothing happened, they resumed pushing on the trapdoor. Evers's and Bauer's faces were slick with sweat, their teeth bared as they used their combined strength to muscle the steel slab upward. Finally the last part of the cut seam gave way with a creak and a loud pop.

Evers groaned as he slid the piece of steel aside, on top of the tunnel roof, and Bauer shined his Maglite on the exposed area above it. An old wooden door with an iron ring handle was revealed in the beam of light, about three feet above the hole cut into the tunnel roof.

"Off duty bank employee we interviewed said this leads directly into the manager's office," Tuck said to the others, keeping his voice down just in case. "If we're lucky, there shouldn't be anything but a thin slab of marble covering this on the other side. Pass up the boltcutters." Schroder brought them over. Tuck held them up for Evers while Bauer climbed down, still directing the intense beam of light at the trap door.

Evers made short work of the old padlock holding the iron ring handle in place. He pulled it free and handed it down, gave an experimental push against the wooden surface. "It's giving," he confirmed. "Shouldn't take much for you to pop it free now."

"Sounds good," Tuck answered. "Come back down."

He waited until Evers had left the ladder before putting his right boot on the bottom rung and looking back at the others. He didn't need to remind any of them what the contingency plans were, or that Bauer would take command if something happened to him.

"Ready?" When they all confirmed in the affirmative he began his ascent while Evers held the ladder and Bauer kept the light steady on the door. The soles of his boots clanged softly against the aluminum rungs with each step.

When he was partway up, Cruz took up position at the bottom of the ladder, waiting to follow Tuck as the second man in line, weapon at the ready. Tuck slipped the EMP into a pocket on the front of his webbing and positioned his body weight on the ladder so he'd be able to use his hands without fear of falling.

"On three," he whispered, knowing they'd all hear him via their earpieces. Heightened by years of operational and combat experience, his situational awareness was honed to a razor's edge. Every sense was intensified as he stood ready to lead his men. He had one shot at this. It was going to be enough.

Bauer shut off his flashlight, plunging them into total darkness.

Tuck pulled down the NVGs on his helmet mount and switched them on. They wouldn't help him here in the pitch blackness but even a tiny amount of ambient light inside the bank would allow them to see everything clearly, lit up in a field of neon green.

He placed both hands against the wooden surface of the door, braced his feet wider apart to give him a solid footing on the ladder. "One." He added some pressure with his arms, relieved when the door moved a tiny bit. Fucker was solid though, and heavy.

Silence greeted him, his teammates' gazes riveted to what he was doing.

"Two." The muscles in his arms and shoulders pulled taut as he put his body weight into it. The door gave a little more.

Nobody moved, the energy in the tunnel suddenly intensifying in anticipation of the assault.

Go time. "Three."

Calling on all the power he could muster, he used his legs to help give him the leverage he needed and heaved with all his might. The wood and marble slab lifted a quarter inch, revealing a sliver of faint light from above. His arms shook from the strain. Gritting his teeth, Tuck shoved the door upward farther, uncaring of the noise it would make when it fell over because it couldn't be helped—he needed both hands free as quickly as possible.

The trap door hit the marble with a deep thud that

shook the floor.

Tuck's eyes darted around the space as they quickly adjusted to the dimness, every sense on alert. The room was empty. He grabbed the EMP from his vest, placed his left hand on the floor and shoved up, scrambling through the hole onto one knee. As he did he snatched his sidearm with his left hand, was bringing it up into position when he caught a flash of movement in the doorway ahead of him.

Time went slo-mo as it always did on an op. His gaze zeroed in on the darkened threshold, locked there.

Disable the vest. Take Spivey down without lethal force.

Everything happened within the space of a few heartbeats.

He raised the EMP device, his entire body tensing as Spivey appeared, wearing NVGs, and came to an abrupt halt between the jambs. The man's attention zeroed in on Tuck, the beginnings of a feral smile spreading across his face as his left hand began to move upward.

Tuck recognized the dead man's switch. He aimed the EMP device and pulled the trigger, holding it down a mere instant before Spivey released his thumb from the switch.

Nothing happened. Which meant the device had worked.

Tuck barely had time for that to register, for relief to crash through him and to see the look of absolute shock on Spivey's face before the man raised his Glock.

Tuck fired twice and automatically ducked down slightly to take himself out of the line of fire just as a round whizzed by, right where his head had been less than a second ago. His own bullets hit home, burying themselves in Spivey's right shoulder.

The man bellowed in pain and surprise and

stumbled back, out of view. A second later his running footsteps echoed in the silence. Tuck cursed and set a hand on the floor to push his body up and give chase. He gained his footing, heard Cruz coming up the ladder behind him, and raced for the open doorway. As he reached the threshold something heavy thudded shut in the next room. The vault?

An ominous foreboding slammed into his brain.

Spivey was out of range. *He's going to detonate the bombs.*

Fuck.

He whirled back toward the trap door. "Get down, everybody down!" he yelled to his team.

He dove for the opening, his chest and belly hitting the floor. He managed to swing around, shove both feet back through the open trap door so he could go backward down the ladder. Someone—probably Cruz—grabbed his legs and yanked hard, trying to get him back into the relative safety of the tunnel. His lower body slid down, then his torso.

The moment his right boot touched the top rung of the ladder, the room exploded.

A wave of searing heat and pressure hit him, knocking him backward into the air. Blackness engulfed him as the world came crashing down around him.

Chapter Seventeen

———◆～◆———

At a roped-off area of the interior perimeter closest to the bank, Celida walked up to Travers, who was speaking to DeLuca and one other man. The newcomer was dressed in tactical gear, an HRT patch on his shoulder.

Travers saw her, lifted an eyebrow and took a step toward her. She didn't recognize the HRT member, but based on his presence here and that he was consulting with DeLuca, she guessed he must be the backup assault team's leader.

She turned her gaze on Travers. "Gunderson talked to Spivey's former Denver PD CO. She's on the phone with his former platoon leader, a master sergeant he was really close with but Spivey still won't answer any of the landlines inside."

The master sergeant was their last shot in terms of finding someone to help talk Spivey down, and maybe their best one at this point. They'd served two tours together in Afghanistan, saved each other's lives over there. Apparently he was one of the only people Spivey had spoken to regularly via phone and e-mail since getting out of the Army.

Right up until a week ago, two days before the bombings had started. The sergeant was shocked by what Spivey had done and wanted to talk to him, plead with him to give himself up. Unfortunately it didn't seem like he was going to get that chance.

Travers sighed and shook his head. "He's too unstable to listen right now. Using a bullhorn is useless at this stage and I don't want anyone breaching this perimeter anyway, it's too dangerous."

Celida slanted a look at DeLuca, whose gaze was focused on the bank as he listened to something else the other man was saying, hands on his hips, posture tense. Were Tuck and the others in position for the assault right now? She looked back at Travers. She had security clearance but protocol dictated that in this case only the director, DeLuca and his crew, and possibly Travers would know when the assault would happen.

It was killing her not to know the details, but he couldn't divulge them to her even if he'd wanted to, for security reasons. The fewer people who knew when the breach would happen, the safer it was for the team.

Travers's eyes softened with understanding. "Won't be long now."

Her pulse sped up and she nodded before he turned back to join DeLuca and the other team leader. On her way back to the command trailer, Celida's phone rang in her hand. When she saw Zoe's number for a second she thought about ignoring it again as she had her friend's previous two calls, then changed her mind and picked up. This lull in the op was driving her crazy, there was piss-all she could do at the moment, and a few second-long convo with Zoe would help calm her nerves.

"Hey." She walked a short distance away from the men and stopped, watching the bank. Tuck and the others could make the assault from the ground or they might try a roof entry. Both were extremely dangerous given Spivey's expertise. A helo op was out because the noise of the rotors would give Spivey too much notice of the assault. Her stomach knotted.

"Hi. I'm watching the news about the bank and knew you'd be on scene. Are you okay?"

"I'm fine, Zo." Just stressed and worried as hell.

"What about Tuck and Bauer, are they okay?"

Celida sighed. "As far as I know."

"Okay, I know you can't share details with me. I just…I wanted to call and check on you, and to apologize for setting you up like that last night."

"Don't worry about it."

"So we're still good?"

"We're still good." It was impossible to stay mad at Zoe and to be honest Celida was grateful for the shove Zoe had given her and Tuck last night. Without that, the ensuing confrontation would never have happened and she wouldn't have shared what was the single most important night of her life with him.

"Glad to hear it. If you see my cousin, tell him I said to be careful. I figured I'd go visit with his dad for a while. If he's having a good day and he's seen the news coverage, he'll know what's going on and he'll worry."

"That's good of you, Zo, thanks." She blew out a breath, still watching the bank. The tension was freaking killing her and as much as she'd love to spill it all to Zoe, she couldn't. And she wouldn't want to burden her friend with all this shit anyhow, because there was nothing Zoe could do to help the situation. "I gotta go, hon. Don't know when I'll be home, so remember that *mi casa es su casa*, right?"

"I'm not at your place, I'm still at Tuck's."

Celida felt her face go blank with surprise. She'd stayed the night with Bauer?

Pushing that thought away, she responded. "Okay,

I'll call you back when I can, but it'll probably be—"

An explosion thundered through the air. The blast wave ripped outward, making the ground roll beneath her feet. Celida gasped, her gaze flying to the bank as she automatically crouched. A plume of smoke rose into the clear, blue air.

Every muscle in her body was rigid, her lungs feeling like they would explode as she held her breath. Had Spivey done that, or was the assault team in there? DeLuca, the other assault team leader and Travers were all stock still, the looks on their faces making her gut sink.

She started to push to her feet. Before she could stand, three more powerful explosions rocked the building with a great roar. This time she hit the ground and covered her head while the earth rolled beneath her and the pressure waves blasted her ears and body. Debris thudded the parking lot ahead of her, smaller bits raining down around her.

When the noise faded she uncovered her head. Her phone lay in the dirt where she'd dropped it. Over the ringing in her ears she could faintly hear Zoe's frantic voice in the background asking what was going on.

Terror slammed through her at the sight that met her eyes. The walls of the bank had crumbled, big pieces of the ceiling missing. Smoke and debris filled the air, and in the gaps the explosions had opened up she could see flames already licking greedily at the interior.

She jerked her gaze to DeLuca. He was on one knee, his face was taut with concern, one hand to his ear as he spoke in a loud voice into his radio. "Alpha team, report." He looked up at the other team leader, shook his head. The other man took off.

Jesus Christ.

Climbing to her feet, she ran to where Travers was frantically talking on his cell phone. He saw her coming, snagged her arm and tugged her, turning his body as if to shield her.

Over his shoulder she stared at the smoldering building, denial and shock slamming into her. As he started to lower his phone she grabbed his arm, hard, and shook him. She knew she should be worried about the hostages but there was only one person on her mind.

"Is Tuck in there?" she demanded, panic slamming through her.

Mouth pressed into a thin line, he met her gaze and nodded once.

Celida stumbled back a step, heart in her throat as she looked back at the smoldering ruins of the bank. Without thinking she took off toward it, her only thought was that she had to get Tuck and the others out before the fire spread.

Travers cursed and grabbed her from behind, lifting her off her feet. "You fucking stay put," he snarled.

Celida twisted out of his grasp and whirled on him, breathing hard. "They're trapped and the fire's spreading. Are we gonna just stand here and watch them die?"

Travers's expression told her he thought they were already dead. "There could be more unexploded devices—"

"He rigged all the doors and windows, which are no longer fucking standing." She was shaking all over, nausea roiling in her gut. "I'm going in there." Pivoting on her heel, she lunged past him.

Hard arms caught her again, twisted her to the ground where he pinned her with his weight. She screeched in outrage but he held her fast. "Goddamn it, just wait. Just *wait*," he snapped when she shoved at his chest, and finally eased up to help her into a sitting position.

It was then she felt the way his muscles were

shaking, realized he was dealing with his own adrenaline surge and didn't want to see her hurt. "Give them a few minutes to make sure," he said, voice tight.

Celida nodded, accepted the hand he held out and let him help her to her feet.

"You can't help him if you're dead. Give them a few minutes to make sure," he said, voice raspy.

Curling her hands into fists so hard her nails dug into her palms, Celida watched helplessly as their bomb techs checked the perimeter. Agonizing minutes ticked past while her heart ached with each slam against her ribs.

Tuck. Tuck, please be okay. She didn't know how to cope with losing him.

One of the techs moved forward with a sniffer dog and Celida caught a flash of movement in a gap in one of the partially collapsed walls. She stepped forward, squinting through the haze of smoke. "Someone's coming out!"

All heads turned in the direction of the bank. A woman was struggling to push her way through the debris. She ignored the bomb techs' shouts to stay still and kept fighting to get out, her hands secured behind her back. Celida could see the shock on the woman's dust-streaked face as she shoved her shoulder against a block of stone that had tumbled down and fell forward as it toppled over. She landed on the rubble-strewn ground outside the perimeter. Cops and agents began running toward her.

Celida took off with them. Her heart beat a frantic rhythm against her chest, her thigh muscles burning with the effort of the prolonged sprint to the ruined bank.

DeLuca and Travers caught up to her, pulled past her as they raced to help. They all drew their weapons. If there were other survivors then Spivey could still be alive in there and they weren't taking any chances.

Thick dust and smoke coated her skin, her nostrils. She coughed, yanked the neck of her T-shirt up to act as a scarf. While DeLuca and Travers swung over a low section of rubble to enter the bank, she hauled herself up and over the first stone hurdle then raised her weapon.

Once inside they all paused to look around. Utter devastation met her gaze everywhere she looked. Flames crackled around what was left of two window frames set into the east wall and around the front doors on the south side. "Back there," DeLuca said, waving them toward the back offices. He knew where Tuck and the others had been.

Fear jolted through her as she took in the wreckage. Those blasts had been powerful enough to practically implode the building. The odds of anyone inside surviving were low.

And yet that woman had made it out. Were other hostages still alive too?

DeLuca climbed over more debris and disappeared from view around the corner with a few other agents. Celida and Travers started after him, climbing the small mountain of stone, concrete and metal. Grit and smoke stung the back of her throat, made her eyes water. She grabbed at a block of limestone and used it as a handhold to pull herself up.

Shouts from where DeLuca had gone brought her head up. Two agents appeared at the top of the pile, a dust-covered man between them. His ears were bleeding, hands still behind his back. Another hostage.

Desperate to help with the rescue effort to locate the assault team, Celida scrambled to the top, unconcerned about the cuts and scrapes on her hands, arms and legs. Once at the top the air seemed to clear a little, the outside breeze carrying some of the dust and smoke away.

She made her way down what used to be a hallway

to the back offices as fast as she could, stopped when she saw the group of agents coming at her with more hostages. She turned sideways to let them pass and then finally realized where they were coming from.

The vault.

Spivey had put them all in the vault and the force of the explosions must have cracked the door enough to allow them to get out. Had the suicide vest detonated everything? Under all this mess they wouldn't find his remains for a long time.

The vault door stood open about a foot, the edges warped. Stone and concrete jumbled at the bottom prevented her from opening it any farther but she grabbed her flashlight from her belt and aimed it inside. More hostages were moving around, some moaning, others silent with shock.

"FBI," she called inside. "I'm here to help you out." And as soon as she helped the hostages to safety, she was going to help DeLuca and the others. She could hear them digging in another room past the vault, at the place where Tuck and the others had executed the breach.

Refusing to allow herself to think about them finding Tuck's body in the rubble, she clamped down on her emotions and focused on her job. She helped two women to the exterior wall of the bank where others were waiting to shepherd them back to the secure perimeter and the ambulances. Their climb up the debris pile was made awkward by their lack of balance due to their bound hands. A quick snick of her pocketknife made short work of that. Travers stopped long enough to help an old woman get down the pile safely then hurriedly climbed back to Celida.

"I'm gonna go back and help clear the rubble to get our guys out," he said.

Throat tight, she nodded and went back for more hostages, moving aside for another agent as he helped a

man pass by. On her way back to the vault, more
hostages emerged from the darkness. She recognized the
security guard and was shocked that he was still alive.
He was bleeding badly from his shoulder, his hands
unbound, face and head obscured by that pale gray dust
that covered everything.

"Over here—I'll help you to the EMTs," Celida
called out.

He flicked her a quick look, shook his head and
turned toward the back offices. "Gotta help."

Before she could go after him, a woman stumbled
out of the vault. Her nose and ears were bleeding, her
eyes were dazed. She blinked at Celida like a
sleepwalker. Celida took her by the arm and led her out,
cut the zip tie holding her wrists prisoner at the small of
her back.

As she turned around, she came face to face with a
man standing in the vault doorway. Like the others he
was covered in dust but he wore nothing but an
undershirt and boxers. And his hands were already
unbound. He held them up on either side of his head,
showing he wasn't a threat.

"I'm Mike Ippoliti, the bank's security guard," he
blurted. "The perp's alive, he just walked out—"

Ippoliti? She quickly scanned his features,
recognized him from the photos she'd seen of him. He
wasn't even bleeding. So Spivey hadn't shot him? He
was right in front of her in nothing but an undershirt and
boxers—

Shit!

Everything funneled out as realization hit Celida
like a cannon blast. Her head snapped toward the ruined
hallway, terror streaking through her.

Spivey had put on the security uniform.

He's going after DeLuca and the others.

Grabbing her radio from her hip to give the others a

warning, she snatched her service weapon from her belt and tore after him.

****

Ken scrambled his way up the pile of debris while the blood roared in his ears, his progress made more difficult because of the searing pain traveling from his ruined right shoulder to his fingertips. He'd wrapped up the wounds with his shirt as best he could before grabbing the security guard's uniform but blood still dripped from his fingertips in a steady rivulet. He wiped at his face with his left hand, clearing away the sweat, smoke and coating of gray dust that stung his eyes and clogged his throat.

When he'd locked himself in the vault with the others and set the charges off he hadn't been sure any of them would survive. The damage out here was every bit as bad as he'd expected. No way that HRT guy had survived, and hopefully a few of his teammates had died too.

Coming through the floor like that was something Ken had dismissed long ago, early in the planning stages for the operation. When he'd come around the corner and seen the guy crawling through a hole in the floor he'd been prepared to die. Whatever he'd aimed at Ken had fried the circuitry in the vest, rendering it useless. Luckily it hadn't affected the rest of his explosives.

But now he had the chance to kill DeLuca too.

His breath shortened and his heart pounded. Urgent male voices floated back to him from the rear office where the assault team had tried to make entry. They were digging, trying to move the rubble away from the opening in the floor.

"Can anyone hear me?" DeLuca's voice called out.

Ken's pulse pounded. He gripped the security

guard's Beretta in his left hand and cleared the top of the rubble pile. It was chaos in here. The stolen uniform had already helped him pass by that female Fed. All he needed was another twenty seconds to get into that back room and kill DeLuca. After that he didn't care what happened.

"Still no radio contact with them. *Fuck*," DeLuca snarled.

Ken's boots slid over the small mountain of broken stone and concrete. He slipped and fell, his wounded arm taking the brunt of the impact. He bit back a howl of pain and rolled to his back, using his feet to stop his descent. Agony washed through him, stealing his breath and hazing his vision.

He couldn't stop. DeLuca was right in front of him, focused on trying to dig his men out. This was Ken's only chance to kill him. The pistol was solid in his hand, his index finger already curling around the trigger in anticipation of taking the shots.

He had only a moment to register the sound of someone scrambling up the pile behind him before he heard the squawk of a radio and a female's urgent voice come through.

"Spivey's alive and headed toward you, dressed in a security uniform!"

Shit! His heart lurched. He snapped his head back toward the vault as running footsteps sounded behind him. She was close and now DeLuca would be armed and waiting for him.

Pushing to his feet, he fought through the pain to make the last desperate rush to get down the ruined hallway. The voices ahead had quieted. The men were likely already coming for him, hemming him in between them and the female Fed behind him, and everyone outside the bank.

He reached the bottom of the pile, thudded to his

knees on the broken limestone. A snarl of pain lodged in his throat, the smoke and dust in the air making it hard to breathe.

The footsteps behind him grew louder. Closer. Bits of debris began trickling down from the top of the pile where she dislodged it.

Ken got up. Took a lurching step toward the back office. So close now. Just another few seconds.

"*Freeze*! Hands in the air!"

Jaw set, Ken whirled to face his opponent. The female Fed had cleared the crest of the pile. She stood above him, feet braced apart and her service weapon aimed at his head.

"Morales, you got him?" a concerned male voice called from the manager's office.

The men back there were moving fast now. Coming toward him. His time was nearly up.

He met the female's cold stare, muscles coiled, ready to spring and make that last desperate rush to get DeLuca. But he'd kill the woman first if he had to.

"*Hands*!" she shouted again, taking a menacing step toward him.

This time Ken didn't hesitate. Time slowed to a crawl, every movement and heartbeat a separate eternity. His hand contracted around the grip of his own weapon, intent on hitting her above the neckline of the Kevlar vest she wore. The sound of his ragged breaths was harsh in his ears. His heart thudded heavy and hard against his ribs as his finger tightened around the trigger.

The woman's gaze never wavered. Her expression was set, determined as he started to raise his weapon.

He didn't get the chance to fire. A bullet hit him in the chest just as his hand began to come up, throwing him off balance as it plowed into the Kevlar vest with the force of a sledgehammer. He staggered back a step, tried to keep raising the pistol into firing position. Pain flared bright and hot for just a moment before another round slammed into him, right through the bottom of his throat.

He dropped back, both hands flying to his throat as the blood spewed up, choking him. Wheezing and gasping, he struggled onto his side, his bleary gaze landing on the Beretta a few feet from him. Dimly he heard the sounds of the men rushing from the back. He reached out a trembling hand, his fingertips straining to find the grip of the pistol lying on the debris.

No air.

His vision went gray, his body spasming in a desperate fight for air. His mouth opened and closed, chest heaving as his lungs tried to suck in precious oxygen.

No use.

His muscles jerked once, then went lax as a loud buzzing filled his ears. His hand fell to the ground.

The woman reached him first. She was saying something, calling out to the men. *DeLuca.* He'd lost his chance to take DeLuca with him.

Through the haze of the pain and that buzzing he was vaguely aware of her kneeling beside him, her fingers pressing to the side of his throat to check his pulse. He could feel it growing weaker. Feel his body fading. The pain began to recede, everything going dark.

Carla and Eli. I'll be with them soon.

Their faces swam before him, their expressions lighting up with pure joy when they saw him. Eli broke away from Carla and started running toward him, arms open and outstretched.

A tear trickled from the corner of Ken's eyes. *I'm coming, buddy. Daddy's coming.*

And then everything went dark.

Chapter Eighteen

Celida looked up from where she was kneeling beside Spivey when DeLuca and Travers came barrelling around the corner of what had once been the hallway wall. Both men stopped short in the haze of dust and smoke when they saw her, weapons aimed at Spivey.

"He's dead," she said, her voice surprisingly steady.

DeLuca pulled out his radio. "Suspect down. Repeat, suspect down." He lowered his weapon, staring at Spivey as Travers holstered his own weapon and came toward her. Celida pulled her fingers away from Spivey's throat and stood, surprised at how shaky she felt all of a sudden.

"You all right?" Travers asked, real concern in his voice as he ran his gaze over her.

"Fine. He never even got a shot off." He would absolutely have killed her if she hadn't taken him out.

She wiped her hand against her pants, trying to clean Spivey's blood off it. Her second shot had opened a gaping hole in his throat. She'd been forced to readjust for a higher shot when her first one hadn't taken him down. He must have taken the security guard's Kevlar vest when he'd taken the uniform.

She couldn't think about all that right now though.

Travers reached for her arm but she pulled back and shook her head, turning her eyes on DeLuca. There was only one thing she was interested in knowing right now. "Did you make radio contact with the team yet?"

"Not yet. We've been trying to dig away the debris from the trap door. Thought I heard pinging down there."

Trap door? They'd breached from beneath the building somehow? Her breath hitched at the thought of them buried down there, entombed beneath a small mountain of stone and debris. "They're alive?"

"Someone is. I think they're banging something against the roof of the steel tunnel to signal us."

Hope expanded in her chest, huge and painful. Her heart hammered as she hurried over the debris to follow the two men. In what had been the manager's office she found four others struggling to clear away the rubble from the trap door.

Her stomach twisted at the sight before her. The damage in here was bad, even worse than the rest of the bank.

She swallowed, terror gripping her as she took everything in. It seemed impossible that Tuck and the others could have survived the blast, let alone all the rubble caving in on them. Were they trapped in all the debris down there? She began clawing at the rubble, clearing everything she could, barely noticing the cuts and scrapes the rock opened up on her hands. All she cared about was freeing Tuck.

Her breath sawed in her ears as she struggled to move the debris. Sweat rolled down her back, down her temples. Some of the pieces were too big to move. The men struggled and strained to clear them, but it was no use.

One of them looked up at DeLuca, sweating and breathing hard as he spoke. "We need heavy equipment in here. No way we're getting through all this, but I think I heard the pinging you were talking about too."

They couldn't wait for equipment, they had to dig them out *now*, and using heavy machinery could bring more debris down on top of them. Whoever was alive down there might be running out of air. "What about accessing them via the entry point?" She threw a worried glance at DeLuca, who pulled out his radio and keyed it.

"Grant, gimme a sitrep," he commanded.

"Just accessing the tunnel now," a male voice came back. "There's a mound of rubble blocking the far end. We can hear someone at the other end but it's pretty faint."

"Well we're not getting at them from here," DeLuca muttered. "I'll get crews in here to pull away the heavy stuff and in the meantime we'll come to you and help clear the tunnel. Emergency responders standing by?"

"That's affirm."

"All right, we're on our way to you."

"Roger."

Celida whirled and rushed back the way they'd come, not waiting for the others. She barely glanced at Spivey's body as she ran back up the pile she'd climbed to get to him. There'd be a lot of bureaucratic red tape for her to deal with later and a mountain of paperwork to accompany it but she didn't give a shit about any of that right now.

Nothing else mattered but finding out if Tuck was alive and then getting him the hell out of that tunnel.

When she emerged from the bank, fire crews were rushing toward her carrying their hoses. She jumped in the back of the SUV DeLuca and Travers climbed into.

The drive was only a few minutes but it seemed to take forever. Cops and ambulance crews stood next to an opening in the sidewalk they'd cordoned off.

Bursting out of the vehicle, she ran for it. The group of men clustered around it parted and she faltered when she saw two men carrying another on a stretcher. She sucked in a breath when she saw Bauer laid out on it, clenched fists pressed to his eyes, his teeth bared in agony. Even from where she stood she could hear his low, animal growls of pain as they rushed him to one of the waiting ambulances.

Her gaze shot back to the tunnel entrance, her heart in her throat. *Tuck.*

A cop held out his arm to stop her but she shoved past him and got her first look at the tunnel entrance. It looked like a regular manhole, with a metal ladder installed into the side of the access tunnel. Below that all she could see was blackness.

DeLuca and Travers came to stand beside her. DeLuca got back on the radio. "Grant, we're here. What's your status?"

"We've got more survivors."

Celida wrapped her arms around her waist and prayed, her entire body locked in an agony of suspense.

"How many?" DeLuca asked.

"Five for sure. Still trying to locate the other two."

Was Tuck one of the five? *Please let him be okay. Please, please, please.*

Another tense few minutes of silence passed and the waiting nearly killed her. Then Grant's voice finally came through the radio. "We're coming out with more wounded—we need three stretchers waiting."

Celida spun around and ran for the closest ambulance.

****

226

Someone was calling his name.

A light slap to the side of his face. "Tuck. Tuck, you ugly bastard, say something."

Evers. Evers was yelling at him.

He could smell dust and burned cordite.

"*Tuck*, come on, man. Look at me."

Tuck peeled his eyes open, winced at the sudden flare of pain in his eyes as the beam of a flashlight blinded him. He tried to raise a hand to shield his eyes, found his arm was pinned. He looked down, found half his body buried by rock.

"Thank fuck. He's still with us," Evers called out. He started shoving at the rocks covering Tuck's body.

That's when the pain registered. Holy fuck, it felt like someone had beaten him all over with a sledgehammer. He sucked in a breath, wriggled to help free himself.

"Just stay still, man. Stay still until we can see how bad you're hurt, okay?"

Tuck let his head drop back down, his helmet hitting with a soft *thunk*. "What happened?"

"You just about got blown to hell, buddy," Evers answered as someone else ran over and started helping with the digging. Schroder, their medic.

"I think I did get blown to hell," he muttered, wincing as one of them dislodged a big chunk of stone and rolled it off his right thigh. He remembered coming through the trap door, hitting Spivey with the EMP. He'd wounded him, then realized he was going to set off the explosives and tried to duck back into the tunnel. His last thought had been *this is it*.

He was extremely fucking grateful it hadn't been.

Tuck took a better look around. Hell, it seemed like half the bank had fallen through with him. "Is everyone else okay?"

"Bauer's hurting pretty bad, they already took him out. Think he fucked up his back. And Cruz got his bell rung pretty good. He's kinda out of it right now. Other than that, I'd say we're all damn lucky to still be breathing."

Yeah, no doubt. When the weight pinning his right arm released, he bent it, fighting back a cry at the pain. Shit, that hurt.

"No, you lie still," Schroder growled at him when he tried to sit up, planting a hand in the middle of Tuck's chest and pressing to hold him down.

"I'm okay," Tuck muttered.

"Yeah, we'll see about that, and I'm trying to pay down more of my tab here, so just gimme a break," Evers said, and finished clearing the rubble away from him. He started running his hands over Tuck's body, checking for injuries. "Think anything's broken?"

Tuck shook his head. "Just really fucking sore."

"I'll bet," Schroder said as he gently palpated Tuck's abdomen. "What about here? Any pain in your stomach, in your chest?"

"Nothing major. Let me the hell up, guys. Fucking Spivey's still up there."

"Doubt he's breathing anymore, man," Schroder said, his teeth a white flash in the darkness. "If it's this bad down here, I can only imagine it's worse up there."

"Help me up," Tuck snapped impatiently. Evers and Schroder both grabbed a hand and slowly helped haul him to his feet.

"You good?" Evers asked, bracing his body against Tuck's as he winced. "Or you want us to carry you out?"

"Just help me walk, dammit."

Evers started leading him down the tunnel while Schroder walked behind them, every step its own separate agony. His entire body was one gigantic bruise, and that was at the very least. A dull throb settled in the back of his skull and the insides of his ears hurt, too.

"Grant, we're coming out," Evers shouted down the darkened tunnel, his flashlight the only illumination.

"Roger that!"

"Grant's down here?" Tuck asked.

"Other team came down to help dig us out. Apparently DeLuca and some others were trying from inside the bank but couldn't get to us."

"So Spivey must be dead then." And all the hostages with him.

"Dunno. We'll find out soon enough. Now shut up and lean on me until we get outta here."

Tuck fell silent and did as he was told. Beat up as he was, there was no way he'd be able to crawl through all this mess on his own.

A faint light at the end of the tunnel appeared, getting brighter and brighter the closer they came to the entry point. Someone dropped down into the tunnel and started toward them. "You guys need a hand?"

Tuck opened his mouth to say no but Evers spoke before he could. "Gonna need help getting him up that ladder," Evers called back.

When they reached the access tunnel Tuck recognized Grant standing there. "Hey," he said.

"Glad you're still with us, brother," the other man said with a grin, then turned to call up the ladder to whoever was waiting above ground. "Last one coming up. Have a stretcher ready."

The next few minutes passed in a blur of sweat and agony as they muscled him up the narrow access tunnel. Hands grabbed him from above and he looked up into Blackwell's face, then DeLuca's. He got several pats on the back and shoulders, all of which sent fresh flares of pain through him, and then he was weaving on his feet as they cleared the way for him.

He looked up, expecting to see a couple of EMTs

bearing down on him with a stretcher, but his heart stuttered when the crowd shifted and Celida appeared. She stopped dead when she saw him, both hands flying up to cover her mouth and nose.

Then she dropped her hands and raced toward him, dark ponytail streaming behind her. He watched her face crumple a second before she reached him and a different kind of pain lit up in his chest. Beat up as he was, there was no way he couldn't reach for her. He held out his arms just as her sob broke free and then she was plastered up against him, face buried in his throat and her arms tight around him.

He flinched at the embrace but held her close, startled and totally humbled at not only the public display of affection from her, but also the way she was sobbing into his neck. As though her heart had been broken at the thought of losing him.

Tuck closed his eyes and pressed his face against her hair, breathing in her scent, so damn grateful to be alive, to have her in his arms. "I'm okay, sunshine," he murmured, not giving a fuck that everyone was staring at them. "I'm okay."

Celida just shook her head as her tears dried up and held him like she was afraid someone would rip him out of her arms. Tuck felt his own eyes sting, smiled a little against the top of her head.

She *did* love him. Maybe she wasn't ready to say it yet, but she did and the proof was right here for everyone to see. It made his heart roll over in his chest.

She'd only calmed a bit more when the EMTs came up with a gurney and made him get on it. Celida wiped at her face and held his hand while they wheeled him over to an ambulance.

"I don't need an ambulance," Tuck protested with a scowl. "I'll stay with you and you can drive me to the hospital to get checked out later."

Celida shot him a hard look, one eyebrow raised. "Not a freaking chance."

He came up on his elbows, fighting a wince as his body protested the movement. Everything hurt. "Seriously, I don't need to be transported."

She set a hand against his vest and pressed down with enough force to make him wince and him lie flat on his back again. "You either lie still and do as you're told, or I strap you down to that thing myself."

A chuckle bubbled up in his chest but he held it back. She was clearly worried about him. "I probably look worse than I actually am."

This time she didn't bother looking at him as she held up her free hand toward him, palm out. "Not even listening to you right now."

DeLuca fell in step with him on his other side. "How you doin', Tuck?" he asked.

"Good. Just banged up. Is Spivey dead?"

DeLuca flicked a glance at Celida, then looked back at him. "Yeah."

"And the hostages?"

"All alive."

He blinked. "What? How the hell did they survive all that?"

"Spivey had them locked in the vault. He detonated everything from in there."

Tuck frowned. "He died in the blasts then?"

Again, DeLuca's gaze slid to Celida, a little smile on his lips. "Nope. Better ask your girl what went down."

Tuck snapped his head around to look up at her, shock rippling through him at what DeLuca was implying. "You got him?"

She nodded, wiped the heel of one hand beneath her eye, and sniffed. "The blasts damaged the vault, so he either shoved the door open or used the code. He put on

231

the security guard's uniform before walking out. It was chaos after those blasts—I didn't even recognize him when he passed me. Then I saw Ippoliti without his uniform and realized what had happened. Spivey was going back to make sure you guys were dead and to kill DeLuca too," she finished, her voice shredding on the last sentence.

Tuck reached out and gripped her hand. "You're badass, Lida."

She huffed out a watery laugh and wiped her free hand under her other eye. "Yeah, right."

"You are."

"Total badass," DeLuca agreed with a grin. "She figured out what had happened, radioed to warn us and took him out with a shot through the throat. He was dead before Travers and I could even get there. Thanks for that, by the way."

Celida shrugged, a flush blooming in her cheeks. Tuck smiled up at her, pride filling him with warmth. "That's my girl." His proud, fierce warrior.

She shrugged again and gave an irritated sigh. "Can we talk about you now? Like, how bad you're hurt?"

"I'm gonna be fine, darlin'."

She shot him a dubious glance. "You better be."

Fighting a chuckle because it would no doubt earn him a punch to the arm and he was already freaking sore enough, Tuck stayed silent as they finally reached the ambulance. The EMTs started doing their thing. Tuck let his eyes close, tried to focus his mind away from the pain as they poked and prodded, cut away his uniform and took his vitals.

"Your blood pressure's good and your pulse is steady," the medic said as he shone a penlight in Tuck's eyes to check his pupilary reflex. "We're going to transport you to the hospital for further treatment and x-rays."

He nodded, knowing there was no way around it. But before the medic could shut the rear doors of the truck, Celida climbed in. She perched on the bench seat beside his gurney and took his hand. Her eyes were puffy and her nose red from crying. As she smiled down at him, she'd never looked more beautiful.

"You coming with me?" he guessed, grinning up at her in adoration. It went against procedure to allow someone to ride in the back of an ambulance with a patient.

She snorted, her expression fierce. "Bet your sweet ass I am."

Chapter Nineteen

———◦∽———

C elida crept up the stairs of Tuck's two-level house, careful not to make any noise in case it woke him, because he was hopefully still sound asleep in his bed. The carpet runner was soft beneath her bare feet as she cleared the top step and made her way down the hallway. The door to Bauer's room at the far end stood open, since he was still in hospital. At the first door on the left she paused, cautiously cracked it open and peeked inside.

In the faint light from the digital bedside clock she could see Tuck outlined against the sheets of the king size bed. He was asleep on his side, facing her, his breathing slow and even. Her heart turned over at the sight of him. She'd come so damn close to losing him today, every time she thought of how easily he could have died in there her body went into a cold sweat.

She slipped inside and eased the door closed. After he'd been discharged from the hospital she'd driven him home in an agency vehicle. He hadn't wanted to eat so she'd helped him into the shower to let the hot water

234

soothe some of the aches in his battered body and put fresh sheets on the bed, then tucked him in and gone back to the field office for a couple hours. He'd want to know the status of his injured teammates as soon as he woke up, so she'd already gotten an update before leaving the office.

When she'd called to check on their statuses, she'd found out Bauer would likely not be discharged for a few days more at least. Cruz was being kept overnight for observation for his concussion but would probably go home tomorrow.

Stepping close to the bed, she glanced at the clock on the nightstand. Just after oh-three-hundred. She'd lain with him for a while when she'd first put him to bed, curving her body around his. He'd crashed within a few minutes of lying down, completely exhausted. Only a few hours had passed since she'd held him but it was still too long. She needed to feel him against her, reassure her psyche that he really was going to be okay.

The moment she eased one hip onto the mattress though, he stirred, opened his eyes and focused on her. "Hey," he murmured, relaxing back against the pillow.

"Sorry I woke you." The mattress dipped a bit as she moved onto it and she set her hand on the side of his face. Her thumb swept across his jaw, his stubble rasping against her skin in the quiet. "Sore?" How in the hell he'd crawled out of that rubble without any broken bones or serious internal injuries was beyond her.

He grimaced and shifted slightly, his restricted movements telling her he was in a hell of a lot of pain. "Yeah."

That he'd just admitted it told her all she needed to know. "Time for another dose of meds anyway." She reached for the prescription bottle on the nightstand, handed him two pills and then a glass of water she'd set there when she'd come to bed last time.

Tuck winced as he sat up on his elbow to take the pills, winced again as he laid back down. Celida took the glass from him, gently smoothed his hair back from his forehead, wishing there was something more she could do to ease him. "You're a bit warm," she said with a frown.

"Nah, I'm good." He took her hand, brought it to his mouth and turned it palm side up to place a kiss there, his lips brushing against the band aids covering the cuts she'd gotten while climbing through the bank and trying to dig him out.

They'd both been through hell today, Tuck receiving the worst of it, but at least they were able to be alone together now. She'd been by his side from the moment he'd come out of that tunnel, including the entire time at the hospital except for when he'd been taken for x-rays.

He was so strong and brave but more than that she'd never forget the look on his face when she'd run to him today. Raw relief and gratitude. The way she'd run to him, grabbed hold of him in front of everyone and held him so tight should be proof of how afraid she'd been that he'd died. And it also had to have told him exactly what he meant to her.

Celida settled under the covers with him and turned onto her side to face him, still touching his bristly cheek. He wrapped an arm around her waist and tugged. She gingerly eased her body up against him. He was bruised all to hell on his arms and legs, and even a few where the body armor had protected his back and chest from the worst of it.

He had to be stiff and sore all over, and those kinds of bone bruises would take a while to come to the surface as they healed. "I'm afraid of hurting you," she murmured, setting her free hand carefully on his naked back. His skin was warm and smooth beneath her fingertips, the muscles twitching as he shifted again.

"Don't be. Need to feel you up against me." Tuck nestled in closer and let out a soft sigh. Celida closed her eyes and breathed in his clean, masculine scent, basking in the moment. It felt good to know they were finally on the same page in terms of being committed to the relationship. She loved him beyond reason, and even though her actions told him that, she knew he needed— deserved—to hear the words from her. She'd never said them to another man.

"I love being up against you. You feel so good." She trailed her fingertips over his back, careful to keep her touch light and soothing but not ticklish. It was like petting a drowsy tiger, all sleek and powerful, lying quietly beside her in the darkness.

"You too."

Quiet filled the room, only the sounds of their hushed breathing disturbing the silence. Celida leaned forward to kiss the tip of his nose, then his mouth, fighting a rush of tears. This man meant so much to her, more than she'd ever felt for anyone else. The words pushed up from her chest, crowded her throat, but got stuck on her tongue. Dammit, why couldn't she say it? She wasn't sure what was holding her back. Fear, maybe. An unprecedented sense of vulnerability.

Tuck turned his head slightly, until his mouth touched her palm, and she felt his smile form against her skin. "You love me," he said quietly against her palm, his voice calm and sure.

Her eyes flicked up to his in the dimness, held. "Pretty cocky while you're laid up, huh?" she said in a teasing tone, at once relieved at his perception and guilty that she hadn't told him herself.

His shoulders moved a little in what passed for a shrug. "You do."

Her lips quirked at the certainty in his voice. "Yeah.

A lot." That terrible sense of vulnerability she'd feared never hit. All she felt was peace, a sense of rightness. It would take her a while to get comfortable saying it out loud, but she'd get there.

The smile widened, his lips parting against her palm. "I love you too, sunshine." He said it so easily, the sincerity in his voice making it sound like an ironclad vow.

She nodded, swallowed against a rush of tears at the admission, but she didn't pull away. No more pulling away from this wonderful man, a man who'd once been her partner on the job and would now be her partner in everything in her life. She couldn't believe how lucky she was.

Celida sighed and stroked her thumb across his chin, over his lips. He kissed the pad of it, let his tongue glide over her skin. Her swift intake of breath ripped through the quiet as a surge of heat shot through her, making her nipples harden. She couldn't help her reaction, even though she knew he was way too sore for sex. But she wasn't about to put an end to this delicious intimacy, the two of them tangled together in the darkness in his bed. Without a word she slid her hands up to cradle the sides of his face and leaned close to kiss him, fitting her lips to his and infusing the kiss with all the emotion filling her heart. He made a deep murmur of approval and kissed her back.

Her hands slid gently through his hair, thumbs sweeping gently over his cheeks and jaw. Reverent, tender touches that showed him exactly what was in her heart.

"You're so sweet. My sunshine," he whispered against her lips, meeting each gentle kiss, seeming to savor the connection as much as she did.

Gradually their mouths eased apart and they lay pressed flush together, enjoying the closeness. His breathing began to deepen, his muscles twitching from time to time as he faded toward sleep. She felt the weight of exhaustion pull her under, her subconscious soothed in the knowledge that she was safe in Tuck's arms and he was safe in hers.

The intermittent beep of his phone finally registered sometime later, pulling her out of a deep sleep. She opened her eyes and sought out Tuck's phone, sitting on the dresser on the other side of the room. Another ding sounded, signalling that someone had left either a text or voicemail. Could be DeLuca, or maybe Zoe or Bauer.

Tuck stirred, lifted his head. She stilled him with a hand on his shoulder.

"Stay here. I'll get it." Bending to give him a lingering kiss, Celida sat up and gently disengaged from his body. Immediately she felt colder as she left the bed, aware that Tuck was watching her as she crossed to the dresser.

She picked up the phone and activated it. The light from the screen flicked on, illuminating her face. When she saw the number on screen even without entering his password, cold condensed in her belly.

Oh shit, *no*. They wouldn't be calling at this hour unless something was seriously wrong. And Tuck had been through so much already. Gathering herself, she crossed back to him, holding out the phone. "I think it's the nursing home."

Tuck immediately sat up, the way his breath hissed through his teeth telling her how much the movement hurt. He took the phone from her and returned the call. Someone answered almost immediately and he listened to what the woman was saying while Celida's heart pounded. *Not Al. Not now.*

She gripped his free hand, watching him worriedly. He didn't say much. A few moments later he ended the call and set the phone down on his lap. His stillness, the total silence that echoed around the room, filled her with foreboding.

"My dad had a stroke twenty minutes ago," he finally said, his voice choked in a way she'd never heard before. "They don't think he's going to make it."

No. Without a word Celida slid her arms around him and rested her face against his neck, holding him close in the darkness, helpless to ease his pain but determined to try. "I'll grab you some clothes then drive us over."

****

Clay's eyes snapped open as a low cry of pain erupted from between his clenched teeth. Sweat popped out on his forehead, a thousand lightning bolts searing from his lower back to the soles of his feet.

Mother of Christ, this was fucking torture. How long was he supposed to suffer like this until they operated?

The gentle scrape of a chair had him turning his head toward the window. He blinked, struggled to get hold of his shallow breathing and clear away the haze of pain when he saw Zoe standing there, watching him. Her golden eyes were full of sympathy.

"Should I get the nurse?"

It took him a second to hear her through the last of the pain as it faded away. Lying very still, afraid to move because the least little movement made him want to chop his own legs off just to avoid feeling that kind of agony, he gave a small shake of his head.

She was frowning now, biting at that full lower lip he'd thought about biting way too often for his peace of mind. "There has to be something they can do. The nurse told me you'd be in a lot of pain once the meds wore off."

At that Clay jerked his gaze to the IV bag hanging above and next to his bed. When he saw the morphine, he blanched a little. "No more," he rasped, fighting the wave of anxiety as it rushed through him. "Tell them no more."

Her eyes widened but she nodded. "I'll tell them. Now?"

He nodded.

She hurried out of the room and he took a slow, measured breath, taking stock. An intense ache flared out from his lower back, wrapping around his hips and ass. And that was when he was lying perfectly still. If he so much as shifted, he was in a world of hurt. And God forbid he sneezed or coughed.

It was slowly driving him insane. He'd tried every trick he knew of to combat the pain, push past it, but the grinding, relentless onslaught was already taking its toll. Seriously, how long did they expect him to endure this? Two fractured lumbar vertebrae and two ruptured disks from the combination of the blast waves and the way he'd fallen off that ladder trying to haul Cruz and Tuck to safety.

He hadn't been fast enough.

His teammates had all come by to see him earlier before going home, and DeLuca too. The CO had offered to stay but Clay hadn't wanted anyone to see him like this. Cruz was down the hall with a severe concussion, Tuck was at home nursing a mild one plus a billion bone bruises and hematomas, and the others were all banged up and bruised to hell as well. Meantime, he was stuck in this damn bed, flat on his back with a catheter plugged into his dick, praying a surgeon would take pity on him and give him an emergency surgery spot.

The door opened and Zoe came back in. Her red-and-black hair was pulled back into a sleek ponytail at

241

the back of her head, and she didn't have much makeup on again. She looked tired, though, and worried. He frowned at her. "What are you doing here, anyway?"

Rather than falter at his brusque tone, she walked right up to the bed and sat on the edge of it, her hip close to his. Her golden eyes stared down at him without a hint of unease. "I told Tuck and Celida I'd stay for a while. I wanted them to go home and get some rest, and I didn't want you to be alone when you woke up."

Something caught in his chest. A funny little twinge he didn't want to examine too closely.

He wiped a hand over his face, rubbed the sweat into the front of his hospital gown. "You didn't have to do that. I'm fine."

She shrugged. "I wanted to. The nurse said to give you these, by the way." She held out a small, clear plastic bottle with a prescription written on it for him.

His eyes picked out the word oxycontin on it, and he felt his blood pressure drop. His sister's downward spiral flashed through his mind in painful, vivid Technicolor. "No, no more drugs." Automatically he shot out a hand to push it away. As he did, his ruined discs let him know how galactically stupid it was by letting loose with a ferocious bolt of agony that seared the entire length of both sciatic nerves, right into the soles of his feet.

When he managed to peel his eyelids apart this time, Zoe was braced over him, worry clear in her eyes. "I'm sorry. I put them away. Can I help? Help shift you or something? God, I hate to see you in this much pain."

He swallowed, fighting the low-grade nausea churning in his gut, and managed to shake his head a little, dug deep to answer without snapping. "No. Thanks. Gotta lie still."

She eased away and pushed the bottle of pills out of reach, tucking them behind a pitcher of water so he

TARGETED

wouldn't have to see them. Tucking a stray lock of brilliant red hair behind one ear, she folded her arms across her waist and studied him. "They've done all they can for now, just trying to manage your pain levels. A few hours ago they called in a surgeon but the neurologist won't be able to see you until first thing in the morning."

They didn't see his case as urgent enough to warrant an emergency surgery slot, but he sure as hell did. "First thing. Clarify that."

"Around seven, I think."

"What time is it now?"

She checked her watch. "Three-thirty."

So at least three and a half more hours before he had a prayer of getting any more answers, let alone an operation. God that made him want to whimper.

Zoe shifted her feet, watched him uncertainly. "Your mom's flying in tomorrow as well. She talked to Tuck and they set it all up. Arrives around noon I think Celida said. She's going to come stay with you while you recover."

Clay hid his surprise. His mom was merely leaving one invalid child for another, then. But he was grateful for the help. If things stayed like this and he remained flat on his back he wouldn't be able to do even the simplest tasks for himself.

"I can stay until she gets here if you want," Zoe offered. "Just in case you need anything."

God, why was she so sweet to him? He hadn't been sweet to her, and his thoughts about her sure as hell hadn't been sweet either. Fantasizing about fucking her a dozen different ways made him an asshole. One, because she was Tuck's cousin, but more like a sister than anything. Two, because he knew he'd fuck her and walk away like he did with the few women he'd gone home with since his divorce.

243

He didn't do it often, but when he did he made sure it was only one night, and he left the moment he ditched the condom in the trash. The woman knew good and well it was just a booty call. No date, no dinner before, no sleepovers and no breakfast the next morning. Meaningless sex was all he could handle anymore and he refused to feel guilty about it. The ability to care had died inside him along with his marriage.

Zoe was still watching him, he realized. Waiting for an answer. "I'll be okay. But thanks," he made himself add. He hated that she was seeing him like this.

She nodded slowly, that golden gaze seeming to delve deep inside him. "All right. If you change your mind though, call me." With that she reached out a hand and gently ran it over his hair. Hair that was currently stiff with dirt, dust and sweat, but she didn't seem to care and her touch sent a wave of tingles flowing down his spine.

She smiled a little, opened her mouth to say something else but her phone rang. Her face went slack with surprise and she dug it out of her purse.

"Hey," she answered, but she was still looking straight at him. "We were just talking about you guys."

Had to be Tuck.

"Everything okay? Bauer just woke up and now I bet he wished he hadn't," she continued.

Not necessarily, he thought, because then he wouldn't have gotten to see her.

But then Zoe stilled. Her smile vanished and her body tensed. "What?"

Clay frowned in concern, watching her closely. Had something happened to Tuck?

"Oh my God, I'm so sorry. So sorry." Her voice shredded and she put one hand to her mouth, her breath hitching in. Her clear distress tore at him. She was too far away now for him to touch her, but he wanted to.

Wanted to take her hand, reassure her that she wasn't alone. "I'll find out what room he's in and call you guys back."

After she ended the call she lowered the phone and met his gaze. It felt like someone had punched him in the heart when he saw the tears gathered in her eyes, the moisture magnifying the gold depths. Goddammit, he wished he could get up and do something. "What's wrong? Is it Tuck?"

She started to shake her head, then stopped and nodded. She pulled in a deep breath, seemed to steady herself before answering. "His dad had a massive stroke an hour ago. He's not going to make it."

Ah, shit. This piece of bad news on top of what Tuck had already been through today? And Zoe loved her uncle too. "I'm sorry."

She pressed her lips together, nodded as she tucked the phone back into her purse. "I'd better get down to Emergency and find out where he is. Sure you don't need anything?"

She was putting up a good strong front at the moment but he knew how upset she must be. Instead of saying he was sure he didn't need anything, he took the risk of setting off his back again and reached out a hand toward her, gritting his teeth at the sudden flare of pain. Her fingers wrapped around his and a grateful smile tugged at her lips.

"Call me if you change your mind about me staying with you," she said, her voice slightly husky. "I'll be back to see you when I can." Before he could tell her no, that she didn't have to come back and see him, she bent and touched her lips to his cheek, above the line of stubble.

He froze at the contact, his body automatically reacting with a flare of heat and an indrawn breath to pull in more of her musky, floral scent. At the sound of

245

his sudden inhalation she stilled too, her lips lingering against his skin that was suddenly a million times more sensitive than normal. Her warm breath gusted softly against the side of his face and her head turned slightly.

Clay didn't dare move, didn't dare breathe while she stayed there like that for a few endless heartbeats. Another two inches and her mouth would be on his and regardless of the state he was in right now, there was no way he couldn't kiss her back.

At the last moment she lifted her head and her lips came down on his forehead instead.

A flare of disappointment hit him, startling with its intensity, and he released her hand when she straightened and pulled away. "I'll be in touch," she murmured.

He nodded, not trusting himself to speak. Alone in his room a few moments later, he could still smell the faint scent of her perfume hanging in the air and realized he already missed her.

Chapter Twenty

———————◦◦◦———————

Tuck parked his truck in front of the church and killed the engine. In the sudden silence he heard nothing but the pings of the cooling engine. The United church loomed before him, tall front doors open to the guests entering. People were already gathered around the front of the building, talking.

Pulling his gaze away from them he did up the top button on his collar and began tying his tie, his muscles protesting each movement. The soreness was a little better than it had been initially but he was a solid week away from being able to move around without pain, and now his whole body was one big multi-color bruise.

He couldn't believe it had already been four days since his dad passed away. He'd been staying at Celida's place rather than his, giving Bauer some peace and quiet to recover after his back surgery. Bauer's mom had flown in from Pennsylvania to stay at the house and look after him. No doubt the big guy was ready to climb the walls to escape.

"Do you want a few minutes alone?"

He glanced over at Celida, seated beside him in the

passenger seat. Her dark brown hair was tied into a loose knot at the back of her head, little pieces of it falling around her cheeks and jaw to frame her face. "Yeah, if you don't mind." He wasn't up to making chitchat with the guests right now and she apparently knew it.

He'd been dreading this day, and now he just wanted to get through it. Once this was all over he and Celida were taking off to Maui for a week. Just the two of them, seven days to heal and spend time together. That was something to look forward to, at least.

Searching his eyes for a moment, she reached over, pushed his hands aside and efficiently tied his tie for him, the sweet gesture touching him inside. Then she popped her door open. "I'll wait for you by the door." Giving his hand a squeeze, she stepped out and shut the truck door behind her.

He watched her walk away, up the stone steps to the front of the church. The black short-sleeved dress she wore scooped just above her breasts and ended at her knees, the soft fabric swishing around her as she moved, highlighting her curves.

He'd always known she was strong, but over the past week she'd amazed him. Yeah, she still had some issues to deal with, but surprisingly the whole Spivey incident seemed to have helped her somewhat. As though being the one to pull the trigger had eased the sense of helplessness that had haunted her and restored her confidence. And she'd been a huge help to Tuck through all of this, a fucking trooper. They both needed this trip to Maui, the time away together.

Blowing out a breath, he pulled the notes he'd written in point form from his suit coat pocket. A single note card, thirteen points. He'd agonized over every single one of them over the past two days, wanting to get it just right. How did he encapsulate the life of the most extraordinary man he'd ever known into a single, five minute long speech?

The now familiar tightening in his throat started up again as he reviewed the list. He'd gone over it at least a dozen times already. He was as prepared as he could be.

Except he still wasn't ready to say goodbye yet. There was a hole inside him now, one he knew would never completely heal.

His father had told him early on after the Alzheimer's diagnosis that when he died he wanted a full casket and a small service. No cremation, no fanfare. Didn't mean his son would bury him without honoring his memory properly.

Tuck slipped the notecard into the pocket and looked back up at the church.

Celida stood on the top step next to the door with Evers and his girlfriend Rachel. Bauer, three days post-op after his spinal surgery, was there too, talking to Zoe. The rest of his teammates were inside already, along with DeLuca and Travers. It meant the world to him that the guys had come out to pay their respects today.

But Celida's presence meant more to him than anything.

Right from the moment on that hellish night when he'd gotten the call, she'd been there. From the race to the hospital where they'd transported his father, through the seven hours after that when Tuck had been perched at his father's bedside holding his frail hand, to those final, rasping breaths.

She'd been there. A quiet, solid support system for him to lean on. A woman who knew how it felt to lose a beloved parent, and knew to let him grieve alone until he was ready to walk out of that room. His sunshine.

When he'd finally found the strength to say goodbye and let go of that frail, cool hand, he'd left the room and found her waiting for him out in the hallway with Zoe. She'd stood and walked to him. Without a word he'd gone straight into her arms and held on tight, drowning in a thick fog of pain that engulfed him inside and out. Afterward she'd driven them back to his place and held him in the darkness, granting him the wordless comfort of her embrace and presence. The next morning she and Zoe had asked him what he wanted done about the funeral, then made all the arrangements while he dealt with the legal paperwork and tied up his father's estate.

Celida had done all that without him asking, and she'd done it while still working her ass off to wrap up the Spivey case. She still faced a mountain of paperwork and a hearing to verify that lethal force had been necessary and justified since she'd been the one to take the fatal shots. He knew without a doubt she'd be cleared of everything, but he couldn't wait to get her on that plane tonight and take her away from it all for a while.

He was the luckiest man in the world to have a woman like her at his side.

Tuck expelled a slow breath and checked his watch. Time to get his ass in there. He'd already seen his father's body, but walking into that church and knowing he was inside that casket was going to be tough.

He'd been so young when his mom died. It had hurt and he remembered crying himself to sleep for the first little while, but back then he hadn't really understood then what death meant and he'd adjusted to his new reality soon enough. Since then he'd gained a lot more experience with death and it never got any easier.

Saying a final goodbye to fallen teammates and friends was hard. Saying goodbye to the man he'd worshipped his entire life, who'd made countless sacrifices for his country and many more to ensure he gave his son everything he could? Tuck didn't even know how to begin.

Picking up the suit coat from where he'd left it on the armrest, he climbed out of the truck. The summer heat and humidity hit him, the bright sunlight reflecting back at him off the black asphalt of the parking lot. He put on the coat anyway, buttoned it up and smoothed his tie down flat.

Celida and the others turned to look at him as he crossed to the steps and climbed them. Evers nodded and stuck out his hand. "Your dad was a helluva man. I'm sorry for your loss."

Tuck shook the hand, nodded his thanks and accepted Rachel's as well. They headed inside and Tuck turned to Bauer. His eyes were bruised black underneath and his freshly-shaven face was pale, the sheen of sweat on his upper lip and forehead likely having more to do with his pain level than the temperature outside.

"Thanks for coming," Tuck said.

Bauer shook his hand. "Wouldn't miss it. Al was a great guy." He stepped back, a slight tension around his eyes and mouth and his stiff movements telling Tuck just how much he was hurting. "I'll be inside. Can't sit right now so I'll stand at the back." He flicked a glance at Zoe. "You'll be okay up front?"

"It's fine," she answered with a little smile. "I'll be with my parents and Tuck and Celida."

Bauer nodded, glanced back at Tuck and slowly made his way inside.

"He should be at home resting," Tuck said.

Zoe snorted. "He should still be in the freaking hospital. But he was coming here to support you come hell or high water. Without taking any pain meds, I might add. Stubborn ass. Personally, I think he just wanted to get away from his mom for a while. From what I've seen, that woman is a force to be reckoned with." She reached up and wound her arms around his shoulders, gave him a squeeze. "See you guys inside."

Celida nodded and cast him a questioning glance. Tuck snagged her hand and led her back down the steps, to the side of the church where they were away from prying eyes.

"What?" She stared up at him with those watchful gray eyes, and his heart suddenly felt full to bursting. "Did we forget something?"

"No." He'd just been delaying something. Something that couldn't wait any longer.

Her brow furrowed. "Don't you dare thank me again. You'd have done the same for me if the roles were reversed, so just stop." She reached out to fiddle with the knot on his tie, even though he knew it didn't need adjusting. "I know how hard this is. I wish I could do something to make it easier on you, and I hate knowing I can't."

His heart squeezed so hard it hurt. He lifted a hand to her cheek, cradled it as he brushed his thumb across her high cheekbone. Her eyes flicked up to his, held. And he was so undone by the emotion he saw there that he couldn't hold back any longer. "I love you," he said simply. "Don't know what I would have done without you these past few days."

Surprise and gratitude registered in her eyes, then a joyous smile broke over her face, filling him with warmth. "Love you back."

Tuck smiled. Hearing the words in return, especially today, made him feel twenty feet tall. Leaning in, he kissed those shiny pink lips, felt her arms wind around him, still careful of his bruises, then the soft give of her mouth beneath his. Melting for him. He kept this kiss slow, gentle, tender, infusing it with everything he felt for her. God, he could just eat her up.

When he lifted his head, her eyes glistened with tears. She blinked, let out a watery laugh and wiped beneath her eyes. "Don't start me already," she warned without heat.

Humming in agreement, he leaned down and kissed the bridge of her nose. Every day he saw more and more of the softness in her. Because she trusted him enough to let him see it. He knew exactly how precious a gift that was.

Exhaling, Tuck tipped his head back to look up at the clear blue sky.

Well, Dad, this is it. Glad you at least got to meet your future daughter-in-law and got to know her a little bit before you left us.

Because Tuck was so marrying Celida one day. Sooner than later if he had anything to say about it. She was his future.

He snagged her hand and laced his fingers through hers. Squeezed. "Let's do this."

She nodded, squeezed back.

Holding her hand tight in his, Tuck walked up those steps, bracing himself for the sight of that casket. It was the first thing he saw when he stepped into the open doorway. The silver casket sat front and center before the altar, a small table with a framed picture of him and his dad beside it, along with a display of his dad's service medals.

The picture was Tuck's favorite, taken at a military event, soon after he'd made Delta. Both of them in their Army dress uniforms, arms draped across one another's shoulders, smiling at the camera.

As he stared at that image, everything else funneled out. His teammates, relatives, a couple friends and a few of the nursing home staff all turning in their seats to look at him. The sweet smell of the roses up front wafted back to him. He stared into his father's eyes in that picture, and the weight of the grief in his chest suddenly eased.

Celida gave his hand a gentle squeeze in silent

support. Breathing deep, Tuck started walking with her up the center aisle to take their seats in the front pew, his gaze pinned on that picture.

Love you, Dad. Thanks for everything.

He was ready to say goodbye and start his future with the incredible woman at his side.

Chapter Twenty-One

When Tuck came back to the cottage from the main building of the resort with a bucket of ice for the bottle of wine the concierge had left for them, all the lights were off. He paused at the end of the path that led to the front steps as the gentle swell of the surf crashed on the beach behind him and a soft, tropical breeze rustling the palm fronds overhead. She'd gone to sleep already?

Tuck climbed the wooden steps of the one-story cottage and stepped onto the porch, a little disappointed that Celida hadn't waited up for him, since he'd only been gone fifteen minutes. On the other hand, sliding into bed beside her and waking her with a trail of kisses down her naked body had its merits.

Inside all was quiet. He slid off his flip-flops and set the bucket on the round table set off to the side of the small kitchen, grateful that he could do so with only a faint twinge from his almost healed shoulder muscles. He still had plenty of interesting bruises in interesting places, but at least they didn't hurt all that much anymore.

He crossed the cool tile floor of the kitchen and hallway with quiet steps, then paused at the bedroom door where a faint band of light coming from underneath it gave him hope that she might still be up. As he reached for the doorknob, he got his answer.

"I'm not sleeping," she called out, sounding alert and wide awake.

With a grin, he twisted the knob. It had been a helluva long day, with the funeral, reception and flight here. Now they could just relax and enjoy each other. They'd spent every night together since his dad had died, and each night he couldn't wait to go home to her, but with so much shit to deal with and him healing they hadn't been able to spend much quality time together. Being able to unwind with her here in this beautiful resort was exactly what they both needed.

The door swung open under the pressure of his hand. He stepped into the threshold—

And froze on the spot at the sight before him.

Celida reclined on her side on the comforter of the king size bed, her head propped on one hand. And she wore nothing but a skimpy black lace teddy, red high heels and a smile.

His mouth went dry, his pulse thudding in his ears as he took in that mouth-watering outfit, the way she'd done her hair so it curled loosely over one shoulder and trailed seductively over one full breast, pushed up to distracting heights by the lace. Lust punched through him, went to his head like a double shot of straight whiskey.

"It's been a long day," she said, trailing her fingertips over one bare hip and down the length of her thigh while his eyes tracked every inch of the movement, "so I thought I'd give you a special turn-down service before tucking you in for the night."

While he stood there with his tongue stuck to the

roof of his mouth and his erection pushed hard against his fly, she rose to her knees with a knowing smile and swung her legs off the bed. God, those fuck-me heels made him hard all over. He couldn't wait to feel them digging into his back as he settled his face between her legs and teased her with his tongue until she screamed.

Her soft laugh brought his gaze back to hers. She rose and took a step toward him, her movements sleek and feline, almost a prowl. Her eyes were aglow with desire, and also feminine power. The woman knew exactly what she was doing to him, and was enjoying the hell out of it.

His attention slid back to the generous swell of her breasts. He could see the outline of her hardened nipples against the fabric, proof that she was as turned on as him. And he knew exactly how much she loved his mouth on them, knew every sweet spot on that luscious body and how to use them to make her writhe and mewl and beg. His cock pulsed at the thought.

She raised one dark eyebrow in challenge, but she was fighting a smile. "I can see what you're thinking, but that's not what I had in mind for the turn-down service." She held out a hand toward him. "Come over here, strip and lie down on your back."

Well, twist his arm… "I think I'm gonna like this sex-kitten side of you." He was so damn hard he hurt.

"Oh, you're gonna *love* it," she promised, giving him a sultry smile that hit him right in the heart.

He erased the distance between them, took her hand and brought it to his mouth for a slow, hot kiss against her palm, his eyes holding hers. He felt a shiver go through her, but then she tugged on his hand and tipped her head at the bed.

Yes, ma'am, he thought, trying and failing to fight a smile. He stripped his shirt off as he rounded the end of it, tossed it aside and shucked his shorts and underwear before lying down. "Now what?" The anticipation was killing him.

She settled next to him on one hip and curled her legs beneath her. Her warm scent drifted up to tease him. "Now you lie back and let me love you the way I've wanted to for the last week."

There was something in her eyes, a deep longing along with the arousal he read there that tugged at his heart. With everything going on they hadn't seen much of each other except at night, and he'd been too damn sore and exhausted to do more than a little making out. It hadn't been nearly enough for both of them. It felt like forever since he'd been buried inside her, staking his claim while she came undone beneath him.

He cupped a hand around the back of her neck, brushed his thumb along her jaw, up over the scar on her cheek as tenderness and need flooded him. She was so goddamn beautiful and sexy. So good to him. He was such a lucky bastard. "Come here, sunshine."

She smiled and bent to kiss him. Heat roared through him the moment their lips touched, so intense it stole his breath. Tuck lifted a hand to grab a fistful of her hair, ignoring the lingering ache in his muscles as the bruised flesh pulled taut. Celida smoothly took over and he let her. He parted his lips to the stroke of her tongue, touched the tip of it to hers. She hissed in a breath and leaned down to brush her breasts against his chest, the soft lace of the teddy brushing over his skin like a caress.

She set her palm flat against his chest and slid it down his body while she kissed him, slow and deep and hot. When her hand closed around the throbbing length of his swollen cock Tuck moaned into her mouth and tightened his hold on her hair, holding her head where he wanted it.

Her hand curled around him, squeezing and stroking in a slow, hypnotic rhythm that had his hips rolling in response. She broke the kiss to nibble at his chin, his throat, her lips whispering over the faded bruises on his chest and abdomen. His cock flexed in her grip as her tongue trailed gently across his skin. He lay there and waited for what came next, savoring the anticipation of her mouth on him.

The cool silk of her hair slid across his belly and thighs as she bent and licked up the length of his erection. A low groan tore out of his chest. His muscles quivered, the need burning so hot he could barely breathe. Then the velvety heat of her mouth enveloped him. His fingers contracted in her hair, holding her tight as he raised his hips to push deeper. Smooth heat, delicious suction as she wrapped her lips around his shaft and flicked her tongue across the ultra-sensitive spot beneath the swollen head.

"Lida, God," he croaked, a fine sweat breaking out across his body. His fingers flexed in her hair.

She looked up at him, her eyes heavy lidded with passion. Then she slid her free hand between his thighs to gently stroke her fingertips across his taut balls and hummed in pleasure as she sucked at him, as though she was thoroughly enjoying herself. Flares of ecstasy rocketed up his spine.

Tuck squeezed his eyes shut and gritted his teeth against the exquisite agony of it. So many times he'd imagined her sucking him off. Nothing even came close to the reality of it. The orgasm was building already, her blissful expression as she sucked him threatening to destroy him.

When the pleasure began to crest, pushing him toward that last climb to release, he tugged gently on her hair. "Stop. Wanna be inside you." As good as this felt, he needed that connection with her. Needed to be buried deep inside her, feel her enveloping him and sharing the same pleasure when he came, giving herself to him completely, nothing held back.

After one last luxurious suckle that put him dangerously close to coming, she raised her head, her lips releasing him with a faint pop as she reached for the bedside table. She shut the drawer, paused only long enough to peel that sexy bit of lace over her breasts then down her hips and climbed up to straddle his lap with a wicked grin.

Tuck's hands automatically went to the deep indent of her waist and traveled reverently up and down her ribcage to her hips, mapping her delectable curves with his touch. The lamp's low setting threw just enough light for him to see the smooth expanse of her belly, the round, full breasts and dark, beaded nipples as she rolled the condom down his length and settled above him.

He reached for her, intending to roll her beneath him, but she stayed him with a hand splayed on the center of his chest. She bent and brushed her mouth across his, her lips caressing before she slid her tongue inside to touch the tip to his. "Just lie still and let me love you," she whispered.

The words made something in his chest squeeze. She was getting more and more comfortable telling him she loved him, and that meant as much to him as the words themselves.

A jolt of desire and need punched through him, making him light-headed. He eased his grip on her hair and struggled to lie still, giving her the control she clearly needed. She sighed as she eased into position, her love for him shining in her eyes.

He cupped those full globes in his palms, swept his thumbs across the hard tips and earned a gasp. She bent toward him, putting those gorgeous mounds at eye level and he couldn't stop himself from leaning up and taking one delicate center into his mouth. Celida moaned softly in the back of her throat and arched her back as she positioned his cock between her thighs and slowly sank down on him. He groaned around her nipple, his left hand going to her hip to clamp tight, prevent her from moving.

Hot. Christ, so hot and wet for him and he'd barely touched her. Slowly he relaxed his grip.

She started to move, rising and falling above him, her body undulating in a slow, sexy rhythm that threatened to melt his brain, her inner muscles squeezing him. One hand braced on his shoulder for balance, she slid the other between her thighs to stroke the bud at the top of her sex.

God, so fucking sexy.

Her fingertips circled slowly and a plaintive, broken moan spilled from her lips. "Ah, Brad. So good…"

He was way beyond the ability to speak, but man, he fucking loved the way she said his name when they were together like this. All throaty and soft, more intimate than anything he'd ever experienced. He let his hands and body answer for him, savoring each hot glide of her core over him, his heart trying to pound its way out of his chest. This was what he'd needed, way more than the meds he'd taken this past week. Celida naked in his arms, her body wrapped around him, holding him deep inside her.

In the background he dimly heard the low buzz of his cell phone on the dresser across the room. He ignored it, because there was no way in hell he was answering it now. As far as he was concerned, the outside world didn't exist for the next week. He slid his right hand from her breast to her other hip, holding tight while he sucked first on one hard nipple, then the other.

The plaintive, husky moans she made had him shuddering, sensation rising to a fever pitch. The knowledge that she was loving the feel of his cock buried inside her and that she was stroking her clit while she rode him frayed the edges of his control. His breathing hitched as she seated him fully inside her and added a slight swivel of her hips.

Staring down at him with pure female satisfaction at the knowledge of his pleasure, how close he was, she did it again. "*Lida*." His voice was tight, harsh. He felt her inner walls ripple around him, her breath suspending a second before her cry of release rang through the room.

Helpless in the grip of the most intense pleasure he'd ever known, Tuck seized her hips and thrust up into her, hard. Fast. Deep as he could go.

With a little moan that made his heart clench Celida bent to kiss him, sweeping her hair over one shoulder. The ends tickled his chest and shoulders as her lips rubbed against his, absorbing his shattered groan, sucking gently at his tongue before licking at it, her body draped over him like a satin blanket.

His balls drew up close to his body, pleasure detonating deep inside him and traveling throughout all his nerve endings as the orgasm finally hit. He arched and moaned her name, one hand tight on her hip and the other buried in her hair. The waves beat through him in an endless tide, gradually fading until he groaned in exhaustion and lay limp against the pillow. The sound of the ocean floated through the open window beside the bed, a rhythmic, soothing surge against the nearby shore.

Celida let out a contented sigh and settled atop him, tucking her face into the curve of his neck. "I've wanted to do that for so long."

He gave a low chuckle. "Feel free to do that again anytime you want. And don't forget that outfit next time, either."

Her soft laugh washed against his skin then she sat up and reached back to slide the high heels off, tossing them to the floor with a quiet thud. She brushed her hair back from her face as she faced him once more, their bodies still joined. "You want me to get your phone so you can call whoever that was back?"

He snorted. "Nope." He didn't care who had called, he wasn't picking up that phone. "Only thing I want for the rest of the night is you."

The soft, loving smile she gave him turned him inside out. "You've got me," she murmured, cupping his jaw and rubbing her thumb across his lips. "Forever."

Coming from her, the significance of that word made his throat thicken. Tuck kissed her thumb and drew her down into his arms, groaning in relief as he hugged her close. "I'm going to hold you to that, sunshine." Because he loved her more than anything and forever was *exactly* what he had in mind.

—The End—

Complete Booklist

Romantic Suspense
Hostage Rescue Team Series
Marked
Targeted

Titanium Security Series
Ignited
Singed
Burned
Extinguished
Rekindled

Bagram Special Ops Series
Deadly Descent
Tactical Strike
Lethal Pursuit
Danger Close

Suspense Series
Out of Her League
Cover of Darkness
No Turning Back
Relentless
Absolution

Paranormal Romance
Empowered Series
Darkest Caress

Historical Romance
The Vacant Chair

Erotic Romance (writing as *Callie Croix*)

Deacon's Touch
Dillon's Claim
No Holds Barred
Touch Me
Let Me In
Covert Seduction

Acknowledgements

Thanks to my poor hubby, who not only does my proofreading of the final manuscript, but has to listen to me endlessly run plot ideas past him. Plenty of our dates are spent discussing plot twists, which is when his eyes will glaze over. Poor guy.

Katie, you're my biggest supporter and cheerleader, and I thank you for all your insight!

Kim, thank you for helping me out of a tight bind and sharing your expertise with me to help this story shine.

And of course to Joan, thank you for helping me make the story all sparkly!

About the Author

NY Times and USA Today Bestselling author Kaylea Cross writes edge-of-your-seat military romantic suspense. Her work has won many awards and has been nominated for both the Daphne du Maurier and the National Readers' Choice Awards. A Registered Massage Therapist by trade, Kaylea is also an avid gardener, artist, Civil War buff, Special Ops aficionado, belly dance enthusiast and former nationally-carded softball pitcher. She lives in Vancouver, BC with her husband and family.

You can visit Kaylea at www.kayleacross.com. If you would like to be notified of future releases, please join her newsletter: http://kayleacross.com/v2/contact/

Printed in the USA
CPSIA information can be obtained
at www.ICGtesting.com
LVHW041024251024
794802LV00003B/20